# About the Author

Joanne Sefton lives in Bath with her husband and two children; she is very short and moderately Scottish.

Joanne always wanted to be an author, but wasn't sure how to go about it. Instead, she studied law at Cambridge and enjoyed a prestigious career as an employment law barrister in London before taking time out to move west and complete her MA in Creative Writing at Bath Spa University.

As well as gaining a distinction in her MA, Joanne has been long-listed twice for the Bath Novel Award and was once a runner-up in a short story competition which earned her a biro with 'West Lothian Young Writer' embossed on it in gold letters.

Alongside her writing, she continues to practise law on a part-time basis and also holds a role as an advisory board member for a social mobility charity. In her spare time she often thinks about going running or gardening and ends up reading books instead (sometimes ones about gardening, so that counts). She has a weakness for fancy-schmancy dining and impractical shoes.

You can follow Joanne on Twitter @Joanne_Sefton

# If They Knew

## Joanne Sefton

avon.

Published by AVON
A division of HarperCollins*Publishers* Ltd
1 London Bridge Street
London SE1 9GF

www.harpercollins.co.uk

A Paperback Original 2018

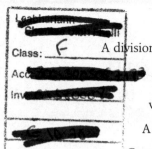
A catalogue copy of this book is available from the British Library.

ISBN: 978-0-00-829445-8

This novel is entirely a work of fiction. The names, characters and incidents portrayed in it are the work of the author's imagination. Any resemblance to actual persons, living or dead, events or localities is entirely coincidental.

Typeset in Birka by Palimpsest Book Production Limited, Falkirk, Stirlingshire
Printed and bound in UK by CPI Group (UK) Ltd, Croydon CR0 4YY

**MIX**
Paper from
responsible sources
**FSC™ C007454**

This book is produced from independently certified FSC paper to ensure responsible forest management.

For more information visit: www.harpercollins.co.uk/green

# If They Knew

# June 1963

*Katy*

S he wondered if there would still be honeysuckle.

From the car window she caught sight of it from time to time – flashes of mottled flowers on the motorway embankment and in the hedgerows – pink and cream against the bright beech and shadowy hawthorn. There had been honeysuckle in flower a year ago; scrambling around the edges of the building site, its tendrils grasping over the broken earth and scattered debris and scenting the afternoon air. It would all be different now. But still, she would like Mary to have honeysuckle.

That was why they were coming today, Mr Robertson had said. It might seem more familiar at this time of year; Katy might be able to remember something new. It was also the last chance before the building was due to open to the public.

Katy didn't want to remember at all.

Last time they had brought her back, it had been in winter. The windows of Mr Robertson's stately old Austin had frozen up while he waited for her. Katy remembered that, and she remembered Etta, wrapped in a fur coat with black felt hat and gloves, standing stiff with malice whilst Katy and the police shivered from the cold.

It had all been different to that first June day with Mary. In winter, there had been no broken earth and no wire fences, no ramshackle no man's land where the site met the farms. By January it was all flat tarmac surfaces, white paint and clean lines. Builders' vans were parked neatly by the entrance, and a pair of window fitters had stopped work to gawp at them, until one of the coppers went over to have a word.

'This is us, then,' Mr Robertson called from the front seat, bringing Katy back to June; back to honeysuckle and the present. Miss Silver, sitting next to her, gave her hand a quick squeeze, as if she were embarrassed but felt she had to do it anyway. There was a copper waiting at the bottom of the slip road. Mr Robertson pulled in, past the signs advertising next week's grand opening of the service station. Moreton Chase it was going to be called – someone had told Katy that last time. The Austin slowed as if to stop, but the young constable waved them on, scurrying to replace the painted wooden traffic cones that were being used to block the slip lane.

As the car swung round a wide bend into the car park, Katy felt her heart beat faster. She didn't want to remember what happened a year ago. She didn't want to feel Mary's weight in her arms. She didn't want to see Mary's face. Instead, she forced her mind's eye downwards, remembering only her own feet in their scuffed school shoes, tramping through the grass and clover on a sunny June morning.

# July 2017

*Helen*

Her phone rang just as the children were finishing their food. Helen answered, then tried to balance the slim handset between her ear and shoulder so she could bend to wipe Alys's mouth, but the child was too quick for her, wriggling off her stool and smearing jammy stickiness down Helen's clean tights. She let her go, too bone-tired to do anything more.

'Sorry, I didn't catch ...' she started to say.

'It's Dad, Helen.'

'Oh, hi, just a sec ...' She paused to push down the door handle for Alys, allowing her to make her escape. Even through the confusion, Helen caught a weight to her father's tone, and registered that it was odd for him to call when he must have known it was the children's teatime.

'The kids on good form then?' he asked.

'Yeah, they're both fine.'

'They're not too ...'

She heard Neil try to shape the question on his tongue and pictured his fingers worrying at the grey hair that was still thick behind his ears. Eventually he gave up, failure escaping his lips as a gentle sigh down the line.

'They're doing fine,' she repeated, making an effort to say it more gently. 'But what about you – is everything okay?'

Another breath down the line – this one heavy, steadying.

'Your mum was up at the hospital today, love.'

Helen racked her memory, uncertain whether this was an appointment that she was meant to have known about. Had Barbara's eye problem flared up again? Was there anything else that she'd mentioned recently?

'Right ...' she stalled.

'It's not good, Helen.'

His voice cracked on the 'H' of her name and she felt her heart jump, then race.

Her father continued, 'She had a mammogram ... They've found a lump.'

*

It was twenty minutes after the call ended when Alys and Barney came tumbling down the stairs. Helen was still sitting at the kitchen table, surrounded by their leftovers. The phone was by her side and she was dabbing her eyes with her knuckles. Barney wobbled on his tiptoes to get the box of tissues from the windowsill before placing it on the table by her elbow. She went to take one but the box was empty – he must not have realised – so she kissed his gorgeous chestnut hair and tried to keep her voice steady to ask him to fetch some toilet paper instead. She hated that they were seeing her like this.

'Mummy? Are you sad because of Daddy?' Barney asked, frowning as he handed over a streamer of toilet roll.

'No, my love, don't worry.' Helen shook her head. 'That was

Granddad. He was phoning to tell us that your Nana Barbara is ill. She might be very ill, and that's why I'm sad.'

'I'm sad too,' said Barney, looking relieved.

'We'll have to go and visit them,' Helen said, attempting a smile. 'You'll both like that, won't you? A trip up north? You can see Granddad Adam and Nana Chris while we're there.'

Alys spoke at last. 'Daddy come too?'

'I don't think so, lovely.' Helen bent to kiss her, which allowed her to hide the fresh tears from Barney. She could smell the jam around her daughter's mouth. 'But we'll tell him we're going. And you'll be able to talk to him on the phone.'

'But we're staying with Daddy on Friday,' said Barney, in his matter-of-fact way. His small brow wrinkled and Helen caught her own father's frown in his expression. 'We're all going to Gambado.'

'You are, are you now?'

Darren had only moved out six weeks ago and already it seemed he was resorting to indoor-adventure-play bribery. That'd be hurting him in the wallet. And did Barney's 'we're all' include *Lauren*? She felt a tension flicker start up by her left eye.

'Gam-ba-do, Gam-ba-do!' Alys was echoing her brother, her voice full of wonder. Gambado might enchant them now, but it surely wouldn't be long before the stakes were upped to Euro Disney, then Florida. Anger at bloody Darren flared inside her.

'Well, now that Nana's ill, I'm afraid Gambado might have to wait for another day. Barney, will you take Alys upstairs please. I have to phone your father.' She realised she'd never called him 'your father' before he left; how quickly they were turning into one of those ex-couples.

He held the phone in his hand for a good minute or so after Helen had hung up. Even after all these years, he still ached for his daughter like a missing limb. He just needed a moment.

Once he'd gathered himself, he'd go back through to the living room, where Barbara would be doing the crossword or sudoku; denial tap-tapping from her pen as she drummed it on the newspaper, fingertips dancing under the shadow of her neat, treacherous breasts.

He put the handset back into its cradle and opened the living room door.

'Shall I put a brew on, love?'

She nodded towards the cup at her elbow, her hands not even slowing.

'No, thanks. I didn't finish the other one, and it's barely cold.'

'Right.' He paused in the doorway. 'Do you mind if I sit with you?'

'Why would I mind, you daft bugger?'

He took a few steps, crossing the floor towards her, then reached out a hand to take the paper from her.

'What are you doing? I'm about to get one.'

'Put it down, love, eh? Just for a minute.'

She sighed, but did as he asked, laying the paper and pen to one side and folding her arms. He sat down beside her and placed a hand on her knee, half expecting her to brush it away.

'I told our Helen.'

'But we agreed we weren't going to worry her.'

Neil shook his head. 'We were wrong, love. I know what we said, but—'

'Well, if you've done it then you've done it.' She cut him

off briskly and went to pick up her pen again. Neil pushed her hand gently down.

'Barbara ...' his voice was shuddering, '... oh God, Barbara. You know I love you so, so much.'

To his surprise, she turned in to him and opened her arms to hold him.

'And I love you, Neil. Always.'

After their embrace, he slipped an arm around her shoulders and she leant in against him, although she'd picked up the paper again, making a show of concentrating on her little scribbled sums. Her shoulders felt narrow, almost bony, and he pictured the cancer already leaching her strength, growing with parasitical single-mindedness.

'I love you,' he said again, almost apologetically.

'So you said. And you'll have plenty of time to say it again, whatever happens.'

'I know.'

He counted to ten in his head.

'Barbara?'

'What?'

'I love you!'

He peered over the newspaper, wondering if she'd laugh or just glare at him, but the look in her eyes was one of pity. His own laugh caught in his throat.

Surely Barbara was the one more in need of sympathy? But then his wife had never been one to conform to expectations.

*Helen*

The drive from London to Lancashire was a total nightmare. They sat in solid traffic for much of the way up the M6, even though it was only Thursday. Alys mostly slept, but Barney barely closed his eyes at all and whined about everything, from the dropped toy he couldn't reach, to the fact that Helen wouldn't turn up the sound on his DVD, to the abandoned trip to Gambado that she thought he'd forgotten about. When they finally arrived at her parents' house, Helen had a pounding headache and a voice hoarse from singing 'Wheels on the Bus'.

'You do look very pale, Helen,' said Barbara, on the doorstep, as though Helen was the one who was ill.

Helen scrutinised her mother carefully. She looked the same. Quite a tall woman, she still stood poker-straight, with her hair neatly coiled into the tight bun that Helen couldn't remember seeing her without, and her brown eyes that always seemed to be somewhere else. While superficially nothing had changed, Helen could see that she'd lost weight, and Barbara had never had that much to spare. Her collarbones looked coat-hangerish and her hands, which were on the large side, looked even more out of proportion. There was a trace of a shadow around her eyes, but when Helen bent slightly to hug her, Barbara responded with her usual tight but perfunctory squeeze. She smelt of ink and mint imperials.

In the fuss of coats and comforters and Alys leaving a shoe in the car, Helen only noticed the envelope on the doormat because she actually stood on it. It was pale green and unsealed, clearly hand-delivered because it simply said 'Barbara' on the front, in what looked like black felt tip.

'There's a card for you here, Mum,' she called.

Both children settled easily enough at bedtime. As usual when they visited, their beds were made up in Helen's old room that they now thought of as theirs. As Helen bent to kiss Barney's head, she remembered vividly lying in that bed, curled up to face the window as he was now.

Ten minutes later, she was downstairs in the living room, clutching a mug of gritty instant coffee. She breathed in deeply and could almost feel the steam easing out her frown lines.

'So ...' she turned to Barbara '... how is everything?'

'I'm fine, Helen, really, I am. I'm sure it'll all be a fuss over nothing.'

'I'm sure you're right,' Helen echoed, 'but I'd rather be here all the same.'

'We don't know much more than when I spoke to you,' put in Neil, who was nursing his cup of tea and standing anxiously by Barbara's shoulder rather than taking a seat of his own. 'We're visiting the hospital tomorrow. She'll see the consultant and get the results of the biopsy they did.'

'I see.' She knew all this already, but it seemed right to hear it again, in person.

'You'll come?' he asked.

Helen looked at her mother. 'Do you want me there?'

Barbara hesitated. 'Well, it might be difficult ... with the children and so on.'

'I want you there,' said Neil. Barbara opened her mouth, but he waved a hand and, uncharacteristically, she shut it again. 'No, Barbara. You know we struggled to remember everything they said to us last time. It'll be good to have Helen with us. She'll know what to ask.'

Helen nodded. 'Of course I'll come.'

The appointment was early the next morning, so Helen put down her coffee to make arrangements for the children. Christine, her mother-in-law, was kind as ever – her voice heavy with regret over the reason for their visit – but Helen could hear a reserve in her tone too. They weren't on quite the same team any more. Dropping the kids off would be the first time she'd seen either Christine or Adam since Darren left.

A little later, with the children's visit to the Harrisons sorted and the three of them sitting glazed in front of a detective show that nobody was actually watching, Helen's gaze caught the two greetings cards on the fireplace. They were both floral designs, with no wording on the front. If it did turn out to be cancer, they'd soon start to multiply.

'What was that note that came in today, Mum? In the green envelope?' She was making conversation as much as anything else.

'Oh, that. It was a card from Jackie at work.' Barbara nodded towards the fireplace.

'Why didn't you put it up?'

'I did.' Her tone was placid, bemused.

'You can't have. Those were both here when we came in. I looked at them when Alys was saying goodnight to you and Dad.'

'It's the one there with the irises. You must have made a mistake.'

'But—'

'You must have made a mistake, Helen.'

Barbara's gaze met Helen's: calm, but commanding never-theless. She couldn't push it any further. But then why should it even cross her mind to pick an argument over a missing card? It was odd, thought Helen, what coming home could do to you.

*

'Did the doctor make Nana Barbara better?' asked Barney, in the car after Helen had collected them from the Harrisons. She was taken aback that he'd remembered where she had been; her little boy was growing up so quickly.

'Well,' she began, 'the doctor can't make Nana Barbara better straight away. But he did explain everything they're going to do to try to make her better. She'll be having an operation soon. Do you know what that is?'

Barney shook his head solemnly.

'They give you some medicine so you go to sleep and can't feel anything and then they open you up and have a look inside and try to take out whatever it is that's making you ill. When they are done, they stitch you back together again as good as new.'

'So then will she be better?'

'Well, then she'll have to recover from the operation, because it's very tiring. Then they'll give her some special medicine. And then she'll hopefully be better.'

In fact, the prognosis had not been particularly rosy. Mr Eklund, the Swedish surgeon who would be operating on Barbara, had gently informed them that the biopsy had confirmed a malignancy in the left breast, and there were pre-cancerous changes in the right one, too. He couldn't be sure how far it had spread before operating, but he thought the most likely scenario was a Stage 3 diagnosis, which would give her, very roughly, a 50/50 chance after chemotherapy. It was a lot to take on board.

'Shall I give Nana one of my drawings?'

'I think that would be a lovely thing to do, darling. Look, I'm just going to call in here ...' They were passing an out-of-town shopping place. The parking was easy and the kids would tolerate a quick trip in. 'I want to get Nana a new nightdress for the hospital.'

When they got back, Barbara's delight seemed out of proportion to the gift.

'That was so thoughtful of you, Helen. You've really cheered me up.'

'And I've called work – the kids and I will stay until after the operation. No arguments. Getting you through this is the most important thing at the moment.'

The glisten on Barbara's eyes was as close as Helen had ever seen her to tears, and the thought of it almost made her well up herself. This Barbara was so different from the Barbara of last night, so hostile and cold over a stupid thing like that card. But then her mum always had been a conundrum. You never knew what you were going to get with her. That way you didn't get too close.

She had plenty of practical issues to worry about, what with trying to hand work stuff over remotely and making a list of the things she'd need to buy for the kids, but still, somehow, Helen found the image of the green envelope was bothering her. She tried to blame it on tiredness, or perhaps her brain was looking for some sort of distraction from the hideous news at the hospital. But what could it be and why would Barbara lie about it? She kept drifting back to those questions.

Much later, when everyone else was in bed, Helen decamped to the back room to reply to some work emails and stuck on the TV for a bit of background noise. It was only when she finished and went to switch the TV off that she noticed the slim edge of green pushed to the bottom of a pile of papers on the sideboard.

She slid the top section of the pile aside and, sure enough, the green line turned out to be the edge of the small envelope that she'd seen on the doormat. The front simply said 'Barbara', written in a nondescript hand with, as she'd thought, black felt tip. The letter looked as though it had never been sealed, and the paper, cheap and green, matching the envelope, slid out easily.

HELLO BARBARA.
CANCER IS TOO GOOD FOR YOU.
DON'T WORRY – I'LL BE WITH YOU ALL THE WAY.
JUST LIKE YOU DESERVE.
JENNIFER

Helen's hands started to shake; the harsh New York laughter from the chat show on television seemed to be taunting her. This was a joke, surely? Yet, on the other hand, it was no kind of joke at all.

She reread the thing twice or more, but her mind couldn't process the words. Who was Jennifer? And what could she mean? Whatever it was, the intention behind it was obviously malevolent. But could it be serious? She started to look at the note itself, mechanically noting the flimsy copier paper, the black felt tip, the careful capitals with a few wobbles – she guessed that the author was using their wrong hand. But none of it took her any further.

After a few moments, the credits music startled her into action. She refolded the note and replaced it in the envelope. Once she'd tucked it away, back under a building society statement, she could almost believe she'd imagined it. She focused in turn on the graduation pictures on the wall and the wedding-present china shepherdess that Barbara hated. This was the normal world. It was more than normal – it was the world of dull, petty suburbia that Helen had escaped. It had nothing to do with threatening notes from anonymous villains. She resolved to confront Barbara again the next day. No matter how frosty or secretive her mother could be, she couldn't simply brush off something like this.

# December 2014

*Helen*

The thing about Darren was he'd always had a knack for giving people what they didn't know they wanted. It occurred to Helen later that she probably shouldn't have been so shocked when he finally managed to turn that talent into hard cash. Perhaps the more surprising thing, she mused, as she tried on her third little black dress and frowned hopelessly at the mirror again, was that it had taken him quite so long. Austerity ground on, and yet here she was, getting ready for a blowout Christmas party that would show the world just how damn successful Darren Harrison was.

The man himself, immaculate in Paul Smith, stuck his head round the bedroom door.

'Are you getting there, Hels? The car will be here in twenty.'

Apparently they were too grand for minicabs these days.

'Okay, thanks, I'm just going to swap this for my black one.'

'I thought you'd got something new during the week?' His brow creased slightly, with just the hint of a frown.

'I didn't find anything.'

The truth was, she'd only managed an hour to dash into a couple of local shops and, ten months after giving birth to

Alys, she still found trying clothes on a miserable experience.

The business was called Date Night. Darren had started putting on these ironic telly-themed singles nights, having got the idea after watching one too many cheap nostalgic box sets. It was the seventh or eighth golden business brainwave he'd had, whilst her dull but steadily more lucrative career in financial-services HR supported them both. Finally, this one had stuck.

In a year, she'd gone from being a career girl in Shoreditch to maternity leave in Chiswick. Going back to work after Barney had felt like a return to civilisation. After Alys, though, Darren pointed out that he could pay for everything now – all the holidays they could handle. Wasn't it better, he asked, for her to be less stressed and for the kids to be raised by their parents rather than strangers? She didn't speak to him for three days after that and at the end of her first day back in the office she drank Prosecco with her friend Amy Stretton. Amy was in CID with the Met Police and, back then, still single. She could be relied upon to opine at length about all men being bastards.

The dress she had settled on for tonight was from the Shoreditch days. It was black, and forgivingly stretchy – although faded from too many washes. Well, surely it would be dark at the party anyway? She added a pair of silver earrings, looked in the mirror and smiled, feeling, finally, like she was herself.

'The car's outside, Hels.'

'I'm coming!'

She quickly kissed her babies – they'd both been asleep for a while – then she popped into the front room to let her parents know they were off. She'd managed to persuade them down for a rare pre-Christmas visit and then Darren had casually informed her about the party. If she was being honest with herself, she'd be more comfortable booking the usual babysitter.

Darren was jiggling his keys against his hip as she came into the hallway; he looked her up and down but said nothing. His smile was flat.

*

Although it was after one a.m. by the time they got back, Barbara was not yet in bed. Instead they found her tucked in a corner of the sofa under the glow of a single lamp, peering at a laptop she had balanced on the arm of the sofa. Her dark bun had always given her something of the air of a ballerina, and she unfurled gracefully from her pose as they came into the room.

'I hope you didn't stay up for our sakes?' Darren's words were polite, but there was something querulous in his tone. He spoke more to the decanter and glass in his hand than to his mother-in-law.

'Of course not, don't worry.' Barbara's own voice was light. 'I'm doing coursework – the time ran away with me.' Helen and Darren had both been mildly amused when she'd announced a couple of years earlier that she was taking an OU course in computing, but although she'd initially shrugged it off as just a tactic to stay one step ahead of the endless cuts and redundancies in local newspapers, she seemed to have really taken to it.

'Were the kids okay?' Helen asked.

Barbara looked momentarily blank, as though she had

possibly forgotten about them, but then nodded. 'Not a peep out of either of them. All fine.'

'Well, I'm going up,' announced Darren, raising his whisky to them. Helen knew she should join him; after all, she had been the one who had insisted on leaving at the end of the party, rather than heading out into the West End, where many of the guests were going to continue their evening. Now she was home, though, she felt suddenly awake. And desperate to take off her heels and have a cup of tea. Barbara declined her offer and Darren slunk off.

'Good night?' Barbara asked as she shut down the laptop.

Helen shrugged. Had it been? She found it exhausting, having to keep track of the employees, the investors, the suppliers, the hangers-on and God knows who else. Over the years, she'd shared little of the day-to-day concerns of her life with her mother – taking her lead from Barbara herself no doubt. She wasn't now about to start dissecting her insecurities about Darren and how she feared the business was changing him.

To be fair, the night had improved when Darren – probably irritated with her defensiveness – had insisted that she knock back a couple of glasses of champagne and led her onto the dance floor, swinging her around to Pharrell Williams. She knew they'd looked good together; they always did. And in the moment, she was 'Happy', just like the song said. The dancing made her feel less self-conscious about whether people were questioning what on earth he was doing with her.

Sometimes she wondered if he ever had crossed the line, and mixed play with the work he was so devoted to. She'd asked him about it once and he'd laughed. He said he'd spent thirty-five years with nothing to recommend him but his smile and his wits; he wouldn't want to be with the sort of woman who might want him now that he had a belly and grey temples and a bit of cash. That was a couple of years ago, though. Back then he wouldn't have slunk off to bed with a whisky. On the other hand, back then she'd probably have mustered the enthusiasm for a nightcap elsewhere.

'Well?' Her mother was still looking at her expectantly.

'Sorry, I drifted off a bit – a bit woozy I'm afraid. It was lovely. The venue was spectacular.'

'I'm glad you had fun,' Barbara said, making Helen feel about seventeen again. Her eyes were on the laptop as it went through its shutting-down processes. It seemed Helen had no need to worry about her mother trying to get her to open up.

'So how's the coursework going?' Helen asked, more to stop her own mind whirring than for any other reason. 'I thought you were finishing up with that last spring?'

'Yes, I did, but then I signed up for some of the degree-level modules. It's fascinating, actually.'

'It's a shame you didn't get into it when you were younger – you could have made a fortune.'

Barbara laughed lightly. 'Yes, it would have been nice to have had the chance. But never too late, as they say – I've got a few little projects I'm dreaming up. Anyway, that's my work done. I think I'll get to bed.'

'Night, Mum.'

But Helen's mind had drifted back to the dance floor, to the moment when a slow Sam Smith number had come on and she'd insisted that she was exhausted and needed to go back to their table for a drink. Darren had nodded and they made their way back across to the low table where their bottle of champagne still waited, half full.

One of the new regional managers glided over, in painfully high sandals that pushed her chest forward.

'Darren! You two were amazing on the dance floor. You kept that quiet!'

'Louise ...' He clasped her shoulder warmly.

'Lauren.'

'Lauren, of course, so sorry. This is my wife, Helen.'

'Don't worry.' She brushed his hand, as if to smooth away his mistake, laughing loudly. 'There's so many people here!'

She'd cornered them for the next ten minutes – despite Darren's smooth attempts to move her on – sharing gossip and gushing compliments.

If he were going to get involved with someone at work, someone like Lauren would be last on the list. So why was the sound of her grating laughter continuing to rattle around Helen's head as she failed to get to sleep?

# July 2017

*Helen*

In the end, she didn't get any chance to mention the note on Saturday. Neil whisked them all off to a theme park for the day, then dinner at the local Italian. 'Take our minds off it all,' he said, repeatedly. Helen grinned for his sake, as much as for Barney and Alys. Barbara's enjoyment, she was sure, was just as manufactured. The thought gave her an unfamiliar sense of camaraderie with her mother – for as long as she could remember, she'd found herself siding with her dad in the face of Barbara's quirks and moods.

On Sunday morning, however, she woke up thinking about the note. It had lurked through her dreams, which had danced from Darren, to her children, then her parents; all unformed and fast-fading glimpses. Each encounter had played out on the sickly green landscape of the notepaper – those black capitals always there but never in focus. In those giddy predawn hours, something fearful woke in her belly, and, once woken, it shifted and clawed about inside her like a rat.

She was still turning the words of the note over in her mind as the grey dawn gradually crept round the edges of the heavy velvet curtains. They were cast-offs from Neil's sister

– Aunt Vicky – given away when she moved to Málaga, to replace the yellow ones that had been up since Helen was small. Good enough for the spare room, her parents must have decided, even though the size wasn't quite right. She'd got used to sleeping here with Darren over the years. Now she was sleeping alone in the big old bed, with no one else to see the patterns the morning light made around the badly fitting curtains.

If only she could show Darren the note. *Her* Darren, not the new, arm's-length, polite-chat-about-the-weather Darren who made her skin crawl. It wasn't that she thought he'd have all the answers, just that she wasn't used to having no one to share things with. They'd met at school and grown up together as an 'us'. Suddenly Helen had to work everything out as 'me'. And everything was bloody tough.

At first, her mind had tricked itself – he was on a business trip, or working late – God knew she was used to not having him around. But now it was more than six weeks, and the reality, the permanence, of his absence was becoming undeniable. All the more so since that awful call with her dad. The old Darren might not have been around when the au pair was sick or when she needed to decide on a holiday booking, but she could be confident that if the world fell apart he'd be there to catch her. Now it had and he was content to see her in free fall.

Gradually, the lumpy shadow-scape revealed itself as her assorted bits of luggage, strewn with clothes and toys and everything else that she'd not had the will to try to tidy up. The green dizzy dreams and the clawing rat seemed to shrivel in the light. It was too bizarre. To be looking at the fresh baked-bean-juice stains on her dressing gown, or the cascade of children's books erupting from a Gruffalo backpack, and thinking that somebody out there was happy her mother could be dying, that somebody out there wanted Barbara to suffer.

*Error*, as the laptop would say. Switch it off and on again. If only she could.

She kept coming up with improbable explanations – the note was a prop from a murder-mystery party, or a handwriting test, or Barbara had written it herself as some sort of weird displacement activity. But why the mention of cancer? And why had it been on the doormat when Helen arrived? There was no simple answer to explain that away.

Finally she heard Alys start up her morning whimper, which, in her usual way, would soon become a chatter and then, shortly after, a wail. As Helen quit the stale bed and pulled on the bean-juice-stained dressing gown, the demons scuttled back to their dusty recesses. She pushed the curtains back, then, still fumbling with the belt of her dressing gown, she headed upstairs.

*

Helen found the blue dress later that morning, when she was going through some stuff in her old room. She'd hoped that one of the dusty boxes stashed under the bed would hold something that might keep the kids occupied for a while.

Of course, she'd packed for the journey in a hurry, with no real idea of how long they'd be staying, and the flaws in her organisation – no charger for Barney's tablet, DVD boxes missing their discs, and Jess the Doll's tragically deficient wardrobe – were now becoming woefully apparent.

It must have been twenty years since Helen had seen that dress. She knew the story of Neil buying it for Barbara on honeymoon in Glasgow and the shimmer of blue – more eastern Med than western Scotland – was instantly recognisable. She found the straps and held it up, letting the layers of satin and chiffon swing free. There were details she hadn't noticed before, or didn't remember: the old-fashioned label, sewn in by hand, the slight discolouration under the arms. Was there a breath of Barbara's perfume, or was that just Helen's imagination?

'Alys!' she shouted, after a moment or two. 'Come and try on this princess dress.'

She knew Barbara wouldn't mind a bit. After all, Helen herself had spent a good year around the age of six tripping around the house in its gauzy layers, the spaghetti straps nicely set off against her utilitarian white M&S vests. She'd called it her cocktail dress. As a child, Helen had liked to imagine Barbara's youth had been spent swishing around sophisticated parties. She had a vague fantasy that Barbara had come down in the world when she married Neil and renounced a life of leisure and glamour and quite possibly even cigarette holders for love, a red-brick semi and her baby girl. She didn't actually have any evidence for this exotic former life, but, in the absence of evidence of anything more prosaic, it was an attractive fantasy.

Alys duly trotted upstairs, but when Helen held up the dress she looked sceptical.

'Which princess?' she asked.

'Not a Disney Princess. Another Princess. Princess Alys.'

'Daddy buy me Belle dress.'

'Did he?' Helen was genuinely puzzled. Alys adored Belle

from *Beauty and the Beast* and Helen couldn't imagine she could have received such a prize and not been full of it for days.

The girl looked sad and a little confused. 'I get it next time, he say, next time, but ...' She faltered, and her big eyes welled with tears.

At home, Helen had had to tell her over and over that Daddy didn't live with them any more. Each time, it cut her up inside and the tears that she managed to hold in when she was with her children spilled out with interest after bedtime. Eventually, Alys seemed to have understood, on some level at least, but the visit up here could only have confused her.

'Blue is for boys, Mummy.' As ever, the three-year-old's train of thought chugged on at pace.

Helen racked her mind for some Disney Princess assistance. 'Cinderella wears blue,' she said, encouragingly.

'Not *that* blue, Mummy – that's boys' blue.'

Helen looked down at the dress, as if noticing its colour for the first time. 'Oh! You mean I should give it to Barney to wear?'

She loved her daughter's laughter, which bubbled thick and sticky in her throat like liquid fudge. Alys liked the joke of her brother wearing the dress and her chortles brought Neil to the door.

'Good morning, ladies,' Neil said, making Alys giggle even more.

'Alys thinks Barney should dress up in Nana's honeymoon dress. What do you reckon, Granddad?'

She expected Neil to laugh along. Instead, he reached out, groping like a blind man. His fingers touched the fabric, but then it slipped out of his grasp and the dress slithered to the floor. He sat down heavily on the bed. Helen cursed inwardly. Of course, she should have realised the dress might upset him. But a moment later he was smiling again and had pulled a toffee out of his pocket for Alys.

He turned to Helen. 'I came to tell you there's a phone call for you, love.'

'Darren?' she mouthed it silently over Alys's head, and he nodded.

'Now, young Alys.' His grasp on the dress was firm this time, and the wet sheen on his eyes had been blinked away. 'The thing you have to know about this dress is that it belonged to a mermaid once. That's why you can see all the colours of the deep blue ocean in it – in fact, I'm sure I once saw a tiny golden fish flickering through just about here ...'

The phone handset sat like a grenade on a chest of drawers on the landing.

'Hello?' She kept her voice low, going into the spare room.

'Hi, Hels. How's your mum doing?' said the voice on the line.

'She's okay. We went to the hospital on Friday. They're going to operate next week. We'll know more then.'

'I was gutted to hear it, really I was.' She could picture him shaking his head, sorrowfully, rubbing the back of his hand against his designer stubble in that way he had. 'Give her my best, yeah?'

'Yeah,' she agreed, knowing she'd say nothing.

'I've been trying your mobile.'

'I know you have. It's not the easiest time, Darren.'

'Yeah, I understand that. But the kids'll be missing me.' As he spoke, she tried to push away the image of Alys's perplexed face, talking about the stupid Disney costume. 'I'm not saying you shouldn't have taken them up there, and we both wanted to deal with access informally, but ...'

*Bastard.* Always trying to come across as Mr More-Than-Reasonable. *He* should be here with his family now, rather than having fucked off with his glossy, giggling area manager. That's what Helen wanted to say, but the words wouldn't come. She'd had explosive, raging, endless rows with Darren each day since he'd left, but only in the privacy of her own mind. When it came to real life, the words would never come.

She realised he was still talking. He was still going on in his calm *let's be adult about this* voice that she'd so quickly come to despise.

'... So I'll come up at the weekend and stay with my mum. Just me, not Lauren – I don't want to make things harder. But I want to see the kids properly, not just an hour over lunch or something. Okay? And I want to speak to them. Are they there just now?'

Helen pressed the handset closer to her ear. Alys's laughter was louder now, but not so loud that he'd be able to hear it down the phone line.

'Mum's taken them both to the park,' she lied. 'You only caught Dad and I because we were finishing the dishes. We're just going to meet them.'

'Right.'

'Yes.'

He sighed. 'Look, call me later – just let me say goodnight to them at least.' His voice might have cracked, or it might have been static on the line. She was learning, to her surprise, that Darren could be a good actor. It was bizarre, thinking back to how she'd always been able to read him like a book.

Perhaps he'd never had the will to deceive her before, or perhaps it was the distance that had opened up between them making it harder for her to really see him the way she always had before. She ached even more for the man she had married.

'I don't want them to get upset,' she said.

'For God's sake, don't make me beg to speak to my own kids, Helen.'

He didn't sound to her like a man who was begging. She felt the familiar lump swell in the back of her throat. This was why she couldn't fight with him: whenever she tried to give voice to her anger, the rage choked her before she could let it out.

'Tomorrow,' she managed.

'First thing.'

She nodded uselessly into the phone, tears running down both cheeks now. Finally she said 'okay' just about loud enough for him to hear, and then hung up.

God knew she didn't want either of the kids to catch her looking like this; they'd seen enough tears. Taking care to be silent, she slipped out of the bedroom and walked down the stairs. She wanted to return the handset to its charger quickly. Whilst she held it, it felt as though she was carrying Darren around, and he would know that she'd lied to him and be able to see her falling apart.

Just thinking about Darren was so painful, yet she couldn't stop herself. She had no reference point for what was happening to her and that left her completely bewildered. As she and Darren had been together since high school, she'd never had any sort of break-up before. And her parents' relationship had always been rock solid. Barbara had her quirks – always had – she was often distant with her daughter and could be sharp with her tongue. Occasionally her claws came out and Helen could remember the odd ring of a slap or the twist of an arm when her mother was angry.

But, even though he could be on the receiving end of her sharp tongue too, Neil had adored his wife with a constancy that was unshakeable. Even more remarkably, he'd had love enough for both of them, so Helen had never felt the need to compete, and never questioned the security of their family.

Now, it looked like her own children were going to have none of that, and she veered between righteous rage towards Darren and anxious guilt about what more she could have done to keep her family together.

Helen could hear Barbara's voice in the kitchen as she came down the stairs. Although the green and inky haze of the dreams had faded, it hadn't left her completely. It occurred to her that if Barbara knew what the envelope contained *before* she picked it up from the doormat, then perhaps there had been others. She'd not thought to look for any until now, and her decision to confront her mother had lost impetus through the bittersweet family outings yesterday. The thought of interrogating Barbara about the note in the midst of the turmoil of a cancer diagnosis made her squeamish. Given how emotionally vulnerable she felt herself – her hands were still shaking after the phone call – it didn't take much to persuade herself to put it off. She was decided; before confronting her mother, she would look for more notes.

In the hall, she replaced the phone on its cradle and pulled out a tissue. She dabbed at her face in the mirror and managed to tidy it a bit. At least she'd learned to avoid wearing mascara these days. Now that she was closer to the kitchen she could hear Barney's voice too. He was explaining the plot of one of the films he watched endlessly. It seemed unlikely she'd be disturbed by either of them any time soon.

She retraced her steps, stealthily, to the staircase. There was a little hotel safe at the back of Barbara's wardrobe, hidden by a clutter of shoes. It contained passports and building society books and pension stuff. Much duller stuff than Helen had hoped to find when, aged fifteen or so, she'd idly observed her mother opening it and gone on to crack the code: 2973. She could still remember it. Would Barbara have changed the code over the years?

The little door swung open smoothly, and that small disturbance was enough to shift the stack of mismatched papers. Even through the gloom, a knife-edge sliver of green caught Helen's eye. Clearly, the note from the other night had not been the first. Again, this envelope simply said 'Barbara'.

From the bedroom, she heard Alys pause to ask, 'Where's Mummy?' Rather than risk them coming out to look for her, Helen stuffed the envelope into the large pocket on her hoodie to read later. After a few seconds, she felt safe enough to carry on. Riffling through the rest of the papers in the safe, she quickly found two more. Then she replaced everything as accurately as she could and stuck the two new envelopes alongside the first in the front of her hoodie. She'd take them back to the downstairs loo to read, where she could lock the door and not worry about being disturbed. If nothing else, this intrigue might give her something to occupy her brain other than the constant, cycling worries about Darren.

As soon as she got to the bottom of the stairs, though, Barney erupted from the kitchen and threw himself at her, without stopping for breath in his chatter. Helen twirled him around and he dragged her back to the kitchen, where she had to enthuse over the half-done jigsaw on the table. Moments later, Neil appeared in the doorway with Alys, who wanted to show off her princess dress.

While Alys performed curtsies, Helen watched Barbara applaud with no sign of sentiment over the reappearance of her dress. Barney talked all the louder for fear of his little sister getting some attention.

Neil moved across to the window, where Barbara stood by the sink with a tea towel in her hand. She let her husband rest his arm across her shoulders for all of three seconds, before she gently lifted it and twisted away.

'Shall I get us all some tea?' Barbara asked, brightly.

*

It was half an hour, in the end, before Helen managed some time alone. The three new notes were not identical to the first, but they were all similar: short and mysterious but written with unmistakable venom.

HELLO BARBARA
THIS IS JENNIFER.
I KNOW WHO YOU ARE.

HELLO BARBARA
I KNOW WHO YOU ARE.
I KNOW WHAT YOU DID.
I'VE COME TO PAY YOU BACK.
JENNIFER

HELLO BARBARA.
DOES NEIL KNOW?
OR WOULD YOU LIKE ME TO TELL HIM?
JENNIFER

There were no dates on any of them, but that was the order that seemed to make most sense, leading up to the cancer one. There was no clue as to how long it had been going on for, nor as to whether 'Jennifer' had approached Neil or done anything else.

Helen had been well aware whilst growing up that her mum wouldn't speak about the past; that she would admit to no family, no history – in fact, no life at all before meeting Neil at the age of twenty. Occasionally, he would call her his girl who fell to earth. Helen had badgered him over it at times, mostly when she was in her teens, but as life unfurled, the mystery seemed minor in the scheme of things. It had become part of the scenery.

'I know who you are,' the notes said, and the words made Helen's blood turn icy, because the truth was she didn't. And she never had.

She tried to imagine asking her dad about it now; her relationship with Neil had always been simpler. He was her dad; he loved her, worried about her and thought she was a superstar. She was his daughter; she loved him, allowed him to bore her with his gardening chat and bought him socks for Christmas. For as long as she could remember, they'd been able to talk easily about just about anything.

But she hesitated, only now realising that the one thing they never really talked easily about was Barbara. Her mind was full of the image of his face, crumpling at the sight of his wife's blue honeymoon dress. The notes would be devastating – doubly so if Barbara hadn't told him about them herself, which Helen was convinced was the case. 'Jennifer' had threatened to tell Neil something – Helen had no idea what – but if she showed him the notes she might well blunder into the very threat that 'Jennifer' was holding like an axe to Barbara's neck. So she was left with the first option she'd thought of. And the one Helen had always found most difficult – trying to talk to her mother.

She folded the notes into their envelopes, tucking them deep in her pocket to return when she had the chance. Then she washed her face as quietly as she could, using cold water to try to subdue the redness. The tears had been close to the surface since that awful phone call with Darren, and her anger on reading the notes had quickly brought them back. When she finally looked human, she combed her hair through, listening to the hum of the house around her and the laughter and chatter of the children with their grandparents.

On the surface, she thought, this looked like perfection. No fly on the wall, or neighbour peeping through the net curtains, would know the different ways in which every heart in this house was breaking.

# June 1963

*Katy*

She recognised the stern, mustachioed face of the policeman who came towards them, though she wouldn't be able to name him. As Mr Robertson opened the door for Katy, the officer held out a pair of handcuffs, gaping open, the metal glinting in the sunshine.

'I don't think we'll need those, thank you.' Mr Robertson's tone was firm, and the other man frowned.

'Protocol—' he began, but Mr Robertson cut him off.

'I have custody of the prisoner. Miss Silver and I are content that nothing untoward will happen, and if it does, then we'll be the ones to answer for it.'

'For the sake of the family, though,' the officer tried again, waving towards a large white estate car, painted with the letters 'POLICE'. Katy supposed that Etta was inside.

'Mrs Gardiner is here to try to find her child, not to see Katy Clery humiliated. You can put the handcuffs away.'

Katy wasn't so sure that she agreed with Mr Robertson on why Etta Gardiner wanted to be there, but the policeman finally did as he was asked. A few of his colleagues had made their way over during the discussion, and Mr Robertson exchanged pleasantries with the inspector in charge. The plan was that they would initially walk across the site onto the adjacent farmland, to the vicinity where it was believed that Katy must have accessed the site a year earlier, coming from the railway station. Katy turned and walked with them, keeping close to Miss Silver so as to not give the police any excuse to pull out the handcuffs again. None of the adults talked to her, although she was all they were talking about.

A few seconds after they had passed the motorway patrol car, she heard its door open and the rustle of a passenger getting out. Risking a glance back, she saw she had been right. It was Etta, not in fur this time, but instead in a black, shapeless dress and jacket, a dark-dyed straw hat pressed low on her brow. Their eyes met, and for a moment Katy thought she saw sadness rather than anger. Then the woman turned deliberately to one side, away from the constable at her shoulder, and spat coolly onto the tarmac. The hatred, when she lifted her eyes back to Katy, was clear.

Katy fought back the tears prickling behind her own eyes and continued to walk forward. Soon the police started to slow. They were nearing the edge of the site. The tarmac of the car park ended, and there was a thin strip of scrub before a wire fence. Someone had cut a gap. There was a neat roll of fencing wire stacked to one side – ready to fix it quickly so everything was shipshape for the grand opening, she supposed.

There were nettles around the fence, and as they made their way into the field, the ground became soft and uneven. Katy, now used to the confines of Ashdown with its paved yard and endless linoleum corridors, felt herself stumble. The smells of the wet earth, of the green grass, buzzed in her mind.

'Well,' said the inspector, suddenly turning to face back towards the service station and the motorway beyond it. 'Do you recognise it? Are you planning to tell us anything, or just to waste everyone's time again?'

# July 2017

*Barbara*

She held the soap out under the shower water. The jets carried away the film of dust and the creamy white surface began to glisten. She turned it over in her hands, waiting for the hot steam to release that unmistakable floral scent. Tesco shower gel was sufficient most mornings, but today something more potent seemed called for. The bar of No. 5 had been eased out of its monogrammed box and pressed into service.

*I'm still me*, she thought, as she worked the soap into the brown marks left on her dry ankles by her sandal straps, and then lathered up her shins in preparation for the razor. Saggier, more wrinkly and more blemished, yes. Bearing scars inflicted both by accident and design. But still, this body was recognisable as the one that had twirled in the blue dress up in Glasgow; still the same body that appeared, bikini-clad, in the Lanzarote beach photos from a few years later. Not to mention the same body seen smothered in sheets in the blotchy hospital shot from the day Helen was born. It hung on the bedroom wall even now, despite years of trying to talk Neil into taking it down.

She'd decided a long time ago that age-related deterioration in eyesight was a small mercy; those stray hairs, liver spots and discoloured veins, which would have horrified her in her youth, were easier to ignore through the forgiving blur of myopia.

*I'm still me.*

Her limbs were firm and strong; she'd been careful not to run to fat, though it was true her back ached now when she bent like this to shave her legs. At least the hairs grew slower than they used to, even if they compensated with random migration – sprouting witchily in unexpected places. All in all, she looked and felt in good nick for sixty-nine. That had been old-woman territory in her own mother's day, but not any more.

Barbara remembered the paradox of the ship of Theseus – not that there'd been much in the way of the classics where she'd had her education, but she'd come across a *Myths and Legends* book in the library during her early days at the newspaper. It turned out that a couple of renewals brought a surprising amount of useful bullshit within her grasp. If every plank on a ship is replaced, one by one, until none of the original planks are left, is it still the same ship? Or the same axe, or broom, or human being?

It was said that our constantly regenerating cells meant no part of our body was ever more than seven years old – or perhaps it was ten? What, then, made these the same feet that had run pell-mell on terraced streets in gaping shoes? What made these the same lips that joined, shaking, with Neil's on their wedding day? What made these the hands that, trembling with fear, had cradled newborn Helen?

It was the pattern, the mould, that was important. Just as each plank of the ship was measured, cut and sanded to fit in its position, so each cell died and another grew in its place, arranged just as before, cheek by jowl with its comrades, directed by God or DNA or both to maintain the thinness of her bottom lip, the flecks of gold in her brown eyes and the bluntness of her stubby fingers. But not any more.

'Cancer' is our word for what happens when the mould breaks.

Barbara lathered her breasts, lifting each one tenderly and committing the weight and tone and pucker of it to memory. Her pattern read 34C, the cells dutifully multiplying and expanding to sprout at thirteen and to swell during pregnancy, just as mandated in their instructions.

Now, though, they'd gone rogue. She had Militant Mammaries. Jihadi Jugs. The pattern had been ripped up, and right now there were thousands (millions?) of manically reproducing cells bulging into colonies of chaos, thrusting aside the law-abiding, structured tissue and making manifest the sins of the flesh.

*I'm still me.* She let the middle finger of her left hand creep over the Lump. *Except for the bits that aren't.* She pictured the glinting edge of a scalpel. Incision. Excision. Fifteen hundred years of medicine and it still came down to this: cut the damn thing out.

When she wasn't thinking of the cancer, she was thinking of the note. Barbara was sure that Helen's sharp eyes had picked up on it. She'd find the others in the safe soon enough – if she hadn't already. That girl gets her sharpness from her mother, Barbara thought proudly, even if her daughter couldn't really be called a girl any more. There was a distance in Helen's eyes, an uneasiness in her smile, that told Barbara she had read the note, and would be asking awkward questions soon enough. Helen's distracted look could just be worry about the illness, especially coming on top of the business with Darren, but Barbara didn't think so. She had a sense about these things.

Of course, the fact the notes were there didn't mean anything would come of them. Anonymous vitriol was easy enough – just look at the internet these days. This was the curtain call for a closing act that Barbara had waited all her adult life for, but she still didn't know if she was ready to take to the stage.

*I'm still me.* She muttered it aloud this time, letting the bitter soap taste into her mouth.

*Still me; but so, so tired.*

That was how she knew the cancer was for real, not the blurry shots from the mammogram or Eklund's careful explanations, but the numbing, bone-aching, deadening tiredness that had her in its embrace, sucking her down like quicksand. She had prepared for this finale well enough. If it was ever going to play out, the curtain was going to have to come up pretty damn quickly.

*Helen*

They agreed that Neil would take Barbara into hospital by himself when she was to be admitted for the operation. That way, Helen could stay at the house with the kids and not have to worry about bothering Chris and Adam again. Chris had frowned when Helen told her, saying: 'I thought you'd want to be with your mum,' but the look in her mother-in-law's eyes told Helen there was more to it than that. She didn't want to give Chris the chance to start pleading Darren's case about seeing the children.

It was afterwards that Barbara would need the support, anyway, once the doctors were ready to say exactly what it was that they had found in there. And later on, when she came home, and would need care that Neil might struggle to provide. Helen had already made a couple of discreet calls to social services, just to check what would be available for them, but Neil had started talking darkly about the indignity of having strangers poking around when you're at your lowest ebb, and Helen knew she wouldn't be able to bring herself to walk away.

So, instead of following up with the council, she had called her boss. It came down to an ultimatum – *give me a sabbatical or I'll walk*. The managers weren't happy, but there wasn't much they could say. Helen told herself that keeping up the mortgage payments was the least she could expect from shit-rat Darren and prayed to God that her bravado wouldn't come unstuck.

Now, the day had come and she was helping Barbara to pack. The master bedroom had barely changed in twenty years and Helen still felt odd going in there. They had never been one of those families who all piled into the double bed on a Sunday morning – like she and Darren used to do with the kids. Whilst she hadn't exactly been forbidden from going into her parents' bedroom, it certainly wasn't encouraged, and it brought back stiff memories of having her hair done on school-photo day or before a birthday party.

'Thank you again for the nightie you got, Helen,' said Barbara, rather formally. 'It is lovely.'

'Let me get it out. Did you put it in the drawer here?'

Helen opened the drawer as she spoke, but had got confused. Barbara kept her nightwear in the fourth one down, and she'd opened the third, full of tights.

'Sorry!'

'Next one down, Helen, perhaps I should just …'

A couple of minutes later, once Helen had managed to pick up the wrong toilet bag and then folded Barbara's spare jumper incorrectly, Barbara insisted on swapping places.

'I'm not an invalid, not yet at any rate.'

'I know … I just want to help.'

'Don't worry, love, it's nice just to have you here.'

Helen couldn't help but notice that her mother was avoiding her eyes as she said it.

She tried desperately to think of some way to start a real conversation. The notes on their sickly green paper swam in her mind's eye. Her thoughts flicked back to a time, aged twelve or so, when she'd sat in this same chair and Barbara had outlined the facts of life in her brisk, hearty journalist's manner. Neil had practically had to push Helen in through the door to have the conversation, and, looking back, she reckoned he'd probably had to do the same for Barbara. Beyond that she struggled to remember any meaningful conversation the two of them had had alone.

'Have you got the list the nurse gave you?' she asked, stalling for time.

Barbara just waved a hand towards a scrap of paper on the bedside table and carried on folding the nightie.

'What books are you taking?'

'I picked a couple up at the library.' She nodded towards a couple of paperbacks on the bed. Helen nearly picked one up to ask about it, but decided she had to do better than that.

'Mum? Are you scared?'

Barbara didn't answer, just carried on arranging the same few bits of clothing in her bag. For a moment, Helen wondered if she'd not really said it out loud, but she noticed Barbara's hands were trembling. Eventually, she sat down heavily on the bed and looked Helen in the eye for the first time since they'd come into the bedroom.

'What sort of question is that?'

Her gaze was hard, almost contemptuous.

'I didn't mean to—'

'Yes, I'm scared.' Her voice was flat.

'I want you to know you can talk to me, Mum, if it helps – that's all.'

'Talking doesn't help, Helen. I'm afraid that's one thing that your dad and I disagree on.' Her smile looked thin and forced. 'If you're trying to tell me you care, don't worry – I know that. I know that I've not always made it easy for you and I know that you care anyway. You've got that much of Neil in you and we can both be grateful for that.'

Helen nodded. For a weird moment, she felt almost jealous of whoever had written the notes. Barbara was so self-possessed, so isolated, it was hard to imagine how she'd ever got close enough to anyone to wreak the harm the author of the note seemed to blame her for.

Helen took a deep breath.

'I found the note, Mum.'

'What note?' Barbara looked up only for an instant. She was winding the cable on a phone charger, ready to add it to her bag.

'You *know* what note: the green one, the awful poison pen thing.'

'So *that's* what you've got your knickers in a twist over! And I thought the idea of me at death's door was enough.' Barbara raised her eyebrows.

45

'Well? What's it all about then?'

She shrugged. 'It's sad really, a young girl in town – well, not so young any more, I suppose – her shoplifting conviction was reported in the paper and I was the one who wrote up the report. She lost her job – I think that's right. I'm not sure of the details. Anyway, she fixated on me, blamed me for making her life fall apart, and started sending notes, threatening to get *me* sacked or to expose me as a liar.'

'So how long's it been going on?'

'Well, it started about ten years ago. I got the police involved first time around, but once you unmask a stalker they tend to be a lot less scary than you imagined. When I found out it was her, I felt sorry for her more than anything else. She's tried it on two or three times since, dropping little poisonous notes into work, or here. There were one or two phone calls too. Then years with nothing in between. She's never gone any further. The best thing is just to ignore it.'

'Does Dad know?'

Barbara's lightness of manner lifted, leaving her tense and rigid once again.

'He doesn't,' she confirmed, with a shake of the head. 'I should have told him first time around – I wish that I had – but I didn't want to worry him. If I tell him now, with all this ... all this other stuff, I don't know what he'll do. That's why I was so cagey about it when you brought it up before.'

She looked up at Helen, assessing. 'And that's what's worrying me. If another one arrives here, when I'm in hospital, and he finds it ... it'll all be so much worse than it needs to be. Would you keep an eye open?'

Helen nodded. 'I don't understand why you don't just put them in the bin, though, Mum?'

'I probably should have, but I threw them out when it happened before. The police told me off – very nicely of course. They said I should keep anything else. I remember a woman officer wagging her finger at me and saying, "You never know". I don't know what she meant by it. I doubt she did, to be honest.' She sighed, wearily. 'So there should be one or two from last time – about three years ago. I could probably put my hands on them if I had to, but I think we've all got bigger things to worry about, don't you?'

Suddenly decisive, Barbara pointed to the jewellery box on her dressing table. 'Put the note in there: the one from downstairs, and any others that come. There's a compartment underneath. They'll be safe there.'

And that was it. Barbara tucked the phone charger down the side of her little wheelie case and zipped it closed.

Helen fingered the notes in her pocket. Were the notes she'd found in the safe years old? Or had they come recently? Barbara's explanation allowed for either possibility, but she couldn't nail it down without admitting to the raid on the safe. She wasn't proud of herself for riffling through her parents' private papers, whether as a teenager or now, and it was her reticence to bring that up that had led her only to ask Barbara about the latest note.

If the notes had been coming sporadically for years, with no sort of escalation, then perhaps her mother was right to ignore it. Helen certainly found that idea more comfortable than the thought that this was something that had kicked off very recently. It was unpleasant, she reasoned, and odd. But not dangerous. As Barbara had said – they both had bigger things to worry about.

# June 2012

*Helen*

All the other NCT mums thought Helen was crackers. Barney was only two weeks old – a red, mewling alien, so tiny his whole being would expand and contract with each precarious breath. Now, rather than sitting back and letting grandparents queue up to fuss over her in the comfort of her own home, Helen was taking Barney to them.

To be fair, she realised they had a point as she packed the car. As soon as the bump became awkward, they had traded up Darren's beloved MX5 for a family-sized Audi. When the new car was delivered, the pair of them had gaped at its interior and laughed when their few lonely shopping bags rolled around and scattered their contents across the felty wilderness of the boot. It had never occurred to them that they would fill the thing, at least not unless another two kids and a decent-sized dog came along. Yet here they were, a few months later, setting off up the M1 on the Jubilee bank holiday weekend, with the boot groaning with baby paraphernalia that they were too scared to leave behind.

But this had been how Helen had wanted it, she mused, as she held Barney's hot little hand between her finger and thumb and gazed down at his snuffling, sleepy form in the car seat. Taking him up north meant she could show him off, but saved her from feeling like she had to play the hostess in her sore and exhausted state. She was sitting beside him in the back and it was all she could do to stop herself from unbuckling him and pulling him close. He'd been a part of her for so long, any physical gap between them seemed somehow wrong.

God knew, she'd survived just fine for long enough without a baby. Thirty-eight wasn't ridiculously old, but given that she and Darren had been together (well, mostly) since high school and married for twelve years, there had certainly been a few raised eyebrows when they'd announced it. Already, though, she couldn't imagine life without this mysterious snuffling bundle.

It was early June and one of the warmest days of the year so far. The daylight seemed to stretch out forever, as if they were chasing the sunset north. That always made the journey feel longer, and this one blurred into a long, fading evening of traffic jams and stops; bad coffee and bored baristas microwaving endless tubs of formula milk; the sound of Barney's crying; that 'Umbrella' song that was never off the radio; and Helen's own seldom-heard singing voice hoarse with 'Twinkle Twinkle'. Finally, the blue signs announced their junction and Darren flicked down the indicator.

'Don't come off here,' she told him. 'I got a text from Dad; go on to the services.'

All the locals used the access road to Moreton Chase as an unofficial junction, but the motorway police closed it from time to time and it was a long trek back from the next official exit if you got caught out.

Even with the shortcut, it was gone eleven by the time they got to Barbara and Neil's, and the hosts looked as tired as their visitors did, though their faces lit up to see them all the same.

'Here's the wee man!' said Neil. 'Bring him in, bring him in. Let's have a proper look. Oh, he's a smasher, Helen.'

The NCT mums had talked about their own mothers being all over their babies. But when Helen went home, it was Neil who held Barney first, who kissed his toes and nudged his pinkie into Barney's hand so the baby's little fingers would curl around it. Barbara stuck the kettle on so Helen could make up a bottle and they could all have a cup of tea that didn't taste of cardboard.

When Barbara finally held him, he reached towards her and did the thing with his mouth that Darren kept saying was going to turn into smiling any day now.

'He likes you, Barbara,' said Neil.

'I think he does.' She smiled down at Barney. 'I also think it's about time he went down for the night.'

Neil held him again, whilst Darren and Helen brought the travel cot in from the car and wrestled it up next to their bed in the spare room. His chest still rose and fell dramatically with every breath, but Helen noticed it wasn't as marked as it had been in those first days. Already her little boy was growing, getting stronger.

'Are you okay?' It was Barbara, passing by with an armful of carrier bags. Helen wondered if her mother would notice the tears threatening to seep from her eyes.

'Deathly tired, that's all.' She smiled. 'It's been a tough couple of weeks.'

She expected her mother to frown, but Barbara just nodded.

'There's nothing harder than coping with a newborn, Helen. You need to be kind to yourself. You and Darren, too.'

'Yeah.'

'I mean it. Don't struggle more than you have to. We can help, and Adam and Christine, of course.'

'We're doing fine.'

'I'm sure you are, Helen.'

Neil opened a red wine he'd been saving and they toasted Barney first, and then, jokingly, the queen. Before long, the glasses were drained. Helen sank into bed, knowing that sleep would take her the moment she shut her eyes and that the next thing she knew would be Barney's mewling hunger dragging her from it.

*Barbara*

Barbara listened for the change in her daughter's breathing as Helen finally succumbed to her exhaustion. For a few moments, she stood by the spare room door, matching her own shuddering breath to Helen's, trying to be slow, trying to be calm. When she was sure that her daughter was asleep, she crept into the bathroom.

The master bedroom had an en suite – Neil had plumbed it in himself ten years earlier and together they'd sponged the walls blue and lavender. The bathroom cabinet was cluttered with stuff that was never used – toiletry gifts that hadn't quite hit the mark and little travel bags that Neil had saved from the occasional business-class flights taken before he retired. Right at the back was a cheap polyester make-up bag. Like everything else, it had gathered a fine film of dust. It wasn't often that she felt the need to get this kit out. She was pleased

51

to note that when she checked over the contents they were immaculate.

Next, she swabbed the toilet lid with a disinfectant wipe, before setting out the cotton wool, the steri-strips, the anti-septic and the pack of blades. Her hands shook as she ripped the cardboard from the packet.

She allowed herself a pause, more breathing and counting to steady herself, but she knew Neil would be back before too long. Of course, he couldn't be expected to understand how difficult she found it to have a baby under her roof. He didn't even know the memories that it brought back. This would help her, just as it had helped when Helen herself was tiny. Neil would hate it but manage to accept it nonetheless, because Neil's best quality was his ability to accept.

The feeling of the blade on her thigh was delicious for an instant, and even after that first golden moment, when the loathing began to pour back in, the sense of satisfaction remained. Now she was steady, now she was in control once more. The blood ran into the shower tray, her anxiety seeping away with it.

She cleaned up quickly, feeling the silvering of old scars under her fingertips as she pressed and wiped the wound.

Later, in bed, Neil's fingers found the neat row of steri-strips.

'Oh, love,' he sighed.

'I'm okay. I won't need to do it again.'

He'd always had a vampire's sense for her blood, and a haemophobe's aversion to it. He drew his hand away abruptly and nestled it in her hair, stroking and soothing – although she was the one who had to do the reassuring. She'd known she would struggle with the baby in the house. These days, she didn't cut often, and she was disappointed in herself that it had come to this, but she'd done what she needed to do. Neil thought the world was about gardens and beauty and patience rewarded. Barbara liked that about him, but in her heart she believed it came down to much less than that – just people doing what they needed to do.

A few hours later they made love, when they'd both been asleep and could pretend more or less to be sleeping still. It was the first time in many weeks, and, in the morning, when the memory of their silent and familiar coupling came back to Barbara, it made her smile. She recalled bittersweet moments from their past, and the fact that Neil was perhaps not so much of a haemophobe as he liked to have her believe.

*Helen*

The next morning, Darren took Barney to meet his other grandparents. They would all be going over for dinner, but Helen's day had been going since four a.m., not counting the two a.m. feed. His suggestion that she try to grab a nap had been welcome, but sleep didn't come easily – partly because Barney wasn't nearby. And it wasn't helping that dawn had been hours ago. Again, she felt the endless daylight was stalking her.

Eventually, Barbara stuck her head around the door. 'Shall I bring you up a cuppa?'

'No. Hopefully I'll get to sleep. Thanks, anyway.'

Ten minutes later she was still lying there. It was bright outside and the closed curtains cast a jaundiced glow about the room without achieving any semblance of darkness. She heard the kettle go on, and the steps on the staircase shortly after.

Barbara edged round the door with a mug in each hand, peering at Helen to check if her eyes were open before speaking.

'I thought I'd make two, just in case you were still awake.'

'Thanks.' Helen gave up and pushed herself up against the headboard. She was slightly unnerved by her mother's thoughtfulness. Barbara was efficient, witty and even generous, but in Helen's experience, her admirable qualities didn't usually extend to anything resembling tenderness. 'Don't suppose you've got any headache pills?'

Barbara quickly fetched a pack from her own bedroom, and a glass of water.

'Are you coping, Helen? I hope you'd tell me.'

Helen went to shake her head but stopped because it hurt.

'It's okay – tiring. Everyone struggles a bit, though – it's normal.'

'Of course it's normal,' Barbara said, even though Helen had not meant it as a question. 'God knows I've never been one for newborns—'

'Haven't you?' asked Helen. She couldn't remember seeing her mother fuss over a baby, but then she couldn't remember there being many babies around. And Barbara wasn't a fusser over anything.

'Better when they grow up a bit ... By mid-thirties it's much easier!'

Barbara's laughter sounded forced, as though she felt this should be an intimate moment and was working desperately to make it happen. Helen laughed along, but a little cautiously.

'You know, Helen, I'll admit I found it difficult to feel close to you when you were younger. Your dad found it much easier, and then you two were so natural together ... Anyway, I want you to know I'm not judging you.' Now Barbara gave a sharp laugh. 'I'm the last person to judge anyone.'

There was a lump in Helen's throat. It was as much to do with her mother's rarely spoken of pride in her, with a vague sense of Barbara's own missed opportunities, as with the fact Helen was knackered, but most of all it was grief for the shared understanding she should have had with this woman, her mother, that they'd somehow missed out on along the way.

Helen wanted to reassure her mother that she did care about her, that she'd always cared about her, even though Barbara had made it as hard as she could. The thoughts and words buzzed in Helen's head but she couldn't marshal them; she couldn't trust herself. She'd always felt somehow that her birth had spoiled things for her mother. That was the conclusion she'd drawn from the never-spoken-about gaps in Barbara's past. And that was why, she reasoned, Barbara could never feel about Helen the way Helen felt about Barney.

# August 2017

*Helen*

Barbara had still been on her laptop when Neil was ready to leave for the hospital. He'd put her bag in the boot, checked the admissions letter twice and was now shuffling by the front door.

'I'm just tying up loose ends. You don't want me taking it with me, do you?' Barbara called down to them.

'What's she doing on it these days, anyway – I thought she'd pretty much retired?' Helen asked her father.

He shrugged. 'Open data. Citizen journalism. Crowd science. None of it makes a jot of sense to me, but she's always got something going on. Keeps her sharp, she says, and I suppose it seems to work.'

They heard the computer power down and then Barbara emerged on the stairs. She and Neil went out to the car. Helen took the children to wave at the window. Neil's face was strained and she regretted not taking the chance to ask him how he was whilst Barbara was busy. Still, it underlined Barbara's point about the notes: he wasn't a man who needed anything extra to worry about.

Pat from next door rushed over to the car with a card in

her hand and both Neil and Barbara looked to be trying hard to seem pleased to see her, without managing to succeed.

Normally, Helen only insisted the kids come to the window to wave when the grandparents had been staying with them and were leaving to drive home. Barney was clearly bored by waiting for them to actually get into the car and couldn't get back to CBeebies quickly enough. Alys, though, was confused.

'Granddad Neil and Nana Barbara go to our house?' she asked, as the car finally pulled away.

'No, Nana is going to hospital for a few days. Granddad will be back later.'

'And Nana.'

'No, just Granddad.'

'Granddad can come to our house.' She was nodding firmly, as if that decided it.

'No, we need to stay here a bit longer. We need to wait for Nana to come home.'

'Daddy come here.'

*God*, thought Helen, *please don't start this now.* 'No ...' she began patiently, getting ready to explain once again.

'Not no!' Alys shouted. 'Daddy come now!'

She was pointing out of the window. Helen hadn't even registered the car that had pulled into the cul-de-sac a few moments after Neil's Nissan had turned out of it. It was a silver Astra, badged up by a hire company.

*Fuck.* Alys was right. He was three days early.

Darren jumped out of the driver's seat and bounded onto the drive, before catching sight of them in the window and veering across the lawn, waving at Alys.

Frantically, Helen strained to see if there was anyone else in the car, but he seemed to be alone. Alys's voice rose to a clamour and by this time Barney had left the television and was hauling himself up to stand on the sofa and see what was going on.

'Daddydaddydaddydaddydaddydaddydaddydaddy.'

'Feet *down*, please, Barney.'

He ignored her and the volume of the children's joyous duet surged ever upward. Darren didn't disappoint, miming his excitement through the double glazing whilst studiously failing to meet Helen's eye.

Of course, she had no choice but to let him come in. After as few terse words as she could manage, Helen left the living room and let the three of them get on with it.

She went to the spare room first, but that immediately felt wrong, so instead she crept upstairs and into the womblike snugness of her childhood bedroom. She sat in the corner of the single bed, leaning against the wall, with Barney's precious blanket tucked between her knees, straining to listen and to keep the tears from falling.

*Bastard. Bastard. Bastard.*

\*

Helen studied the lilac, swirly wallpaper she'd picked out when she was fourteen, trying to match up the ghostly, faded squares with the posters and pages ripped from magazines that had once decorated her walls. Michael J. Fox over there, later replaced by John Squire. George Michael, replaced by John Squire. She pictured the various incarnations, trying to switch off her brain.

Eventually she heard his footsteps on the stairs. He'd lasted about forty-five minutes, which was more time than he'd spent alone with Barney and Alys together in as long as she could remember, not counting soft play. He opened the door without knocking and walked into the room. She stayed hunched up on the bed, looking over his shoulder instead of directly at him, but still catching the look of mild pity as he gazed down at her.

'What the fuck do you think you're doing turning up here?' she asked.

It wasn't brilliant, but she was proud that she had managed to spit it out, past the lump in her throat and the decades of conditioned politeness. Darren didn't answer immediately, probably weighing up his options.

'They're my kids. I had to see them, Helen. I didn't have any choice.'

'Well now you've seen them.'

She was going to add 'fuck off', but in the end it seemed too crude, too teenage. The pair of them fell into silence. Then Darren dropped down to a sitting position, closing the door to lean his back against it and laying his long legs out across the only stretch of carpet in the tiny room where they fitted. He should know. Years ago, he used to play guitar sitting like that for hours, while she was revising or reading or just watching him. Hard to believe it was the same person.

'My mum said Barbara's going in today, that the op's tomorrow?'

'I'd like you to leave.'

He bit his lip and then put a finger to it. For a moment, she sensed he was about to slam his hand against something, but he seemed to hold himself back.

'I miss you, Helen.'

She said nothing.

'I know I chose this, I know it's my fault. But that doesn't mean I don't miss you. We grew up together, didn't we? No one knows me like you do, and I know what you're going through as much as anyone can. I'm sorry about it, Hels, I really am.'

'Are you asking to come back?'

Now it was Darren's turn for silence. He wriggled an index finger into the pile of the carpet and stared at the holes he was making.

'We've been through all this,' he whispered. 'You know it's not been right for ages. This is better for both of us.' But then he rushed on, whip-quick, as if to head off any disagreement from her. 'But the point is I can help you. And I want to. For the kids. And for us, for everything we were. You've got to let me, Hels.'

She shouldn't have agreed, she thought later.

In truth, she didn't agree. She didn't say anything. But her silence was acquiescence enough.

She let him bring her a cup of tea and put the kids in front of a film. She let him sit on the single bed next to her, the weight and the smell of him on the homely sheets just as intoxicating and incongruous as it had been twenty-odd years earlier. She poured out the details of surgery and staging, metastasis and Macmillan nurses. She even told him about the green notes. He seemed perfectly happy with Barbara's explanation about the teenage shoplifter. 'There are some fucked-up weirdos in this world, Hels.' He laughed. 'That's one thing you learn running a dating business.'

The words had come out of her like a dam burst, but Darren caught every last drop, and mopped them up and dealt with them like he mopped the tears from her cheeks. She didn't even need to tell him where to find the tissues. Was it just a performance for her benefit? To persuade her to let him see more of the kids, or to soften her up for whatever he and Lauren were planning next? She felt she ought to be more cynical, but she was too exhausted and wrung out to do anything but accept the sympathy on offer.

Her friends were far away and had their own worries. They'd all drifted apart since they started having families – literally as well as metaphorically, as they had moved out in different directions to various London suburbs. She missed the gossip and the laughter, but Darren had always been her emotional anchor. In her twenties, she'd provided the shoulder to cry on as her friends went through dating disasters and relationship break-ups. Now, finally, she was the one in need and the only confidant she'd ever needed was the one whose betrayal was ripping her to shreds.

Eventually, after a snack with the kids and about four cups of tea, and after he'd taken off his socks because he always preferred bare feet, and after Helen had finished one box of Kleenex and, shamefully, got him to refill the screen wash on her car, he said he should go.

They agreed he'd have the kids on Thursday, assuming Barbara's operation the day before had gone okay, and take them somewhere for the day. Both Barney and Alys had been very forbearing whilst their parents sat alone upstairs and that pricked at her – between her and Darren they were turning them into diplomats. On the doorstep, Darren paused awkwardly and she let him falter, but he turned away without a kiss, or a handshake, or any touch at all. She thought about the way they'd been in the bedroom and wondered if different rules applied there. Barney and Alys waved the Astra off quite happily, without asking any questions.

'Was it nice to see Daddy?' she asked.

They both nodded and 'yes-yessed' enthusiastically.

'Daddy smelt happy,' said Barney, quietly.

'Really? What do you mean?'

But he just shrugged and tried to grab a piece of jigsaw from Alys's hand.

It killed her that even Barney could see Darren was happier now. Happier having abandoned his family. Happier without her. Happier with carefree, bright-eyed, not-yet-thirty Lauren.

\*

Neil went back to the hospital at seven the next morning. It was Wednesday already; tomorrow they'd have been away from home for a week and she had no idea when they'd be going back. She tried to occupy herself with washing the kids' clothes and making a list of extras she should pick up for them from the supermarket, whilst waiting for news from the hospital. Neil sent a text when Barbara was going into theatre and then one when she came out; another when she'd started to come round from the anaesthetic and another when they'd let him in to see her in the recovery room. It had all gone 'by the book' he said, though Helen guessed those were Mr Eklund's words, or someone else at the hospital. They'd get the first proper update on what they had found on the Thursday ward round, by which point it was expected that Barbara would be well enough to take it in.

It was early evening by the time Neil was able to report that Barbara was back on the ward. They'd planned for him to come home then, but when it came to it, he didn't want to leave her alone. Eventually, Helen persuaded him that he should drive back around the kids' bedtime and that she would go in and sit with Barbara through the night. When he came back and she saw him in the flesh, she was glad she'd insisted. He looked wearier than she remembered ever seeing him. The day had clearly taken everything he had to give.

As soon as she'd kissed the kids – both sleeping soundly, thank God – he was gently hurrying her out. She insisted on delaying long enough to make sure he ate the pasta bake she'd left for him, and wondered bleakly whether anyone would get so concerned about her by the time she was Barbara's age.

It was going dark by the time Helen arrived, and the strange, unnatural half-light of the hospital corridors made her feel suddenly weary. Barbara was in a half-private cubicle set back from the main ward. The young nurse on night duty explained that visitors were allowed in tonight because she was just out of surgery. Soon she'd be moved into the ward itself and visiting hours would have to be observed.

The heels of Helen's ankle boots clipped loudly on the few steps between the ward door and Barbara's cubicle, and she peered anxiously into the gloom, hoping she'd not woken up any of the other patients. The nurse left as soon as Helen was settled in the chair, closing the ward door carefully behind her and slipping off, rubber-soled, into the shadows. Helen had no chance to ask her anything.

Barbara lay there like a storybook invalid, her head back against the semi-propped pillows, eyelids lowered and hands folded on the blanket. Her skin had an oniony look, translucent, papery, unhealthy. It was as if the operation had somehow removed a layer of her. Helen was shocked by the difference from the previous day, when she'd looked whole and wholesome – give or take the odd liver spot and the dark circles under her eyes.

She sat down in the plastic armchair and laid her hand over her mother's. She couldn't decide if Barbara was too cold or if she herself was too hot. Barbara's eyelids didn't flicker. By now, Helen had tuned in to the shallow sound of her breathing. She let herself fall into its rhythm.

# June 1963

*Katy*

The honeysuckle made no difference; Katy couldn't tell them anything.

The builders and their machines had changed the very shape of the earth. It had been moulded and flattened and moulded again, like the sandpits in the infant school.

'Well, did you come in to the left of the oak, or the right of the oak? The damn tree's not moved!' The sergeant with the moustache was making no effort to hide his annoyance.

Katy could remember there being trees; she didn't know if the one he was waving at had been one of them. She wanted to tell him that she'd been terrified and panicking. That she'd barely slept and it was the furthest she'd ever gone from home on her own. When she thought about that day, it was through a fog of guilt, the horror of what she'd done weighing down on her with each day she got older, each day she spent at Ashdown. Mr Robertson might understand, but she knew this man never would.

'I only remember there being a road sweeping up ahead of me,' she said, and the muscles round her mouth twitched oddly as she fought back tears. 'There was a bank of loose earth and stones. That's where ... that's where ...'

'It's okay.' Miss Silver stepped closer, patting her arm.

'It's bloody well not okay,' interjected the policeman. 'How far from the site perimeter was this road? How far did you have to walk to get to it?'

Katy shook her head. She couldn't answer.

'How was the road orientated? Which direction did it go in?'

'I don't know.' Her lips formed the words, but there was no voice.

The man's face was in hers now. She could see the smattering of ginger hairs in his brown moustache, and the spittle catching at the corners of his lips.

'There were signs bloody everywhere; what did the signs say? How high was this banking? How far were you from the building itself?'

Eventually it was over. The little group picked its way across the field and back to the car park, the policeman muttering darkly about not having any more of this sort of little jolly. Katy managed to keep her silence, though a few tears escaped down her cheeks. They didn't sting like they had in the cold of January. The inspector went ahead to where Etta Gardiner stood, the same constable still by her side. Katy couldn't hear what he said, but she heard Etta's loud gasp and saw the inspector's white handkerchief flutter as he pulled it out to comfort her. Although they kept a good distance away, Katy's cheeks burned as they walked past, feeling Etta's gaze track her all the way to the Austin.

That was it. They wouldn't be back in time for dinner and would have to get something on the road, Mr Robertson noted with a strained cheerfulness. For a moment, Katy imagined running. Never having to go back to Ashdown with its menace and melancholy and stink of boiled cabbage. She could bury her face in the smell of the wet earth and go to sleep cradled in the scent of honeysuckle without ever waking up.

She didn't run. It would give the creep with the moustache too much satisfaction.

As Mr Robertson made heavy weather of turning the Austin, she caught a final glimpse of Etta through the window. There was a man beside her, his slim, slightly hunched figure unmistakable. Simon Gardiner handed his wife a posy of white narcissus and linked arms with her to walk towards the fence where Katy guessed the flowers were to be laid. Etta leant in to him as they walked the few steps, almost collapsing in his arms as they drew to a pause.

*White for innocence*, Katy thought. *If only you knew, Etta Gardiner.*

The Austin wheeled round abruptly and the tableau was gone.

Katy made a silent vow. *One day I'll show her what he is. One day I'll show everyone.*

# August 2017

*Helen*

Giving up on sleep, Helen had gone to get a coffee. It was after two a.m., but there was a twenty-four-hour kiosk in the main foyer. She strolled around the deserted tables to stretch her legs, nodding to a couple of medics on their break. She paused to look at a gaudy poster about the fundraising efforts for a new cancer centre.

Not wanting to be away for too long, she returned to Barbara's ward, still clutching her paper cup, and slipped through the doorway. A nurse was bent over paperwork at a small desk that had been empty before. She lifted her head to smile and Helen caught the faint scent of toothpaste as she walked past. The late shift at the hospital was giving way to the early one.

In Barbara's cubicle, the figure in the bed looked exactly the same as when Helen had left her: still lying on her back, the same shallow breathing lifting the cellular blanket only a touch with each inhalation. Helen felt an unexpected surge of relief.

She settled herself, then simply sat and held Barbara's hand, just as she had done before. She was achingly tired, and her mind felt dull. How many people were awake in this building just now? she wondered. There must be babies being born here – as she had been born here. There must be other grown-up children holding the hands of parents and wondering if their time together was coming to an end. Did any of them feel only numbness instead of the grief and worry that she'd expected to feel? Did this distance and lack of feeling make her a bad daughter? No, 'bad' was the wrong word – an unnatural daughter, that was more what she felt. And if she was an unnatural daughter, was it her fault or Barbara's?

She swept back through her memory, looking for moments of love, special times that she and Barbara had shared, trying to conjure some missing fondness, almost in the way that, as a child, she found thinking of her neighbour's dead cat helped to stop her getting the giggles when she was in trouble with a teacher.

There were certainly happy images. Her disbelief when she was allowed the biggest chocolate sundae in the world at an ice cream shop in Italy. Jumping the waves on a beach in France the day after a thunderstorm. Her tenth birthday party, which had been a surprise, with all her school friends jumping out from behind the sofa when the family returned from a 'grown-up' celebratory pub lunch.

Her childhood, on the whole, had been a happy one. But in every mental picture her dad's face was clearer – shining with joy, sharing her laughter, showing tender concern about some childhood malady. Neil had worked full-time until his retirement. Barbara worked on the newspaper only two days a week when Helen was in primary school, a little more after she went to the high. Those hours together had made little imprint on her memory, it seemed. The best she could

69

recall was that they were filled with books and TV and homework. That she kept out of her mother's way, without really knowing why. Or was it Barbara who had been keeping out of hers?

There was a movement from the bed and the limp hand Helen had been holding gripped back. When it was clear that Barbara was waking up, Helen manoeuvred the bed and the pillows to prop her up a bit, and then held the glass that she'd filled to her mother's lips.

'So how do you feel, Mum?'

'Okay,' she said, then sipped again. 'Sore.'

The nurse from the desk appeared, gently tugging the curtain back.

'I heard your voices,' she said. 'Doing okay this morning?'

'Just sore,' Barbara repeated, and the nurse nodded sympathetically. 'There's a painkiller in your drip, but I can get you a tablet too if you can take it. And breakfast will be around in an hour or so. I'll tell them just to try you on some toast for now.'

Helen wasn't sure if Barbara had heard. Her eyes closed slowly and the rhythm of her breathing changed.

'She'll be dozy after the anaesthetic,' said the nurse, a little unnecessarily.

Helen nodded. She was so tired that she was still nodding to the nurse's back as she replaced the clipboard in its holder and walked off down the ward.

*

Neil turned up about half past ten. Darren had picked up the children as arranged and Neil had jumped in the car the minute they'd gone. He was just in time to see Barbara's third session of dry-heaving. Just the smell of the toast had set her off and she'd not had much peace from it since.

'Oh, love,' he said, bending down to hold her shoulders as she shuddered over the paper bowl. 'That's it, that's it, there you go.'

When it was done, she fell back on his arm and let him lower her down to the propped-up pillows. A thread of spit trailed from the corner of her mouth, and she was too exhausted this time to even take a sip of water.

'It's the anaesthetic,' Helen told him. 'The nurse says it should pass in twenty-four hours.'

Neil grilled her for more information that she didn't have. The consultants hadn't done their rounds yet and it was pretty obvious that Barbara wasn't really in a state to take anything on board anyway. Helen really wanted to ask him about Darren and the kids, but he brushed off her first attempt, telling her they'd both slept like troopers and gone off happily this morning – Darren was taking them to some soft play centre apparently. She didn't want to seem uncaring, focusing on her own children rather than on Barbara, so she bit her tongue.

It was a shock for Neil to see his wife looking so fragile, Helen could tell. Having been there since Barbara woke up, she'd had more of a chance to get used to it. If anything, Helen felt there was perhaps a little bit of colour coming back to her cheeks – when she wasn't throwing up, obviously. But Neil looked dismayed, and even as Helen filled him in on what time Barbara had woken up and what the nurse had said, she could see his wide eyes darting back to the bed, taking in every detail.

71

Eventually, Barbara opened her eyes, smiled at him, and gestured for the water.

'You never could keep away,' she whispered.

'Of course not. Oh, Barbara ...' he bent to kiss her cheek, '... you're looking wonderful, love. You're going to be out of here in no time.' He said it fiercely, as if he could wish it hard enough to make it true. Helen couldn't meet his eye, but she saw that Barbara did. She wanted to be happy for her mother – for them both – but all she could think of was that Darren wouldn't be there to say that if it was her.

They made some desultory conversation about the weather and then about the two new families in Neil and Barbara's street and the building work they were planning. Barbara could nod, or make the occasional comment, and Helen and Neil felt like they were entertaining her. After a while, the trolley came round with some pasta and tomato sauce – nominally this was lunchtime – and Barbara managed not to be sick, although she asked them to swap it for toast. A little later, she even ate a few mouthfuls.

'We could bring you something in,' offered Neil. 'Some nice biscuits, or a jam sandwich? Those cheesy crackers? What would tickle your fancy?'

Barbara looked a little green.

'I think she just needs a day or so to recover her appetite,' Helen said. 'We'll have plenty of time to bring stuff in.

'Shouldn't you be getting back to the children?' Barbara asked, probably just to try to change the subject away from food.

'Darren's taking them out for the day. To be honest, though,' Helen said, taking her opportunity, 'I could really do with a shower. Do you both mind if I—'

'No, no, no,' her parents flustered in unison. 'You get home, love,' continued Neil. 'Get a bit of kip if you can – it'll do you good.'

*

In the bathroom, she saw Barbara's cake of Chanel No. 5 soap sitting on the windowsill. It was carefully placed on a folded flannel, drying in the sunshine so that she could rewrap it in its embossed tissue paper and slip it back inside the plastic soapbox and then its cardboard box; but she must never have gotten round to completing the task. The sight of it caught Helen off-guard; she'd forgotten all about that little ritual of her mother's.

She didn't have to pick up the soap to smell it; the perfume still hung heavy in the warm, close air. Gulping it down as her breathing turned ragged and the tears came, somehow the scent had thawed the numbness that had consumed her in the hospital.

There was no point in trying to stop it – Helen let her crying keen out unchecked through the empty house. The ugly, screeching noises seemed to scratch at the walls like trapped wild beasts. In some distant, unmoved part of her mind, she registered mild surprise that she could sound like that. Then she carried on anyway.

The shame of it was that the crying wasn't for Barbara, or even for Neil, though that was part of it. She was crying for herself; for the loss of her mother, for the sort of mother she'd never had in the first place, for the family that was slipping away from her. She'd never bargained for this. She didn't deserve it. She wailed, like Alys might, simply because it wasn't fair.

73

The shower helped, though, and once she was calmer, there was some small comfort to be had in being able to take time to dry her hair properly, to smooth on some body lotion and file her nails, but she was constantly remembering that the time was hers only because Barney and Alys were with Darren. She tormented herself with the thought of what a wonderful time they would be having, of them not wanting to come back, and, worst of all, of the inevitable moment in the future when Darren would insist on them meeting *her*. Whilst she could just about stomach the thought of the kids being happy in the company of their father, she felt very different when she pictured a perfect, nuclear family unit that she wasn't part of.

Gradually, the thoughts took on a relentless, tinnitus-like quality, thrumming incessantly through her over-weary mind. She tried to take a nap but was too strung out to sleep; then she picked up her novel, but put it down again after reading the same paragraph three times.

Barbara and Neil still had a VHS player. Eventually, Helen put on a second pair of socks, retrieved a pack of custard creams from the kitchen and looked on the shelf for her old copy of *Dirty Dancing*. She had to blow the dust off the case before she opened it. It felt surreal, putting on a film (and not a cartoon) in the middle of the day, with the sunlight streaming in the window, but she just prayed that her teenage favourite would give her racing mind a break.

The custard creams were finished before Johnny and Baby even got to the watermelons. It worked as well as Helen could have hoped, suppressing the thrumming of worries in her mind.

Then the call came from Neil.

'Helen?'

'Yes?'

'It's your mum – you've got to come quickly.' The panic was clear in his voice.

'What is it?'

'She's being sick—'

She felt her shoulders relax a fraction and jumped to reassure him.

'They said it was the anaesthetic, Dad. I think it's normal, for some people anyway. Have you spoken to a nurse?'

'It's not normal, Helen, she's bringing up blood. They're talking about intensive care. You need to just get here.'

'I'm coming.'

It was a fifteen-minute drive to the hospital, but it took an eternity. Her heart pounded all the way, with the thought of Barbara in pain and Neil anxious and afraid. She had no idea whether she really should be panicking. Nobody had suggested things could go badly once Barbara had come out of the recovery room and back to the ward – at least not in the short term. Surely she was in the best place and whatever it was they could hook her up to a machine and get it 'stabilised', as they always said on the TV?

Helen had recognised from that first trip with them to Mr Eklund that Neil was finding the hospital difficult, that he felt out of his depth and – there was no other word for it – terrified. She still had hope that her dad had just had a panic, that she'd get there to be told it was a fuss about nothing, and her parents would be sitting in the cubicle happily watching some quiz show or cookery repeat on the mini bedside TV.

She found a parking space near the main door – she'd

already bought a weekly permit for her own car and insisted on doing the same for Neil's – and hurried in.

They weren't watching TV. As soon as she entered the ward, she could see the hubbub of people around Barbara's bed. There were eight or nine of them clustered into the little room, some bent over her, two holding IV lines, and Neil standing a couple of footsteps outside the door, looking smaller than she'd ever seen him.

'Helen!'

She gave him a hurried hug, and then turned to look through the glass at Barbara. If she'd looked bad before, she looked deathly now. Her skin was chalk-like, paler than the white sheets that she was lying on. She was wearing a breathing mask, which seemed to cover most of her face, but her eyes burnt out above it, bloodshot, widened and, above all, scared.

Neil pulled Helen back when she tried to step into the room.

'They said not to. They need the space.'

She was still taking it in as she stepped back – the extra lines now attaching her mother to various machines, and the ominous red-brown stains on the bed. Then a woman in civvies – an open-neck shirt and some tailored trousers – turned away from the bed and stuck her head out of the room.

'You must be Mrs Marsden's daughter? I'm Rebecca Evans. I'm a consultant here. There's a trolley on its way to transfer your mother to the intensive care unit. She should be fine, but we need to take the precaution. I'll have to ask you and Mr Marsden to stand back please.'

The woman gestured towards some chairs by the nurses' station, but Helen had no intention of being herded off into a corner.

'First, tell me what's going on? This morning she was doing fine. They said she just needed to get the last of the anaesthetic out of her system. Surely she can't have had a reaction this late?'

The woman shook her head. 'It's not the anaesthetic. I can't—'

She stopped speaking as the main ward doors opened and two men wheeled a trolley through at speed. She waved her hand towards the chairs again and this time Helen stepped backward. Without even bothering to check if she'd gone, the consultant turned back to the bed, barking out incomprehensible instructions to the nurses and porters. The transfer was made in seconds, despite all the tubes and wires that Barbara suddenly seemed to have coming out of her.

Three or four of the nurses hung back. Barbara was out of their hands now. The others advanced down the ward together, surrounding the trolley like it was some kind of battering ram, with Ms Evans setting a brisk pace in her low heels.

The eldest of the ward nurses came over to where Neil and Helen were standing.

'They'll let you know when you can see her,' she said. 'Come into the office; that way we'll be ready when they buzz for you.'

She had a kindly, grandmotherly way about her, and they followed meekly, walking the length of the ward with the eyes of all the patients and visitors moving silently with them. Geranium Ward clearly wasn't used to seeing much in the way of medical high-drama.

Helen and Neil sat down and the nurse quickly left, saying something about getting someone to make them a cuppa. She seemed to recognise that they needed a bit of privacy. The office smelt of mints and bleach, with just the faintest trace of cigarette smoke. *I'd take one*, Helen thought, *if someone offered.* She'd not smoked since her teens.

The wall was decorated with a single, faded Monet print in a Perspex frame that reflected all the movement from the ward. Life didn't stop because of a visit from the crash team. There were still bedpans to be dealt with, antibacterial protocols to follow and endless charts to be checked off and stuffed back into their clipboards.

'She was bringing up blood, Helen.' Neil's voice was low, and he looked at the floor rather than her. 'Not just a bit – it was just gushing out of her. Coming from her nose as well, even one of her ears at one point.'

Helen thought back to the stains she'd seen on the bed. How awful.

She just couldn't understand it. There had been no suggestion of any cancer in Barbara's digestive system. No one had mentioned any side effects or surgical complications that could look like this. And it had all seemed to be going so smoothly, completely 'by the book', as they'd all been saying yesterday. She didn't know what to say to Neil. She was the one who had read all the leaflets, gone online; she was the one who was meant to know what to expect, and nothing had – nothing could have – prepared her for this.

There was a niggling voice in her head that said maybe there was a reason for that. Could it be that this was something more sinister than a symptom or a side effect? Jennifer, whoever she was, had promised to make Barbara suffer. And Helen doubted she'd suffered anything in her life like the last few hours. What if the notes weren't just empty threats? What if this time Jennifer meant it for real? Helen felt giddy. Was she putting two and two together and getting eleven? Or should she listen to the instinct screaming at her that this was anything but an accident?

She reached out for Neil's hand, and he let her take it, though his eyes remained fixed on the tight brown weave of the carpet tiles.

# May 1990

*Helen*

Spike Island wasn't actually an island. It was a bit of land jutting out into the Mersey estuary, with the St Helen's canal slicing down one side and a great view of a power station. Helen's heart thrilled with anticipation for the gig. The thing about Stone Roses songs was that they were totally different to any other music she'd ever heard. The guitar riffs didn't play in her ears, they flowed through her veins.

She gazed around at the mass of people, all heading in the same direction. Many had Roses T-shirts and, as the crowd thickened, older men materialised with armfuls of cheap knock-offs for those who didn't.

'Tenner a T-shirt, two for fifteen quid.'

'Buying or selling, buying or selling.'

Helen grabbed for Darren's fingers as the crowd pressed in on them, but it was just a bottleneck and soon they were through and heading towards the stage. He dropped her hand so he could rummage in his pockets for Rizlas. She glanced at him, still struggling to believe that the fittest boy in the year had picked her. His T-shirt skimmed his flat stomach and broad shoulders, his dark hair giving just a hint of a shadow through the thin material. She felt her cheeks flush.

The music from the PA was thumping, but nobody was dancing. Instead they sat or roamed around in little groups, checking their watches and shouting to their mates. They'd only come forty minutes south – the first time Darren had driven on the motorway by himself since he'd passed his test the month before – but somehow this felt like a very different place. The strangest thing, she realised gradually, was the accents. She'd never heard so many Liverpool accents before. These kids didn't have the hard, nasal voices of the ticket touts, far less Harry Enfield's slapstick Scouse. Most of them spoke in a gentle, sing-song way. It was nice. They sounded like her mum.

'I wonder if there are any Kiplings here,' she said to Darren, quietly.

'What?' He just sounded confused.

'You know; my mum's family that she never talks about. She's got a Liverpool accent; if I've got cousins or whatever, they're probably Scousers.'

Darren pretended to scan the crowd. 'Nope, don't see your long-lost twin. Oh! Wait a minute ...'

He'd picked out an ageing hippy with pink dreads and mud splattered up her mirror-embroidered skirt. She had one hand out, leaning against one of the filthy toilet blocks, and she looked as if she might fall down without it.

'Ha ha.'

'Come on, Hels, your mum is a bit weird, isn't she?'

Was she? She'd never thought of her as weird before he said it. 'How do you mean?'

'Like, just *odd*, you know.'

'Tell me.'

Darren looked uncomfortable. He stubbed out the last of his joint and began to scratch at his forearm.

'Forget it,' he muttered. 'Let's get some of those chips you were on about before.'

It was almost nine o'clock by the time the band finally came onstage. As the tension built, the two of them had pushed forward along with the rest of the crowd. The sky was darkening and there were lights – red and purple – picking out parts of the stage and the throng of fans Helen could feel the beat thumping in her chest and see it pulsating through the bodies around her. Everyone was psyched. Everyone knew that this was colossal. They'd tell their grandkids they were here.

Then the band ran onto the stage, waving their arms and lapping up the applause, Ian Brown kicking a football into the crowd like a returning hero. Everyone around them surged forward even more. Helen didn't scream, but she gasped, involuntarily, and then felt her own intake of breath echoed by twenty thousand more around her. As one, the crowd sucked the air from the Merseyside sky and for a fraction of a moment it seemed that everything was still – the lights stopped swinging, the smoke rolling down from the stage seemed to freeze and Helen felt her own heartbeat trip over itself. She felt Darren's arms around her, anchoring her. She knew he was The One. She wanted to make this last forever.

*Neil*

Nothing could have prepared Neil for the exquisite torture of witnessing Helen shrug off childhood and become – almost – a woman. He felt it most when he saw her dressed up on a Saturday night, giggling with her friends, the lot of them thinking their tiny skirts and mascara-weighted eyes were great and not realising it was the innocence underneath that made them gorgeous. They were good girls, even a bit naive, and they handled themselves like a bunch of kittens dancing through a minefield.

That night, he waited up for her. He'd tried not to, then made excuses to himself that he was just not feeling tired, that he may as well watch the match he'd recorded at the weekend.

When the car pulled up, he was dozing, but he sprung to his feet in an instant, frowning as he peered into the street. A moment later she was clattering through the door.

'Dad! What are you doing waiting up?'

'Just snoozing, love. I dozed off.'

'You worry too much.'

'Quite right, I do. Who's that anyway? It's not Darren's car.'

She hugged him, the same fierce squeeze she'd had as a child. It seemed like moments ago.

'Just a bunch of girls,' she said, emphasising the *girls*. 'They're from round here, at college in Leyland. Darren and I got separated; it was all pretty manic.'

Neil swallowed back the interrogation he wanted to launch into. The important thing was she was safe. The rest could wait.

'So ... the concert was good?'

'*Gig*, Dad, you call it a gig.'

'The *gig* was good, then?'

She squeezed him again, and when she stepped back and looked up at him, her eyes were bright as electricity. He thought about the article Barbara had pulled from the Sunday supplement a few weeks ago – telltale signs your teen is on drugs. There was something about dilated pupils – or was it narrow pupils? – he couldn't quite remember.

'Well, I can't wait to hear about it, but I think I need to get my old bones to bed now.'

'Me too.'

By the time he'd put away the few dishes from the draining board, locked up and cleaned his teeth, he could hear gentle snoring already coming from her bedroom. He crept in and stroked her forehead, pushing stray hairs off her make-up-smudged face. He could still see that little girl's face underneath. His precious gift from Barbara, who had never wanted children, but loved him enough to agree, eventually, to just one. Neil had always known he had to get it right with Helen. There would be no second chances.

## Helen

The day after the gig Helen was in her bedroom, supposedly studying Franco's Spain for her History A-Level, but mainly humming guitar riffs, when Neil stuck his head round the door.

'Fancy coming out to the greenhouse and giving me a hand with the tomatoes, love?'

She frowned. 'I should be revising.'

'And are you?' His question went unanswered. 'Come on, a half-hour break will do you good. You can get back to it fresh.'

'Go on then.'

She wasn't good company. The memory of the night before was still fizzing inside her like sherbet. She didn't have much to say, then she giggled into the tomatoes.

'What's got into you, Duckface?' asked Neil. 'Laughing at nothing? First sign of madness, you know.'

'Nothing's up. And don't call me that.'

'What? Mad?'

'No. Duckface!' He always called her Duckface.

'Right you are, Duckbum.'

'I was just thinking about the gig, actually. You see, Dad, most of the people there had Liverpool accents – they reminded me of Mum. Where *did* she grow up? Do you know that much?'

Neil's head jerked forward as he bit down on the twine he was using to tie up the tomato plants. She winced at the noise it made as he found a weak spot and shredded the fibres in his teeth. He always did that and it always went through her. He handed her the short length and she tried to ignore the fact that it was still wet with his spittle at its end.

'Can't help you, love,' he said, once five or six lengths of twine had been bitten off. She caught the hint of a frown pass across his brow.

'It just feels weird, you know, knowing nothing about Mum's side. I've tried to ask her, but she just clams up, even when it's something for school. She says she's left them behind and we're her family, us and Nan and Granddad and Auntie Vicky. She says that's all the family she needed.'

Neil must have noticed the disappointment in her face and his voice became gentler.

'Look, your mum never told me much of her family, neither. And if there was anything I ever did know, it wouldn't be my place to tell you. But that only means that you're even more special to her. Think what you've got and what she's missing, eh? For whatever reason. Don't be hard on her.'

'All right, Dad.'

She pushed away her thoughts about her mother and concentrated on the tomatoes. Their viny smell was almost overpowering in the greenhouse – the smell of Neil and summer for as long as Helen could remember. Now it was mixed in with her own cheap body spray – vanilla and something.

'Hels!'

The shout made her look up. Darren was framed in the back doorway, looking annoyed and cradling his forearm across his chest.

'Darren's here, Dad, I'm going in.'

'All right, Duckbum, thanks for helping.'

'Hey,' she called to Darren, breathless from rushing up from the greenhouse. 'Come up to my room?'

But Darren shook his head. 'I'm going into school this afternoon. Special revision class. I just came over to check you'd got home okay.'

'Right. Well I did.' She waved her hands as if to say 'here I am'. He could have just phoned if he didn't have time to stay. And he hadn't bothered with any other revision classes as far as she was aware.

'What's up with your arm?' she said, noticing that he was still holding it.

'Nothing.'

'Don't talk crap.'

'Accident. I was talking to your mum before I came out. She was waving her Silk Cut around and I got in the way.' He unfolded the arm from his chest and turned it to show her the neat red branding of a perfect cigarette burn. It wasn't the sort of burn you got from a glancing touch. She looked up at him, horrified at what her mother must have done, and at a loss for what to say.

'It was my job to bring you home last night, Hels,' he told her, firmly. 'I should have done better.'

# August 2017

*Helen*

'I'm sorry to have to inform you that it seems there may have been a medical error in relation to your mother's treatment.'

'An error? What do you mean an error?' Helen felt her guts lurch. She'd been praying that her worries were ridiculous, repeating it, convincing herself. The doctors would come and tell them that her mum had had a rare side effect or allergic reaction or something, that it was all very distressing but nobody was to blame. 'An error' wasn't in the script. 'An error' was only an error if you didn't know that someone had acted deliberately.

Ms Evans met her gaze steadily. 'She was being given heparin. It's an anticoagulant, which means it thins the blood and prevents internal clotting after surgery.'

'Right.'

'Well, the symptoms she showed – the bleeding – that's the classic result of a heparin overdose. When we tested, we found the levels in her bloodstream were many times higher than they should have been. It's administered via pre-filled syringes with different doses.' For the first time, Ms Evans faltered and glanced at one of the colleagues sitting next to her. 'Our initial check seems to show two additional doses were logged on your wife's records. We've undertaken an audit of the drug stocks on the ward, and that also seems to show two extra syringes have been used.'

They were in another office in the hospital, though this one was much plusher than that afforded to the nurses on Geranium Ward. Ms Evans sat behind a large, modern desk, flanked by Mr Eklund and one of the senior hospital management team. Helen felt herself gripping the edge of the desk.

'How come?' said Neil. 'How could this happen?'

Ms Evans glanced again towards her colleague, who had taken pains to introduce herself as Linda as they had entered the room.

'That, Mr Marsden, we do not currently know,' she said, speaking very slowly. 'The hospital will conduct an internal investigation. We will appoint a liaison officer who will keep you abreast of all the findings. Depending on the results, we may have to consider a referral to the Care Quality Commission.' She paused for breath. 'I can assure you – I can assure both of you – we will do everything necessary to get to the bottom of this.'

'Too damn right you will!' said Neil. 'My wife came in here with cancer. You lot are meant to cure her, not ... not let some incompetent student kill her off.'

'I *totally* recognise the depth of your feelings here, Mr Marsden, we just—'

Neil bristled through Linda's attempts to soothe him, but Helen found herself zoning out. Her dad had assumed it was a horrible mistake, but then he didn't know about the notes. An icy fear spread through her body.

'What happens to Mum in the meantime?' she asked, forcing herself back into the conversation.

Ms Evans took over again. 'Well, she's very comfortable now in our High Dependency Unit. We're going to keep her there to be monitored for another couple of hours, but I'm sure we'll be able to release her back to Geranium Ward to continue her recovery very shortly.' She rushed on. 'I believe that Mr Eklund is confident that this episode won't materially delay her recuperation from surgery or her planned discharge date.'

Mr Eklund had his elbows on the desk and was holding his hands in a prayer position, with his chin resting on his thumbs. He rocked forward, slightly, apparently nodding his agreement.

'Back on the ward?' Helen said. 'But what if it happens again?'

The three of them looked at each other. It was Linda who finally spoke.

'I *totally* understand your concern, Mrs Harrison, I really do. But you must understand that this type of accident is incredibly rare. It's very, very unfortunate that your mother has had to suffer this, but, believe me, the chances of it happening again are absolutely zero.'

'Have you found the person responsible then?'

'You mean the member of staff who administered the drug?'

'Of course, that's what I mean.' She heard the anger bubble up in her voice, making it sound cracked and alien.

'Well, as I said, we're going to conduct a thorough—'

'You mean "no"?'

'Well—'

Helen glared at her.

'Not yet,' she admitted.

'So you don't know who did it; therefore you can't have a clue as to why. You can't be sure it was an accident, and even if it was, they might make exactly the same bloody *mistake* as soon as she's back on the ward.'

Linda opened her mouth, but Ms Evans put an arm out to silence her.

'With respect, Mrs Harrison, what happened today has been a great shock to everyone on the ward.' The consultant spoke briskly, but with some warmth. Linda gaped beside her as she carried on smoothly. 'It hasn't happened before, and I'm sure they will *all* be doubly careful from now on. There's no doubt that your mother's medication regime will be followed to the letter. We have increased the staffing on the ward, and I will arrange for all her medication to be administered with at least two staff present, which I hope will ease your mind and theirs.' She paused, tapping her long nails twice on the table. 'I can't imagine for a moment that we're dealing with a deliberate action, but you are absolutely right that we can't exclude the possibility until the investigation is complete.'

'Well, I suppose that's all we can ask for, Helen, isn't it?' said Neil, before Helen had a chance to reply.

He sounded so weary. Helen's own anger towards them all flared again for putting her father through this. But she couldn't come up with any better plan. She wondered if she should tell them about the notes, but she couldn't do it now, with Neil here. She'd google the hell out of it as soon as she got back to the house, she vowed, and go back into the safe or through whatever papers of her mother's she needed. She'd do whatever she needed to get to the bottom of who Jennifer was and whether she was finally making good on her malicious threats.

Out loud she simply said, 'I suppose so.'

The three hospital staff nodded in unison.

'Do you both want to come and see her again before she moves back to the ward?' Mr Eklund asked gently.

'There's one more thing,' Ms Evans cut across them as they murmured their agreement. 'Until the investigation progresses, we can't allow Barbara to have any visitors without a member of staff being present. The hospital is very keen to make this as easy as possible for you all. We'll ensure that we make someone available whenever you are here.'

'You couldn't think that one of us would ...'

'It's not my job to think anything like that, Mrs Harrison. We have to ensure we're doing everything to protect Barbara as well as yourselves.'

*

Barbara was okay. They'd stopped the bleeding and she didn't have the breathing mask on any more. She smiled and talked to them a little, though her voice was so weak that it was a strain to try to make out what she was saying. Darren was meant to be dropping the kids back at six, so at five-thirty Helen told Neil she'd have to go. She promised that she'd pop in again in the evening, after Neil had returned to the house.

'Don't worry,' Barbara said, pausing with the effort. 'Expect I'll be asleep.'

'I'll come. I want to make sure you're okay.'

Barbara smiled and Helen could see every crack in her lips as they moved. They looked painful, but that must be the least of it. It seemed to Helen to be a knowing smile; that something passed between them in that glance about the notes, about Jennifer, and about the real reason why Barbara's recovery had been so horribly derailed. But, as ever with her mum, Helen just couldn't be sure.

She made her way to the car park, wondering about what Barbara made of it all and whether she feared for what might happen next. One thing was for sure: Helen could sit beside a hospital bed twenty-four hours a day and still have no idea whether the tablets and injections the nurses were dishing out were benign. *You just have to trust them*, she told herself. She hoped it was enough.

When she arrived home, the lights were still glowing on the old VHS player – she'd not switched it off properly in her rush. The anxiety that had plagued her earlier in the day was gone, replaced by a hollow, flat absence of feeling. She'd run out of energy, out of everything.

She went to the kitchen intending to make tea, but ended up pouring a glass of wine instead. A text message sounded on her phone. It was Darren, breezy and late. It would be another half-hour before the kids were back. She didn't know whether to be grateful or angry. He had the nerve to put a throwaway kiss at the end of his message.

At least the extra time gave her opportunity to snoop around a bit without Barney and Alys getting in the way. She'd already tried Google, but there was so little to go on. There were twenty or thirty hits for her mum, all connected to her work for the local newspaper. Most of the archives weren't online, so she didn't have to trawl through thousands of articles, but it also meant she had no chance of finding the story that Barbara said had kicked it all off in the first place. None of the results produced anything that seemed to explain the notes, and adding 'Jennifer' to the search didn't help either.

Now, it was time for a more traditional approach. First, she went to the safe, but it was only the pension details, mortgage certificates and insurance policies that she'd known were in there all along. There were no extra notes that she'd missed, and nothing else that seemed relevant.

The house had a loft conversion; the whole thing was pretty much used for storage, but at least it was less spidery and easier to get into than a proper attic would have been. Plus, if Neil did arrive back earlier than expected, she could say she was looking for extra bedding or something.

There were boxes and boxes of papers from Barbara's newspaper days. Cuttings were neatly clipped, some even pasted into scrapbooks. Everything was bundled with elastic bands and labelled with dates and references. Some of it was self-explanatory – her employment contracts and payslips, for example – whilst a rummage through some of the files with more cryptic labels, such as 'Forshaw Corruption' and 'Zeilig Ten', showed that they seemed to be long-running research files for stories that Barbara had been working on. Helen stuck with it for about an hour, getting grey and grimy with dust despite the outwardly clean appearance of the room.

By the time another text came from Darren to say he was on his way, she was getting increasingly disheartened, and with the ebb of the adrenaline, her exhaustion came back all the harder too. Aside from a few passing references, she'd found only two Jennifers in the files – one was an elderly woman who had been badly hurt in a street robbery and the other a woman who worked at the Borough Council in the late 1960s and seemed to have fed Barbara some information about controversial planning bids over a couple of years.

Neither fitted in with the story Barbara had told about the shoplifter, and neither had any apparent motive for wishing her ill, or, in fact, for getting in touch with her now at all. That said, Helen had gone through only two of the boxes; there were about fourteen she could see and there may even have been more stashed away in the eaves area. Barbara kept things roughly in order and Helen had gone for the early dates because that seemed to fit with what Barbara had said about her first contact with this woman, but it was still like searching for a needle in a haystack.

She skimmed to the end of the second box and then reluctantly began to pack the contents away before hurrying downstairs to wash the grime from her hands and face. So much for Sherlock Holmes, then.

A glance at the clock showed it was just gone seven. She went to double-check the time of Darren's text where he'd claimed he was on the way back, but before she got to it she heard the noise of his hire car pulling up outside.

Alys was slumped asleep in her car seat and Barney looked shattered.

'We've had a great time, haven't we?' enthused Darren.

'I can't wait to hear about it. You can tell me everything while we get your PJs on, Barney. Darren – can you open this door? It'll be easier if I lift her out and carry her straight inside.'

Barney tugged at her jumper as she tried to turn towards the car.

'No PJs, Mummy, dinnertime.'

She glanced up towards Darren, but he quickly turned away.

'Darren! They *have* eaten?'

'We had quite a late lunch ...'

'You are kidding me?'

Evidently not. He still had the nerve to ask to come in and talk about 'the next few days', but she gave him short shrift, promising to call when the kids were in bed. As he drove off, she edged towards the front door, hung with the spare clothes bag and various toys, as well as the dead weight of her sleeping daughter. At least she'd left it open.

There was no point in waking Alys. It was unlikely the lack of one dinner would trouble her.

Barney whinged his way through some cheese on toast and a Petit Filous. He told Helen they'd fed chickens, painted each other's feet and ridden in a helicopter. Any or all of them might have been true – she simply didn't have the energy to try to work it out.

She hurried him through his bath, teeth, story and song as quickly as they could both manage. When she bent over to kiss him, he wrapped his little arms tight round her neck, as always.

'Night, night, darling,' she said.

'I love you the best in the whole wide world, Mummy.'

For the first time in the whole day she felt good, but then instantly guilty. She pushed the guilt away, though; it wasn't her making him pick.

When she went back downstairs, there was a text from Neil saying that Barbara was sleeping peacefully, and one from an old school friend, Julie Hendricks, who'd got in touch when she'd heard about Barbara. They'd exchanged a few messages, and Julie had offered to have the kids if Helen needed. Her girls were roughly the same age, she said. They'd keep each other entertained, no problem. At least Julie would probably feed them, Helen mused. She decided she'd reply tomorrow, when she had a clearer head. She switched on the telly and collapsed in front of a repeat of a Saturday night talent show.

She hadn't realised she'd fallen asleep until the noise of Neil opening the lounge door woke her up.

'Helen?'

She made some sort of grunt, then managed to ask about Barbara. He said she'd been asleep for the last few hours of his visit.

'She needs her sleep, though, to get over everything she's been through,' he added.

Helen nodded. 'Of course she does. I still can't believe what happened.'

'Well, it's all behind us now, love, that's the important thing.'

'Yes,' she said, feeling far from convinced. She'd found nothing to disprove Barbara's claim that the notes were nothing to worry about, far less anything to suggest that the author of them was responsible for the 'error' at the hospital. But still the icy feeling clawed around in her stomach and her instincts told her that something in her mother's life was very far from how it should be. She thought again about telling Neil directly about the notes, but Barbara's warnings rang in her mind. God knew he'd had enough surprises for today. Tomorrow, perhaps, that would be time enough.

'I'll go back in then,' she said. 'You didn't park behind me?'

'No, love. But is it a good idea? You're yawning – look.'

'S'okay. I was dozing just now.'

'Well, if you're sure.'

She checked on the kids before she went out, worried that

with the living room door shut she might have slept through Barney waking up for a wee, or even Alys deciding she was hungry after all, but they were both sleeping perfectly. She kissed their warm foreheads and said her goodbyes to Neil, stepping out into the chill of the evening with the fug of sleep still heavy about her. She remembered her promise to call Darren, but it was far too late now. It would wait until the morning.

*

Geranium Ward was familiar now. Even in the half-light of a hospital night shift, she could clearly make out the nurses' station with the glazed office behind it, each institutional armchair and each cantilevered hospital table. The blue flickering light of a TV screen lit up two or three of the beds, but most were in darkness. Although she didn't know any of the patients' names, she'd begun to recognise their faces. No doubt if they were awake some would have recognised Helen too.

There was one chair pulled out slightly beside Barbara's bed. As Helen slipped into it, she could almost pretend that Neil's warmth still lingered. Across the narrow ward, an older woman in burgundy settled herself with some knitting in a chair at the foot of an empty bed. Helen's cheeks had burned as she waited at the nurses' station for a chaperone to be found, but at least the vacant cubicle meant the watcher could observe her with a degree of sensitivity.

'It's me, Mum,' Helen whispered, but Barbara was sleeping soundly, head tilted back and mouth open in an unselfconscious snore.

She sat there for a while, fighting the urge to check her

phone, or switch on the television. Her plan was to stay for only half an hour or so. It was the least she could do to focus on Barbara, she thought. Even if her mother didn't know she was there.

Gradually, more and more details resolved themselves in the gloom. She picked out the shapes of the get-well cards on Barbara's locker, a water bottle that rested, forgotten, on the nurses' station, the sheen of the laminated sign above the alcohol hand-rub.

Her gaze shifted to the foot of Barbara's bed. The clipboard leant drunkenly in its holder, as if it had been put back in a hurry. She only meant to prop it upright, but as soon as she bent closer, she spotted the envelope. Her first instinct was to look around for movement, as if she might spot the receding, shadowy figure of a poison postman. But, of course, there was no one to be seen. The envelope was presumably left there hours ago, pushed under the bulldog clip with sleight of hand, so Barbara would have no idea which of the bustling medics had left it, and whatever nurse came round next would think a well-wisher had visited and move it to the bedside table, or even hand it straight over if Barbara was awake.

The name *Barbara* was written in large, confident letters on the green envelope. Helen paused for a moment, then pushed a nail under the seal.

> *SO SORRY TO HEAR ABOUT YOUR SETBACK.*
> *WHAT A NASTY ACCIDENT. GET WELL SOON.*
> *JENNIFER*

The paper trembled in her hand. She looked at the frail sleeping figure on the bed and once again struggled to imagine who could hold this awful grudge against her. The knitting needles gently rattled behind her and rage flared that the hospital was spying on her and her father whilst the real villain seemed to waltz around with impunity. Who was to say that the knitter herself didn't hold some grudge against Barbara? Or wasn't in the pay of someone who did? If Helen confronted her with the note now would she herself be accused of writing it? Helen knew only one thing – precautions or not, she needed to get Barbara away from this hospital.

Plans whirled in her mind, but for now she let her mother sleep. It didn't take a doctor to see that sleep was what Barbara needed most. She texted Neil to tell him she'd decided to spend the night in the hospital. The questioning reply she'd expected didn't come – his response was a simple 'okay'.

Unable to let herself sleep, and too tired to do anything else, she simply sat, letting the minutes and hours wash over her like a slow tide.

Just before five, Barbara stirred a little, and her eyes flickered open. No doubt she would have returned to sleep given the chance, but instead Helen grasped her arm and whispered urgently.

'There's another one, Mum.'

When she was fully awake, Helen passed her the note.

Barbara stared at it, almost as if she was looking through it rather than reading it. Eventually, she let her hands sink back onto the bed.

'It's just to scare me, Helen; try not to worry.'

'You were in intensive care yesterday, Mum. Someone poisoned you; that's more than a scare.'

She shrugged. 'Maybe it's a better way to go than cancer.'

'But you've got every chance. Loads of women survive breast

cancer. This is different, this is ...' Helen struggled for words, '... criminal.'

Barbara gave a sharp sigh, as if she was too weak to snort in disdain. For a long moment, they just looked at each other.

'You've got to tell someone. They have to know there's a danger. They've got to move you.'

'There *isn't* a danger; it's a nonsense and no one poisoned me. There was a stupid mistake and this girl's got wind of it. That's all. I won't have your dad worried by it.'

That was what Helen used to settle it. She told Barbara if she didn't agree to say something to the medics, then Helen would show Neil the notes herself. They decided that Barbara would ask the nurses about discharging her as soon as they came on shift, that she'd claim to be too worried by what had happened to stay there, and they'd give the same story to Neil, with no mention of the poisonous little green messages. It was an alien feeling, conspiring with her mother. They'd never had secrets together, and certainly not from her father. Helen had heard of situations where serious illness brought family members together. She didn't imagine it often came about like this.

*

In the end, the hospital made arrangements to transfer Barbara at NHS expense to a small private hospital nearby called St Aeltha's. Helen suspected that Linda had a hand in the arrangements and that she was hoping to smooth over the consequences of what she imagined to be a random, almighty balls-up.

St Aeltha's didn't normally deal with cancer patients – it was all set up for hip replacements and knee ops – but it meant Barbara didn't have to come off the drip prematurely, as she'd threatened them she would do in order to go home. She'd have a private room with remote-control curtains and proper armchairs for visitors. More importantly, there was no staff crossover between the two hospitals and a very switched-on head of security – they were home to the orthopaedic surgeons of choice for the professional footballers from Manchester and Liverpool.

Barbara travelled by ambulance, with Helen following along behind. Whilst she was in the car, she realised she'd got a voicemail from Christine: a two-minute guilt trip full of *understanding* about how difficult everything must be for her at the moment and how Darren only wanted to help. And so did she and Adam. They all wanted the best; Helen just had to stop freezing them out, apparently. She deleted it.

When they arrived at St Aeltha's, the receptionist waved the elaborately written daily menu in front of them – clearly it was a source of some pride – but Barbara's arrival was too late for her to be able to select from it and she ended up with a slightly limp-looking chicken salad. Neil turned up with Barney and Alys about five minutes later.

'It reminds me of the time we flew business-class,' Barbara said, prodding at the salad. 'Much promised, but what arrives doesn't quite merit the fanfare.'

'Well, I'm just thankful to see you've perked up enough to complain about it,' said Neil. 'And anyway, it might not be gourmet, but it looks a hell of a lot better than the rubbish they've got in economy.'

'Or in this case down the road in the General,' Helen added.

'Exactly. Plus ...' Neil carried on, picking a knife off Barbara's tray and waggling it for emphasis, 'you don't have to pay for parking *here*.'

'Well, that's typical,' said Barbara. 'The people in here are the buggers who *can* afford to pay for parking!'

The kids laughed along, with no idea about what they were laughing at. The room was decorated in a deep rose colour, every touch thought through to conceal or diminish the resemblance to a hospital and make you believe you were in a boutique hotel. If Helen squinted through half-closed eyes, she could almost imagine that nothing was wrong; they were just a family crammed into a small, plush living room, enjoying each other's company.

There was no chaperone. Helen didn't know if that would change if she or Neil visited alone, but there was also no nurses' station, no drugs trolley that might be left unattended for a moment or two, no opportunity. She wondered briefly whether it was only Barbara that the hospital had considered in agreeing to the move, or whether they were also happy to have her and Neil off the premises and no longer their responsibility.

'You've been up almost the whole night,' Neil said, interrupting her thoughts. 'Why don't you go home and get some rest. I'll bring these two along later.'

Helen was missing the kids. It seemed like too long since she'd been able to have a lazy snuggle on the sofa with her babies, but she also knew she was running on empty.

'Okay, Dad,' she agreed, 'don't keep them for too long.'

'Course not.'

She did her round of farewells and hugs and walked slowly out to her car.

All the way home she racked her brains about what else she could do to try to track down whoever was behind the notes. She would scour the internet for every Jennifer in the district. She would call her friend, Amy, who was still in CID. She would call Barbara's old editor. After all that she would call Darren and tell him exactly what she thought about his mother's interference and his own lack of responsibility in bringing the kids home unfed. She would stop at Tesco and buy a chicken to roast so that when Neil brought the kids back from the hospital they would come through the door and find the air filled with the scent of everything-is-okay.

In the end, she missed the exit for Tesco on the roundabout, and by the time she realised, she couldn't summon the energy to go back. When she got home, the thundercloud of a migraine was quickly descending. It was all she could do to open the front door, choke down some paracetamol and crawl under the duvet.

*Barbara*

Finally alone in the plush nest of her new room, Barbara lay back and allowed her broken body to be cradled by the thick mattress and luxurious sheets. Without her glasses, and feeling tired and headachy, the pink and crimson shades of the room bled and blurred into each other. The fabrics deadened the noise, especially after the busy clatter of the General, and the air freshener had a heavy floral scent, which seemed studiedly non-clinical. Overall, she had the impression that she was nestled in the heart of an enormous flower. It gave her a welcome feeling of being small and hidden; able to deceive herself that what she did now – whatever she had done in the past – none of it really mattered.

Her mind wandered. She thought of her cutting kit – odd, as she hadn't needed it in years – not since the first time

Helen brought Barney to see them. When she was younger, using it had made her feel clean. The flow of blood had swept away her faults and flaws, and with it her anxiety, even if it only lasted an hour or two. She had the same feeling lying here.

If only she wasn't so tired, though. Her usually sharp mind felt fuzzy and hazed; she couldn't trust it. But alongside the haze there was a new sense of clarity too, somehow, a distance or a disconnect that let her mind travel into places she'd kept sealed off for years. She let her thoughts run, unfettered by time or inhibition.

Over fifty years ago a butterfly had flapped its wings; now there was a hurricane to be reaped.

# June 1963

*Katy*

They stopped after an hour or so, at a roadside pub. Miss Silver went in and returned ten minutes later with some sandwiches wrapped in paper. 'It took a bit of persuading,' she told them. They all ate in the car, but Mr Robertson wouldn't drive and eat at the same time, so they stayed in the parking area.

The sandwiches were roast beef – from the carvery, Miss Silver had said. Katy didn't know what a carvery was and didn't want to ask. The smell of the beef was wonderful and her mouth watered fiercely, but the meat itself was tough and the bread and juices soon melted away in her mouth, leaving tasteless, leathery wodges that were painful to gulp down.

Once they were moving again, Miss Silver passed back a slim bottle of lemonade with a smile. 'Here's a rare treat,' she said.

Katy tried to return the smile, but the other woman had turned away already.

She sipped the lemonade, watching the scenery whip by. It was rugged now. There were stone walls and grey blobs of sheep with faces she couldn't make out. It was late afternoon and the sun had dipped slightly, but the heat through the glass was still intense, and the atmosphere in the car was sticky. Katy tried to ignore her fuzzy head and the growing restlessness in her stomach, but eventually she could no longer pretend to herself that it was settling.

'Stop, Mr Robertson! Please, I think I'm going to be ill.'

It took a minute or two to come, and for that she was grateful, because she'd have been mortified to sully his pride and joy. She hung her head between her knees, a couple of gorse bushes shielding the sight of her from any passing traffic, and Miss Silver held her hair back and muttered softly. The air was much cooler outside than it was in the car, and briefly Katy thought she might get away with it, but just as she was allowing herself to be hopeful, it came. The spew was brown and pink from the beef – the last beef she'd likely see in a while, she thought, as she stepped carefully away from it.

There was no wall along this part of the road. The tarmac just gave way to scrubby moorland, offering nothing to sit on. Miss Silver manoeuvred her to lean against the wheel arch at the back of the car – Katy wouldn't have dared otherwise, but she sank against it gratefully, taking a moment to steady herself in the fresh air, before swilling out her rancid mouth with the last of the lemonade. A few minutes later, Mr Robertson was tapping at his watch and she knew she had to get back in.

'Try to sleep, Katy,' called Miss Silver from the front. 'We'll be back at Ashdown before you know it.'

*And wasn't that the rub?* Katy thought to herself, saying nothing.

No matter how unwelcome, sleep came, brought by the

steady purr of the Austin's engine and the thrum of tarmac under the wheels. Her sleep, for once, was dreamless. Unless the blurry memory of Eric Robertson carrying her through the corridors of Ashdown, murmuring a lullaby and tucking her under the thread-worn sheets and thin blue prison blanket was itself a figment of Katy's weary imagination.

# August 2017

*Helen*

Helen woke up in the middle of the afternoon befuddled and disorientated, imagining herself in her own home and struggling to make the fuzzy details of the room fit her expectations. Her mobile was ringing, and she answered it automatically, before her spinning mind had had chance to fully right itself.

'We need to talk,' he demanded.

She screwed up her face into the phone like Alys might. Darren was not a person she wanted to be dealing with at that moment.

'I've been up all hours, Darren. They've moved Mum, and ...'

'You're not returning my calls. It's already Friday and I need to be back in London by Monday. I've got a right to see my kids, Helen, and that's where they live, remember?'

'You saw them yesterday. You didn't feed them dinner, *remember?*'

He sighed. 'It'd be nice if you could let something go, just for once in your life. Anyway, I can't hang around up here on the off chance it suits you for me to see them for the day. We need a plan, Helen, we need to talk like adults about this.'

Eventually she agreed to meet in a Starbucks at an out-of-town shopping place. Best to get it over with whilst the kids were still with Neil at the hospital, she reasoned, and sent Neil a text to tell him she'd pick up some supermarket pizzas whilst she was there. Before she went, she put in a call to Amy, but it went straight to voicemail. A dig around the internet for anything about psycho-shoplifter-Jennifer was equally unfruitful. The local newspaper's online archive only went back to 2002. They obviously hadn't got round to uploading the back catalogue. Beyond that, the details she had were too vague to produce anything meaningful via Google.

As she drove, she wondered whether Darren really had to go back for work, or whether it had more to do with Lauren. Helen pictured her calling him from the bedroom of the maisonette he'd rented, toying with her designer heels and purring at him to come 'home'.

By the time she arrived, he was already at a table, with two mugs steaming in front of him. He looked rough, she thought, with a flash of surprise. His hair was flat and in need of a cut and he had a couple of spots on his forehead. Helen knew that she was hardly going to be winning grooming awards herself any time soon, but at least she had good reason to look awful.

He nodded towards the coffees. 'Flat white, yeah?'

She nodded back.

'Funny,' he said, 'I only come to Starbucks when there's nothing else on offer, but it always tastes better than I expect it to.' He looked around but didn't pause long enough to give her time to speak. 'All this used to be fields, didn't it? And wasn't that old flooded quarry round here somewhere?'

'Still there.' She pointed across the car park, where a narrow turning led to a lane, which looped around the back of Next. 'It's a canoeing centre now.' As she spoke, she remembered Tuesday night when he came to the house. Had the pair of them fallen together into that easy intimacy just out of habit and circumstance, or had Darren orchestrated it all along? Well it wouldn't happen again.

'But we're not here to talk about canoeing,' she said, in deliberately flat tones.

'No. The thing is, Hels, I've got to be back in work next week, like I said. I'm not happy just leaving Barney and Alys here. It's not their home; it's not what they're used to. I want to know when you're planning on bringing them back.'

'I don't know. I told you on the phone, Mum had a scare. She's had to move hospital. It's all up in the air at the moment.'

'Then let me take the kids back to London.'

Her mind was flying. He was going back to work – he'd said as much. He worked fifty-hour weeks. For God's sake, he'd forgotten to *feed* them the other night.

He was still speaking, though. 'Mum's going to come with me for a couple of weeks and I've made some calls. Paola from nursery is interested in a nanny job. I'd rather they came with me to the rented place, but if you want me to move back into the house whilst you're still up here then that might work too …'

'They're not going.'

'That's not a discussion, Helen; you've got to be rational.'

'I never offered to have a discussion. They're not *fucking* going.' She might have known bloody Chris was cheerleading him on in this; that must have been what her voicemail had been leading up to. Helen could cheerfully string up the pair

111

of them given half a chance. Instead, she banged her mug down on its saucer. The coffee slopped over the edge and Darren reached across one of the blatantly eavesdropping retirees at the next table to grab a handful of paper serviettes, which he then handed to Helen with an extravagant sigh.

'I don't want to start getting lawyers involved, Helen.'

'So don't then.'

He sighed again. She was trying to sound confident but her insides were somersaulting and she felt sure he'd guess that too. Forcing herself to take a deep breath, she scrabbled for a way to defuse things.

'Look,' she stalled, 'when are you actually going back? Is it settled?'

'I'll go Sunday night,' he said. Two days' time.

'You can see them tomorrow, take them out again – they enjoyed it.' As she spoke, he was nodding. 'Try to give them dinner this time,' she continued. Perhaps she should have bitten her tongue, but she couldn't quite manage it. 'Mum's full pathology reports are due back from the lab on Monday. We'll have much more information about the prognosis by then. I'll drive back with the kids on Tuesday – maybe Monday night if Mum and Dad don't need me. We can speak on Tuesday night, talk about what's going to happen going forward. You can see them on Wednesday whatever happens.' She paused. '*If* you can get the time off, of course.'

'And if you're coming back up here, then you'll leave them with me?'

*Not a chance in hell*, she thought. 'Maybe,' she said. 'I'll think about how it might work. Do you have a number for Paola? I'd need to speak to her before you firmed anything up.'

'Of course.' He was eager now. 'We could interview her together when you're back in town.'

'Maybe.'

*

Neil and the kids were back from the hospital by the time Helen got home. Barney and Alys were making Neil give them donkey rides around the living room. He rubbed at his knees a bit after he stood up, but it struck Helen that he looked happier than she'd seen him at any time since Barbara's illness had begun. She settled the kids down at the kitchen table with the pizzas she'd brought back, and while they ate, she and Neil washed and dried the few dishes that had accumulated by the sink.

'It seems like a great place in there, Hels. I mean, I'm all for the NHS, but she's going to get properly looked after now, like a film star or something. It can only do her good, can't it? When the food's nice and you're not being woken up in the night by someone raving with dementia three beds down?'

'I suppose so, Dad.' Helen was concerned about how the small private hospital would cope with a real emergency, especially if it happened out of hours, but she knew it was a worry she'd have to live with. She had no intention of breaking her promise and telling him about the notes, nor did she want to put in his mind the worry that the heparin incident might happen again.

She sat down at the table, helping Alys scrape the last bits of food onto her fork and listening to Barney chatter about what name they might give to the pet dog he was convinced he was going to get for his birthday.

'Right, then,' she said as they finished their yoghurts. 'We've had supper quite early tonight and you've done a lot of watching telly over the past couple of days. Who wants to do some painting?'

They both cheered. It was their favourite thing and normally something Helen tried to avoid because of the mess, but she'd been determined to have a nice time with them this afternoon. They were used to having the best of her and now, just when they found themselves in a strange place under unsettling circumstances, she'd simply been plonking them in front of DVDs or waving them off with other people.

Helen had to wipe the purple paint off her fingers when the doorbell went; she knew that Neil had gone for a shower. She opened the front door to a large woman, about Barbara's age, wielding an exuberant bunch of flowers.

'Jackie!'

'Helen, love, it's great to see you.'

Jackie Miller was a senior reporter on the local paper that Barbara had worked for since Helen was a child. She and Barbara had known each other for donkey's years, and for as long as Helen could remember, Jackie was the closest thing Barbara had to a friend. She stepped into the hallway, handing over the flowers and asking about Barbara. Helen dealt with it on autopilot, suddenly realising that this could be her chance to put her mind at ease about the notes. Jackie was exactly the person who might have some answers, and here she was on the doorstep. Thankfully, the note from the hospital was still in her handbag, hanging up right next to them.

She could hear the hum of the hot water booster – Neil was still in the shower. Quickly, she retrieved the scrap of paper and handed it over.

'I need to talk to you about something, Jackie. Dad doesn't know.'

The older woman quickly scanned the note. 'Nasty. What's it all about then?'

'Well, Mum says it was a story she was on years ago. A girl convicted for shoplifting, but she was unbalanced, and came after Mum. Mum said the police were involved, but decided she was harmless. She said there'd been a couple of episodes, and it seems to have started up again when she got ill.'

Jackie was frowning. 'I don't see it, Helen. I mean, of course your mum would have covered some magistrates' court stuff, but not that much. But if this kind of thing had gone off, I'm sure she'd have told me about it, and Geoff would have told the whole office. Especially if the police were involved.'

The cold fear kicked up several gears. Jackie had been a chance for reassurance but instead she was pouring cold water on the one explanation for the notes that was just about okay.

'But why would she lie to me about it?'

'Your mum's a dark horse, Helen.' Jackie shrugged. 'I never said she's lying, I just said it's odd.'

'Did she ever tell *you* about her family – I mean her own family, her childhood?'

The question came on impulse, tossed over her shoulder as Helen stuffed the note back into her handbag, trying to stop her hands from shaking. There had been nothing to suggest that the notes were connected to Barbara's blank past, but still ...

Jackie flushed.

'I already said she was a dark horse. I think that's a question for her, don't you, love?'

The disappointment in Helen's face must have been evident,

115

because Jackie quickly carried on, in a mollifying tone: 'Look, would it help if I looked up the newspaper's hard copy archives, see if I could find this story you're talking about?'

'That would be amazing, but wouldn't it take days?'

'We've got a card index. I've got the name Jennifer – though a surname would be better. And I can search the magistrates' court stories. It won't be watertight, but I can have a dig if it makes you feel better?'

Helen nodded, but then Neil appeared at the top of the stairs and Jackie called up a hello. She stayed for another few minutes, chatting to Neil before making her excuses.

When Helen returned to the kitchen, Barney's painting was almost finished. A blue strip of sky butted up against a yellow ball of sun, and clustered underneath were a handful of figures. 'That's lovely, Barney.'

'That's you, Mummy ...' he pointed, '... and me and Alys and Daddy and ...'

He had painted his perfect family with the four of them, all four of his grandparents, his teacher, Peso from *Octonauts* and the pet dog he refused to be persuaded Helen was never going to buy for him. To an outsider, it might have been a random juxtaposition of lines and blobs and circles, but he knew exactly what everything was and pointed to the same places on the page as he named everyone in his picture for Helen, then for Alys, then, later, for Neil.

'If Nana dies, Mummy, she could still be in my picture,' he told her, as he filled in the obligatory strip of green grass along the bottom.

'Ye-es,' she answered, carefully.

'She would be here,' he said, pointing to the greeny-blue sky, 'in heaven.'

'But for now she's here,' Helen said, firmly, pointing squarely in the human tangle below. Thankfully, Barney nodded without pursuing the point.

At bedtime, she stayed with Barney for a good fifteen or twenty minutes after he dozed off, knowing Alys was already sound asleep. She sang him the songs she had learnt when he was a fretful baby. Now, his body was lengthening away from its baby shape, stretching almost daily, or so it seemed. He could hold a conversation and would be mortally offended if she tried to feed him. But now, with that sheen of sweat across his brow, his little fringe matted down and his thumb wedged between his lips; now he was still her precious baby. She breathed deeply to inhale his scent when she bent to give him a final goodnight kiss.

*

Downstairs, Neil was watching a football match with a beer. He seemed engrossed, even wearing the glasses that he only usually bothered with for driving.

Helen looked at the screen. 'Is that Bolton?'

'Nope. Spurs. It's a friendly against some Italians.'

He didn't bother much with football, especially if it wasn't Bolton. She supposed it was natural for him to try to take his mind off everything that had happened to Barbara, though.

'Have you got any lager in the fridge, Dad? I think I might join you.'

He glanced at the pint glass in his hand, as if noticing it for the first time.

'I've got ale, love; there might be a couple of Beck's kicking around the garage if you look. I don't buy the fizzy stuff these days.'

Helen left him with the commentators discussing the prospects for the opening weekend of the Premiership. Not fancying a trip to the cobwebby garage, she went to rummage in the back of the drinks cupboard.

Her mum could die, she thought, and the headlines would still be about the start of the football season. It amazed her that Neil had somehow managed to stay tuned in to the real world, even in this small way. But then, Neil didn't know about the notes.

'I was wondering if there was anyone we should be getting in touch with?' she said, delivering the prepared line as nonchalantly as possible, keeping her eyes fixed on the men lethargically booting the ball around the pitch.

'Hmm? What do you mean?'

'Mum's family. You know, is there anyone who should know that she's ill?'

He gave her a quick, sharp look before turning back to the telly. 'But you know she's not got any family other than us, Duckface,' he said.

'I know the pair of you never talk about it, but there must be someone. Even if they're all dead; she didn't just land from Mars.'

'She may as well have done.'

'What do you mean?'

He just sighed.

'Come on, Dad, I'm an adult, I've got my own kids – whatever it is, you might as well tell me.'

'Wait – they've got a free kick.' He pointed at the screen. 'This could be their chance.'

'You're changing the subject.'

'I'll tell you after.'

They sat in silence as the Italian defenders marshalled themselves into a wall and the Spurs striker fluffed his opportunity and then had a go at one of his teammates.

'Well?' Helen asked, once the game had resumed, leaving the commentators speculating on what use the manager might be planning to make of the rest of the transfer window.

'Well what?'

'You said you'd tell me after the free kick.'

'Oh, Hels.' He put his pint down and turned to face her. 'I would, I honestly would, love, but there's really nothing to tell. When I met your mum she lived in a hostel. It was run by the church.'

'Like, an unmarried mothers' home, or something?'

He gave a sort of shrug.

'Not specifically. Thing is, in those days, girls stayed at home until they got married. At least around here they did. There weren't that many options for anything else. Pretty much all the girls in the hostel had jobs. They were just girls who couldn't stay at home because their parents had died, or there was no room, or no work where they came from. They'd be in flat-shares now, nobody would bat an eyelid, but back then a girl on her own was a cause for suspicion. The hostel was blooming strict, for the good of the girls as much as anything, I suppose, to protect their reputations, but people were still a bit snide about it. You know what folk are like.'

'So why was Mum living there?'

'I don't know, love.'

'You must have asked her!'

'Of course I did.'

'And in thirty-odd years she never told you?'

He nodded. 'Thing is, Duckface, you don't keep asking for

thirty-odd years, do you? Your mum made it clear early doors that she had made a fresh start and she wouldn't brook anyone prying about what had gone before. Me included. Once you've got the lie of the land, you take it or leave it. I took it. I just got on with life.'

'So why do you *think* she was there?'

He sipped his pint. At least he looked as if he was genuinely racking his brains.

'She'd come from Liverpool,' he said. 'You could tell that by her accent, and she mentioned a couple of things. Plus, she never wanted to go there. Even when *Miss Saigon* came on and she'd talked about how she wanted to see it, she wouldn't go to Liverpool for it.'

'So, something happened there?'

'It must have done.' He paused. 'There were people she used to be in touch with. Professionals. Officials. That sort of thing. One bloke called Abe, I remember. It gradually died away over the years.'

'So who were they?'

'I don't know. I always imagined she had a "past". You know, people still talked about fallen women in those days. There were charities that managed it, put the children out for adoption, set the mothers up with a "new start". I thought maybe it was that sort of thing that she'd got caught up in. You forget how interfering people could be in those days; so much has changed in a short time. Back then, it was almost Victorian – the control some people took over others, supposedly for their own good.'

'But she never actually told you that was what it was?'

He shook his head. 'No. The closest she came was when we were expecting you. She was worried that she wasn't a fit mother; that "they" would take you away. I reassured her – over and over again – that I wouldn't let that happen, and that she could tell me about the past, whatever had happened, but she never wanted to. Of course, no one ever threatened me with taking you away.' He gave a sigh. 'I don't even know how much of it was in her imagination.'

'But what about trust? How could you marry her, if she kept secrets from you?'

'I suppose I trusted her enough not to need to know.' He took a long swig of his beer, and she thought the conversation was over, but then he turned to her again. 'When I fell in love with your mother, Helen, I fell for her entirely. Body, mind, soul, everything. I knew I'd make whatever sacrifice I needed to be with her. Looking back, I'd do exactly the same thing all over again.'

'And that's it?' She tried to keep her voice measured. 'You love her, so she owes you nothing. You love her, so it doesn't matter that her life is ... is ... *a fraud*. And if her life is a fraud, then what about mine?'

'I never did any of this to hurt you, Helen. I know that she didn't either. Maybe I should have tried again when you were older. I can see it was important to you.'

Finally, he lowered his voice, glancing at the door, almost as if he was expecting his wife to burst in. 'I think there is a family, Helen. I picked up the phone once or twice to a woman who sounds a bit like your mum. She always made some excuse, but I'm sure it's a sister. And then I started checking the phone bills. There's a Liverpool number she rings, maybe a couple of times a year. I asked her about it once and she said it was about the house insurance. But I know it's not.'

Helen felt a tremor of excitement. This was new. After three decades of living with silence, finally this was something.

'Did you ever try to find out who the number belongs to?'

'I wasn't about to start spying on her after all that time.' He looked rueful. 'Like I said, I hadn't really thought about it in years. Lately ... with all this ... I've been so worried about her, I never even thought about ... the Liverpool thing.'

He gave her a look that reminded her of Barney's expression when he was uncertain, when he needed Helen to tell him what to do.

'I think we should see if we can find out, Dad.' She tried to keep her voice steady, calming. 'We won't tell anyone she's ill, certainly not before we see the doctor on Monday, but perhaps then ...'

'But she'll phone them herself if she wants them to know, won't she?'

'I don't know, Dad. And what if she doesn't want them to know? Or thinks she doesn't? We could end up doing her *and* her sister a lot of good if we put them back in touch.'

He grunted. 'I could end up hung up from a lamp post by my balls, you mean!'

She had to giggle, and after a moment he joined in. 'I won't let that happen, Dad. *If* we do anything, I'll make sure she knows it was my idea. After all, if she does have family, they're my family too remember, and Barney and Alys's. Mum will know it was me who wanted to look for them – she can't really blame me either.'

'Hmmm.'

'So you'll find that phone number for me? And help me try to find them?'

'What if she was hiding from something? What if she's in danger?'

Helen bit her lip, the image of the notes and the blood-stained hospital bedding flashing through her mind. If danger was looking for Barbara, it seemed pretty clear it had already found her.

'I'm sure she's not,' she lied. 'Not if it was all so long ago. And she's in the best place, isn't she, like you said.'

He sipped his ale. 'All right. I'll get out the phone bills.'

Helen wondered what her aunt would be like. Were there other siblings too? Probably she had cousins. She remembered the time she and Darren had driven down to Spike Island to see the Stone Roses and she'd been scanning the crowds for someone who looked like Barbara. Not so wide of the mark, perhaps.

# October 1975

*Barbara*

The call had come into Barbara's work on a wet October morning. The newspaper receptionist transferred it through the classified desk with a chill disapproval, but Barbara only really paid attention when she mentioned the name of the caller.

Sonia claimed she'd not been able to ring any earlier. The funeral was tomorrow.

'My God. How did it happen?' Barbara asked, stretching the cord on her phone to turn away from the open-plan office.

'The big C,' whispered Sonia. 'It seemed quick, but she must have guessed and kept it to herself. She went into hospital last week.'

'Were you with her?'

'Yes, me and our Kevin.'

'Did she say anything?'

Sonia sighed before answering. 'Not about you, she didn't.'

Barbara paused. 'Good,' she said, clenching the telephone wire to stop her hand from shaking. 'It'll be at St James's then? What time does it start?'

'You can't come.'

'I didn't say I was.'

'Aren't you?'

'I could slip in at the back. She was my mother too.'

'Exactly. Do you not think people might be looking for you?'

'Let me worry about that.'

Sonia hung up soon after and Barbara left her desk to make a Nescafé in the privacy of the cubbyhole office kitchen.

'Shall I get you one?' Jackie Miller called over. She was the new junior reporter and she acknowledged Barbara's more senior status with frequent offers to brew up, something none of the men, however new and eager, seemed to think to do.

'Thanks, Jackie, I'll go this time.'

Tomorrow's ads had already gone off to be set, so Barbara could afford to neglect the desk for a few minutes. If she closed her eyes she could picture her mother as she remembered her best. Cheeks dry and burning with shame under her peroxide blonde curls; her characteristic bluster and certainty diminished by the formal surroundings; her good clothes out of place against the sombre flannels of the welfare workers and the police uniforms. Then, Barbara had blazed with shame for the disaster she'd brought down on all of them, her mother most of all. Now, that shame had diminished, and she saw all the things that her mother might have done to save her, if only she'd had the wherewithal to know how.

Still in the kitchen, she took a sip of the coffee and then lit a cigarette. Deliberately, she focused on the image of her mother's face. Not across the distance of that awful day, but close up, as it always had been in her childhood. Her mother's voice. Her beleaguered laughter. Her almond-essence, baking-day smell. Barbara pushed herself, testing, but it was okay.

There was no pricking of tears or catch in her throat. The cigarette had settled the trembling in her hands. It was just the shock that had made her shake, the adrenaline, nothing deeper than that. She looked out of the window as she finished her cigarette; no point in wasting it.

The newspaper offices were in the centre of town. In the street below, people went about their business: travelling in cars or buses, shoppers with packages and umbrellas, mothers with prams, old folk with sticks. It was as if nothing had changed. *And it hasn't*, thought Barbara, stubbing out the cigarette and smoothing down her dress before heading back to the desk.

*

She didn't work on Thursdays, so in a way the timing was good. But it did mean that she'd have to take Helen with her. She turned to where her daughter was sitting at the kitchen table, a plate of toast and banana in front of her. The girl stared at her with her solemn grey eyes and Barbara had the familiar sensation that there was an older, wiser being inside. One that was judging her and would inevitably find her wanting.

'You'll come with me on an adventure, hey?'

At two years and a few months, Helen stared back mutely, before returning her attention to her banana. Barbara hoped the food would keep Helen busy while she rummaged in the wardrobe for a black dress she'd bought for Neil's dad's funeral. That was before she got pregnant. Frank had died in his fifties, his lungs weakened from the pneumonia he'd had in the war, he said. Barbara reckoned forty years of chain-smoking unfiltered cigarettes might have had more to do with it, but who was she to begrudge a dying man a little satisfaction?

Her own mother would have been sixty-seven by now. It took her a moment to work it out. Not too old, really, but then Joyce had been one of those people who seemed made to be young. Barbara tried to imagine what she would have looked like in her sixties but came up with nothing more than a peroxide blur and a harsh web of wrinkles where the fine lines round her mouth would have carved themselves deeper.

She tried the dress on quickly. Fortunately, the fit was still good. She grabbed a pair of black tights that she could put on downstairs and went back to the kitchen.

'Wan' down now.' Helen dangled a leg as though she might be about to jump.

'Okay. Just let me wipe those hands.'

'Down!'

'Yes. In a minute.'

Barbara fetched a cloth from the kitchen sink and smeared it around Helen's mouth and hands, before lifting her off the stool and setting her down on the tiled floor. The girl wandered off through the open door and Barbara followed her into the lounge, tights balled up in her hand in the hope of a chance to put them on. The days were long but the years were short – that was the piece of wisdom one of the neighbours had passed on about motherhood. Well, she could vouch for the first part. The first weeks and months after Helen's birth had felt like a black abyss.

Now, with her return to work, a bit more sleep at nights and a routine to their week, she hoped she was gradually clawing her way out of it. But nothing came easily. At the start of each day, the time she would spend with Helen unspooled ahead of her like an out-of-control rope, slippery and cumbersome with length. But despite the feeling that there was boundless time to fill, whenever she actually tried to do anything – get Helen ready to leave the house, make a phone call or even go to the toilet – the rope whipped round, grabbing her ankles and tripping her up. She felt such pressure to get it right: for Neil, to whom the child meant the world; to show Abe and the others that they were right to trust her; to try to prove to herself that she wasn't some sort of monster.

There had been brief golden moments, a few whilst she was pregnant, a few just after the birth, where it even seemed to be working. But Helen had seen through her. Helen knew, and, gazing at her judging eyes, Barbara knew that she knew. She carried on with the pretence in the hope that one day it wouldn't be a pretence. But also because there was no other option. She coped and she worked and she cut herself and she made love to her husband and she prayed that one day she'd be able to love her daughter too.

'We're going to go for an outing today,' she said, brightly, holding out Helen's little red jacket.

'Swimming!' Helen was gleeful.

'No. Not this time.'

*

She changed her mind a hundred times and back on the drive south towards Liverpool. There was no good reason for going – it wasn't as if her mum would know if she was there. And Barbara had done her own grieving over the loss of Joyce a long time ago. She believed what she'd said to Sonia – that no one would recognise her. She glanced in the rear-view mirror at the dark-dyed hair curling out from under her headscarf. But there had to be some chance; after all, she was family. Perhaps it was silly to take the risk.

But then another part of her argued that she had a right to be there. That Joyce was still her mother as much as she was Sonia's or Terry's or Kevin's. And then there was the niggle of curiosity. To see her siblings, perhaps even some of the nieces and nephews she'd never expected to meet. Perhaps, she allowed herself to believe, some of them might even be pleased to see her.

The one thing she didn't allow herself to think about was *him*. She knew he'd moved out of the area. She was pretty sure he was living near Stoke. Working at the newspaper made it easier to keep track of him. No reason at all why he would come back for her mother's funeral. She twitched in her seat, trying to shake the shiver from her spine.

The roads into the city were fairly quiet, but it had been raining steadily for most of the day and the heavy trucks were kicking up a lot of spray. Whatever tinny pop song had been playing on the radio faded out and she caught the intro for the news. That must mean it was half past one already, and the Mass was due to start at two.

The announcer's voice was sombre. Police investigating the disappearance of Eileen Larkin, the little girl missing from Preston, had found a body. Barbara glanced at Helen, slumped soundly in her car seat, before turning the volume up. They weren't saying much more. The girl had been found up on the moors, only a few steps away from the main road, but hidden amongst some rocks. Barbara looked out at the driving rain and shivered again. She turned the radio off.

The roads got narrower and more congested as she made her way into the city and then turned south again, towards the river. She parked the Imp a good distance away from the church, in a street that looked very similar to the one she had lived in but was almost half a mile in the wrong direction.

'Come on, Helen, we're here.'

The girl was groggy from sleep and clung warily to her mother, deliberately lifting her feet up each time Barbara tried to set her down on the pavement.

'We don't have time for this, Helen.' The Mass was due to start in two minutes. Barbara had planned to be late, but they were a good fifteen minutes away at the speed Helen would walk. Eventually she got the girl standing and began to pull her along in the direction of the church. For a moment, she worried that she'd forget her way through the maze of terraces, but the street plan was engraved on her memory.

She felt her eyes flicker around involuntarily as she walked. She was looking for him, although she tried to tell herself she wasn't. She jumped when a man of similar age and build rounded the corner just ahead of them. He wasn't the one; didn't look like him at all really – even his hair was a different colour.

As they walked, the photo of poor Eileen shown on the television news the previous night, flashed through Barbara's mind. There was a mother out there who'd wish she could have held her girl tighter.

As she'd hoped, the service had just started when she got to the church. The door had been left open and very few mourners turned to look at the latecomers. Barbara had lifted Helen into her arms, hoping to keep her quiet, but also because she could duck her head down and there would be little for anyone to see but the child and the headscarf. Her heart was thudding; the sense of fear rushed up on her, threatening to overwhelm. She slipped, shaking, into a pew just as a hymn began – 'O God, Our Help in Ages Past' – and could almost hear her mother's reedy voice in the congregation. They'd had the same hymn at her father's funeral, she realised, shuddering at the recollection.

The inside of St James's struck her as if she'd been there yesterday. She could already feel the wooden kneeler, cold against her bony knees, and see the blush on Our Lady's cheeks as she gazed down at the motley, penitent assortment. Her mother's profile formed in her mind, brow furrowed with concentration and lips forming the well-worn words, as if she was a wind-up toy. As a child, Barbara would peek through her lashes, her sidelong glances often meeting Sonia's, or one of the boys', but she had never caught Joyce with her eyes open whilst she prayed.

Barbara and Neil didn't attend church, but the blast of the organ and the hum of the voices still felt utterly familiar. Barbara intoned automatically as she flipped through the hymnal, mouthing the familiar words in the hope it would steady her. *You wanted to come*, she reminded herself, trying to quell the growing urge to walk out.

When the hymn was over, two men shuffled up to give the eulogy – her brothers Kevin and Terry – both of whose eyes seemed to linger on her as they flicked their gaze up and down from the text of their readings. She felt herself grow hot with what she hoped was paranoia and bent down to busy herself with Helen.

The church was full. It seemed Joyce was well liked still, or well known at any rate. After the men the priest, whom

Barbara didn't recognise, rose to deliver his piece. She supposed the old Father would be retired, if not dead himself; he'd seemed about a hundred when she was a schoolgirl. This new Father (although he may not have been new at all) spoke in a soft Irish brogue, which meant she had to lean forward in order to catch the official version of her mother's history. Did she recognise the woman he spoke about? Not really. It could have been anyone's mother – caring, loving, made a delicious stew.

Eventually the service drew to a close and she heard the scuffle of the double doors being opened. She moved back into the shadows where she could watch the new Father emerge at the head of the procession. Behind came the family. Terry was first, with his arm round a hard-faced woman who Barbara just about recognised as his wife, Bernice. He wasn't wearing his age well, Barbara thought. He looked plump and his skin was flushed red in a way that looked more permanent than this recent bereavement would account for.

Behind him were Sonia and Kevin, each with a partner, and then a gaggle of kids of all ages. The children hadn't been put in black for the funeral, but they all looked stiff in their Sunday best, the boys in grey trousers that flapped at their ankles and the young girls in pale blouses and dark, jewel-coloured velvet pinafores, quickly covered by bright plastic rain jackets. One or two older ones hung back together, looking sullen and restless.

'Your cousins,' breathed Barbara into Helen's ear.

Hefting Helen in front of her again, Barbara followed, at a distance, to the graveside, placing the girl down in the shelter of an ancient cherry tree.

She'd planned to wait until the rites were finished and the

crowd had dispersed, to spend a little time at the graveside alone with Helen. It would be nice, she'd imagined, to feel that she'd missed her mother only by a short while, that perhaps Joyce's spirit still lingered, that she would know the pair of them were there. In reality, the sight of the slick, dark soil and the wet-earth smell that hung in the air were making her nauseous. Even as the crowd thinned, she shifted, restless and wary as an animal pacing near a fire, both fascinated and repelled by the grave.

There was one figure who didn't head towards the church-yard gate: Terry. Even with her eyes averted she could sense his lumbering gait, feel the intensity of his stare.

'Didn't think you'd have the brass neck to show up here.' His voice was low, rumbling with menace.

'She's my—'

'Yeah, well she's dead now, in't she? There's nothing else to see and you're not wanted.'

'How do you know what Mam wanted? Or what Sonia wants? Or any of the kids? The kids would want to know they've got a cousin.'

He leant back, assessing her, a hum of indecision on his lips.

'You were always a contrary one. You can't be intending to march around glad-handing the neighbours or else you'd not be skulking around here. I know you've been in touch with our Sonia.' His voice hardened. 'You shift yourself, now, or I'll get onto that husband of yours ...' he nodded towards Helen, '... assuming you are married to her dad, that is. And then we'll see who wants to know what.'

She could feel her cheeks burning and her throat choked with rage. Saying nothing, she grabbed Helen and marched

133

towards the gate, holding her head high. The few remaining mourners were clustered around the priest in a tight, black knot. The new Father was chatting to them, patting hands and giving out sweets to the kids.

As the gravel path reached its closest point to them, Barbara caught a movement in the corner of her eye. It was Sonia. Their eyes met for half a second before her sister turned back to the grave.

*Neil*

That night, Neil lay awake listening to the wind rattling the fence panels and the distant thrum of the motorway traffic. He'd caught something amiss almost as soon he turned his key in the lock. Barbara was too subdued – normally after a day at home with the little one she'd be clamouring for adult conversation. He would laugh at how the words flooded out of her.

She had Helen ready for bed and brought the girl down for a goodnight kiss.

'Daddy!' She grinned and held her arms out to him, not looking at all tired.

'Hello, sweetpea, how's my little Duckface?'

They rubbed noses and she chortled, her little face lighting up.

'Daddy'll come and read you a story in a minute,' he told her.

'It's no trouble, Neil, I'll get her settled.' Barbara's tone was light, but the comment puzzled him. She was normally very keen for Neil to have as much to do with Helen as possible, particularly when she'd had a day on her own with her.

'I want to, love. Don't worry, I won't get her excited. I'll just get changed and then I'll be through.'

He knew Barbara well enough to recognise the quick pursing of her lips and see that she wanted to argue the point, but she shrugged and led Helen out to the stairway without saying anything more. Neil eased his work shoes off; he'd find out later what was bothering her. Or else he wouldn't and the world would keep on turning regardless. He'd learnt to accept that sometimes there would be small mysteries with Barbara.

'Grrrrr – look who's coming to eat up, Helen!' Down on all fours, he nudged her bedroom door open and roared, rolling his neck like the cinema lion.

'Lion! Come here, Daddy-Lion!' She shrieked with laughter as he stalked across the floor.

'You said you wouldn't get her excited,' scolded Barbara. But she was smiling, and, still growling, he butted her knees until she moved aside, letting him pull back Helen's blankets and growl onto her flat, wriggling belly whilst she screamed with delight.

After a minute, he sat back on his heels, laughing himself and out of breath.

'Okay, which story?'

He was reading her *The Snow Queen*, and they both loved the strange landscapes and colourful people that Gerda met on her travels. As he flicked through to find the page he'd stopped at the night before, he could hear Barbara on the landing, taking washing off the radiator from the sounds of it. She was still there as he read, telling Helen about the fierce little robber girl and her doves. Helen preferred the princess of the previous chapter. Eventually, Neil heard Barbara's footsteps on the stairs. When he heard the kitchen tap come on, he gently closed the book.

'What did Helen and Mummy do today?'

She looked blankly at him.

'Gerda went to the forest – what did Helen and Mummy do?'

'Went to the big church.'

'Did you?'

But she was looking away from him now and rubbing her eyes. He finished the story, stroking her hair with one hand and holding the book awkwardly in the other.

'Night, night, sweetpea,' he whispered, and there wasn't a peep out of her as he pulled the door to and made his way downstairs.

Lying in his own bed, he wondered again if he should have asked Barbara what Helen meant and pushed until he got an answer. Instead he'd just accepted the cup of tea she'd made for him and sat down to watch her busying around peeling potatoes and grilling the chops.

All of Barbara's energies seemed to be focused on the spuds. She'd not taken him up on any of the little bits of conversation he'd tried. Finally she'd looked over to him. 'Do you want these mashed or just plain boiled?'

'Just boiled. It's easier, love.'

He went to take another mouthful of tea, but then realised he'd already finished the mug. He felt very tired all of a sudden. Exhausted. Maybe he should speak to the boss, ask to cut down on the overtime a bit. Maybe they should look into booking a holiday. They'd not been away properly since the year Helen was born when they'd gone to Devon for a week.

With a little effort, he stood up and went to the sink to start soaking the pots whilst Barbara dished up. He'd poured a glass of water for each of them and pulled the rattan table-mats out of the drawer.

'That lamb smells good, love.'

'I'd hope so. I went to that butcher's in town after work on Tuesday. They're not cheap.'

'Worth it, though, when it tastes like it should.'

Even as he'd sat there, Neil had felt as if they were reading the lines out of some family drama on the telly, his wife as distant and artificial as a second-rate actress.

She would come back to him, though.

That was what he'd told himself in the kitchen, and that was the mantra he repeated late at night as he tried to summon sleep. There had always been times like this, and he liked to tell himself it didn't worry him so much now as it had at first. There was that tiny, unknowable fragment of Barbara that would always remain hidden from him. Most of the time it didn't make any difference; he could just forget about it. Then, from time to time, there was a day like this, when it was there, a shard of ice needling its way between them, but not to be talked about. Was Barbara the Snow Queen? No – he quickly dismissed the thought – Barbara was more like poor little Kai, tormented by the speck of glass that had found its way to her heart.

Eventually, Neil slept. His dreams brought him images of the moors and of melting ice, but the morning brought back a little of the old Barbara. And each morning after brought a little more, until, within a week or so, he could imagine that nothing had ever been amiss.

# August 2017

*Helen*

Darren came to pick up the kids just before ten in the morning. Helen said as little as possible to him as she handed them over at the front door. It wasn't quick, of course – as always there had to be a pair of shoes on the wrong feet, Barney's must-take toy rabbit that contrived to get lost and, finally, a rush back through the house to say goodbye to Granddad. Barney and Alys's chatter camouflaged the awkwardness, though, and soon enough Darren was able to whisk them off in the hire car. They waved happily back to her, leaning forward against the straps of their car seats.

Neither of them had asked if she was coming this time. Were they getting used to it?

She noticed that Christine was in the passenger seat, but she didn't get a wave from her. Helen could see her silhouette, bending round into the back, reaching as far as the seatbelt would let her to fuss over her grandchildren.

Neil had stayed away from the hallway. He'd not spoken much about Darren since the split. Helen surmised that her father was far too cautious to confess he'd never liked her husband, but over the years she'd formed a good sense of what he felt about him. Darren's charm – his one great gift that served him so well in life – had never been an asset as far as Neil was concerned. He wandered downstairs a few moments after Darren had driven off.

'Where's he taking them?'

'Some farm park place, up the motorway.' She hadn't asked the specifics, if he'd mentioned the name she'd forgotten it. She flushed with a brief panic, but then decided her concern was stupid. They'd never tracked each other's movements when they were together.

'You going to try to catch up with some sleep then?'

'Hmmm, probably. I could meet you later at the hospital?'

'Yeah, that sounds good. At least we don't have to worry about visiting hours now she's in St Aeltha's.'

'Before you go, Dad?'

'Yes?'

'Could you have a look for those phone bills for me?'

There was a flicker at the corner of his mouth. Did he regret telling her about the phone calls? Would he refuse now? But, no, after a moment he nodded and explained where she'd find the files of old BT bills.

'You'll have to look through a few years,' he said. 'There's not many 0151 numbers, though – you should be able to scan through quite quickly.'

'Great.'

'Promise me you won't call it, Helen?'

She paused for a heartbeat.

'I won't.'

He kissed her on the cheek and was gone.

*

As Neil had said, scanning through the phone bills was easy enough. She stuck on the radio and sat with a pile of paper about three or four inches high beside her, gradually working through it and moving each one into a 'done' pile that slowly, slowly, crept taller. Whenever she saw a Liverpool number, she jotted it down with the date next to it, and then if it came up again, she put the new date down next to the old one.

By the time she'd gone back to the start of 2013 she was convinced she had it. There were six calls altogether, one each year in December or January, and two extra ones in June 2016 and February 2014 – the 2014 call was just a few days after Alys had been born, Helen realised with a jolt. Besides that number, there was one other possibility that came up a couple of times, but a quick Google search confirmed it was a shop selling gardening supplies. Neil had seed catalogues galore and had been known to hunt the length of the country for a new breed of tomato or rare dahlia tuber, so that was easy to explain. No other Liverpool number appeared more than once.

But what to do now? She googled the number, hoping that would give her some clue without breaking her promise to Neil. Nothing came up, which was disappointing but not a surprise. Private household numbers didn't tend to be broadcast on the internet, after all. Next, she tried to see if she could find the BT phonebook online, but it was only searchable by name, not by number.

Finally, she decided she would call. She didn't feel great about directly going against the promise she'd made to her dad, but, realistically, this was the least of what she was keeping from him. She'd never forgive herself if Jennifer managed to seriously harm Barbara and she'd held back from doing something that could have prevented it.

She rehearsed a little speech in her head, but still her fingers shook as they punched out the numbers, and she worried that whoever answered would be able to hear the nerves in her voice. People hung up so quickly on junk calls, she'd have to get to the point if she was going to have any chance of finding out anything useful.

Her mind spun, wondering who would answer. Would it be a relation she'd never known about? Someone who knew her mother's past? Could it even be Jennifer herself on the end of the phone line?

After three rings, an answer service cut in. Frustratingly, it was a pre-recorded phone-company message, so it gave her no information about who she'd got through to. Or, rather, *not* got through to. She reeled off her speech, giving her name and explaining she was the daughter of Barbara Marsden, maiden name Kipling, and if anyone in the house knew Barbara she'd be very grateful for a call on her mobile. Inevitably it sounded slightly garbled, but she felt it came out better than she'd feared.

It felt like an anticlimax. How long should she wait to get a call back? And what else could she do if it didn't come? Finally, she remembered her idea about enlisting some back-up from Amy. Their friendship went way back to uni; Helen was sure she'd want to help out if she could.

She got through to Amy straight away.

'I think I can help. I'll try a reverse-phone look-up, as long as the number's not ex-directory it's fine. You could probably find a company to do it for you, but they'd charge.'

'And if it is ex-directory?'

'Well, if it was an enquiry I'd have other options, but I can't abuse my access.'

'I get it, but—'

'Look, chances are it'll be fine. Wait till the problem happens before you stress about it, yeah?'

'Okay, thanks, Aims, I do appreciate it.'

They made their promises to try to have a proper catch-up soon, and then Helen was alone again, stalled and running on empty. When her phone rang, she grabbed it.

'Hi,' said a female voice.

'Amy! That was quick.'

'Um, sorry, it's Julie.'

Julie? Helen's mind rattled through the possibilities. Of course, Julie Hendricks. She felt a slump of disappointment that it wasn't Amy, but of course it wasn't realistic to expect to hear from her so soon. Helen had tried to call Julie after their text messages, but they kept on missing each other.

'My fault – I thought you were someone else, sorry.'

'Oh, shall I go, only—'

'No, I'll hear if she's trying to call. She said it would be a while.'

'Oh, I don't want to bother you,' she said. 'You've got so much on your plate. I just thought I'd see how things were.'

'Of course, that's kind.'

There was a silence. Helen realised Julie was waiting for her to fill her in on the gory details about Barbara, or Darren, or both. She was tempted just to tell her where she could stick them, but something made her hold back. She wasn't exactly drowning in friends and support at the moment, and Julie's offer to look after the kids could be a godsend.

'Mum's recovering well from the surgery. We've got to go in on Monday to hear about how far it's spread.' That was bland enough, no need to mention the move to St Aeltha's and the reason behind it. She took a breath. 'Look, do you fancy a drink tomorrow afternoon? We could take the kids somewhere with a beer garden. It'd be great for my two to have some company.'

'Sounds perfect – the shop's shut on Sundays, so I like to try to do something with the girls.'

They settled on a pub and a time and then Julie had to get back to her desk. She worked for a travel agency and had a honeymoon itinerary for Nepal and Tibet to get on with.

After Julie hung up, Helen checked her missed calls just to make sure there was nothing from the Liverpool number or from Amy. While she scrolled down the screen, a series of huge yawns overtook her, her jaw stretching so wide it was actually painful. She decided that trying to get that nap might be a good idea after all.

Amazingly, she managed to get some sleep and then to squeeze in a quick trip to St Aeltha's before Darren dropped off the kids. Neil and Barbara both seemed relaxed there, with Barbara looking much better. There was more colour in her cheeks and she chatted calmly with her visitors. When Neil stepped out of the room, Barbara confirmed that there had been no more notes.

Refreshed by her nap, Helen felt the sense of threat that had surrounded her begin to ebb away. For the first time in days, her shoulders dropped just a little and her earlier worries about Jennifer faded a little. Nothing more than coincidence and paranoia, she comforted herself, with real hope that it was the truth. The hospital move had clearly been the right thing to do.

Although she'd been dreading another encounter with Darren, when it came to it, he dropped the kids off without much fuss and dashed away again. He was going to the pub with some old friends, she picked up from Barney. Darren himself hadn't bothered to mention it, even though she must presumably have also counted them as mates once upon a time. So much for his pressing work commitments, she thought, but then at least he'd managed to feed the children this time. She decided she might just go out for a walk to try to clear her head.

She got her own trip to the pub the next day, sharing a slightly shivery picnic table overlooking the play equipment with Julie, who had been to the place before and wisely brought a fleece jacket. She also produced four foil-wrapped chocolate medals from her handbag for Barney, Alys and her two girls, dishing them out on the pretext that it gave each of the kids a chance to be a winner.

'What a great idea – they're all thrilled with them,' Helen said, as the kids rushed off brandishing their bounty.

'I just spotted them in Tesco and thought it would be nice.' She shrugged.

For a moment, in the sunshine, with a gin and tonic in her hand and a bit of adult company, Helen almost felt normal again. Julie was very easy company. They talked about the kids mainly, but also TV and bits and pieces of celebrity gossip.

'Your two are very polite,' Helen said, as Julie's eldest, Evie, came to the table for a quick drink before dashing back off up a climbing frame.

'Thanks,' she said, laughing, 'they have their moments.'

'Don't they all!'

Alys was sitting with them, playing contentedly enough with a couple of toys Helen had brought from the house.

Barney was tagging around after Evie and her sister Lexie like a Labrador puppy. They were six and eight and happy to throw him the odd bone, so he couldn't be happier.

As Helen relaxed, she found herself opening up about Barbara. Not about the heparin overdose, but about the diagnosis and the operation and the chemo she was psyching herself up for.

'So tomorrow's the big day then?' she asked.

'Yes, I think so. It's all so new, such a rollercoaster … I don't want to build myself up for it and then find that it's not what I expect. Everything they tell us is always so hedged around with ifs, buts and maybes.'

'I'm off work tomorrow morning,' she said. 'If you want me to have the kids you only have to ask.'

'Could you?' It had been worrying at her. She clearly couldn't take them into the appointment. She'd thought that she'd have to leave them with Chris – assuming Darren actually had gone back to London – but the idea hardly filled her with relish.

'Of course, they'll just play out the back. It'll be a diversion for my two – stop them fighting.' She turned to Alys. 'You'll be no problem, my angel, will you?'

'You're a superstar. Really, I can't thank you enough.'

Helen took her address and they began to wind things up. Helen, Barney and Alys waved goodbye to Julie and the girls in the car park before finally making it back to their own car.

'Can I play with Evie and Lexie again?' Barney wanted to know.

'Actually, darling, you can. You're going to go for a little visit to their house whilst Mummy sees Nana at the hospital tomorrow.'

'Me too!' shouted Alys.

'Yes, you too.'

There was a chorus of cheers.

Helen's phone rang when they were almost back at the house. A London number, not one from her contacts. She pulled up sloppily, blocking someone's drive.

'Yes?'

'Hi Hels, it's Amy.'

She had to turn to hush the kids before she could concentrate on what Amy was saying.

'... really sorry. I can't tell you anything else. Just don't go there.'

'What? Alys was making a racket. I didn't catch you?'

'I should have left it alone, Hels, it's my own fault.'

'What's your fault?'

'It was ex-directory, so I ran it through the PNC – the police computer – just in case. I can't tell you who it belongs to, but you should stop trying to find out. It might put someone in danger. Something triggered when I checked it. Now I'm being hauled into the Chief's office tomorrow.'

'What do you mean it triggered something?' Helen was confused, still half-distracted by the kids, but fighting a sliding sense of dread. 'Are you saying the number belongs to a criminal or a terrorist or something?'

'I said, I can't tell you. I shouldn't even have told you that much – that's why I'm not on my own phone. I shouldn't be telling you anything, but I couldn't let you go blundering into ...' She trailed off.

'Into danger?'

'Perhaps. Look, I've got to go. Take care.'

The line went dead. Helen's mind was racing. How could

146

tracing a phone number be dangerous? What was Barbara mixed up in?

'Want bint,' whined Alys, from the back.

'Mint, mint, mint,' agreed Barney.

Blindly, Helen groped for the half-pack of Polos in the glovebox.

They were only two streets from the house, but suddenly she couldn't face being back there. She needed some time to think about what was going on. After dishing out the Polos, she swung the car around and headed back out of the village.

Her seatbelt was suddenly too tight, trapping her heart like a hummingbird flapping uselessly against it. Her clothes were itchy and she was breaking into a sweat. She turned the aircon to max and tried to breathe, watching her knuckles change colour as she alternately tightened her grip on the wheel, making herself relax.

Forcing herself to breathe, she tried to straighten out her thoughts. Amy said someone could be in danger. Barbara had almost died. If that didn't count as danger then what did? Of course, it could just be a coincidence that Barbara had a mysterious past, with some sort of family (presumably) in Liverpool, whom it was dangerous to try to track down, and that she also had a stalker who she had upset years ago whilst working at the newspaper and who had suddenly now decided to get serious. But it was a very big stretch.

Wasn't it more likely that whatever Barbara was caught up in now was completely tied up with whatever had happened in the past that she would never speak about? That would explain why Jackie had seemed sceptical about the stalker story.

It was suddenly all the more real, now, and Helen was

convinced that what had happened at the hospital wasn't simply a horrible mistake. Those awful notes weren't just a prank. Helen had always been a bit of a daydreamer, but Amy was straight down the line. Helen couldn't remember ever hearing panic in her friend's voice like that before. The more she went over it in her head, the more certain she was; this went right back into her mother's past, before her marriage, when she was still Barbara Kipling. Whoever Barbara Kipling really was.

Peace reigned in the back seat, but of course it wouldn't last. There was a ten-minute loop out to the motorway. She'd do that and then head back, she decided. She wouldn't say anything to Neil tonight. Or to Barbara for that matter. But after Mr Eklund had said whatever he had to say tomorrow, then she would make sure she got some answers.

Just then, her phone pinged again. A text message from Jackie Miller. *Sorry, Helen, no luck with the archive.*

*What a surprise*, thought Helen, *because it looks more and more like my darling mother has been leading me right up the garden path.*

# June 1963

*Katy*

The morning after the trip to Moreton Chase, Katy was allowed to have a lie-in. Maureen Stephenson came knocking at eight-thirty a.m. with two mugs of lukewarm tea and a couple of slices of toast – no plate – on a plastic tray.

'They wouldn't give me any jam. Said if you wanted any you'd have to go down for it.'

Katy shrugged. 'The jam's shit anyway, in't it?'

'Yeah, you're not wrong.'

'Thanks, Maureen.'

She didn't know she was ravenous until the smell of the toast hit her nostrils. Then it suddenly felt as if she'd left a black hole in her stomach when she'd spewed up at the side of the road yesterday.

Maureen sat silently, watching her friend slurp and munch, examining her with those sharp green eyes that missed nothing.

'Well?' she said, as the last mouthful slipped down.

'Well what?' replied Katy.

'What happened? Did they find the kid, or what?'

'Nah.' Katy made her answer sound nonchalant, but the

truth was she had tried her best. She wasn't bothered about Etta, far less Simon, but she felt Mary deserved better. If she was honest with herself, she wanted it to please Mr Robertson too, but there was no way she'd admit that to Maureen, or anyone else.

'So no early parole then?'

'No.' Katy gave a snort of disdain at the idea. She couldn't help but notice Maureen's stifled look of glee. Should she be flattered or upset? she wondered. Not that it mattered.

Maureen wanted more details about the outside – what she'd seen and heard and eaten – but Katy brushed her off impatiently. 'It wasn't a bloody trip to the zoo, you know.'

'All right, keep your knickers on. I'm just interested.'

There was a pause, and in the distance the sound of a bell.

'I've to tell you you've got till first break,' Maureen remembered. 'I've to go now. Although it's art, and old Foster will be late as always.'

'He was there this time.' Katy spoke faintly, as if daring Maureen to hear it.

'Who?'

'*Him.*'

'What, the bastard Gardiner?'

Katy laughed bleakly. 'Yes, the bastard Gardiner. Who else?'

'He's got a nerve on him.'

'He has,' Katy agreed, but her tone was thoughtful. That was Simon all over, she thought, though she'd never put it into words until now. The nerve of him. He managed to do all sorts because no one would believe it. A brass neck like a fucking giraffe. A brass neck to hang him.

# August 2017

*Helen*

Somehow, after everything that had happened and the hulla-balloo among the St Aeltha's staff about accommodating a visiting consultant (albeit for only half an hour), the much-anticipated meeting itself seemed flat.

'The surgery confirmed what we had suspected regarding staging,' began Eklund, once the pleasantries had been dispensed with. 'It's Stage 3, but not a bad Stage 3, if I can be a little less scientific.'

'So, now it's chemo?' asked Barbara.

Eklund nodded, then went on to explain the drugs involved and the cycles of pills and injections that Barbara would have to go through.

'And if I decide not to take it?'

His brow furrowed. 'Most people ask about that after we've discussed the side effects. It might not be as bad as you may be imagining from TV and the press, Mrs Marsden.'

She shrugged. 'So tell me about the side effects and then answer my question.'

He elaborated for a few minutes on white blood cell counts, sickness and diarrhoea, hair loss and so on. It was a well-worn speech, but he had the grace to look uncomfortable when explaining that a drop in platelet levels could cause her to bruise and bleed more easily. She merely nodded.

'There is no evidence of metastasis,' he went on. 'There is a chance ...' and here he gave a shrug that seemed more Gallic than Scandinavian '... that you will make a complete recovery, even without treatment. It is, however, a small chance. It's much more likely that microscopic colonies of cancer cells remain in your body, and that without intervention they will develop – whether slowly or quickly – into further tumours. Chemotherapy will certainly slow that process and may well, if we're lucky, prevent it altogether.'

'I see,' said Barbara.

Eklund hazarded that she was considering alternative therapies instead and launched into another well-rehearsed lecture on how they could be beneficial for quality of life but should be viewed strictly as complementary to the Gold Standard medical approach.

'Don't worry, Mr Eklund, I'm not a tree-hugging veggie loon.'

A thin smile flitted about his lips. 'You put it so succinctly. I'll tell my secretary to book you in for the chemo clinic then.'

But Barbara shook her head. 'Not just yet.'

She didn't elaborate, not when Mr Eklund asked her, and not after he'd left.

Afterwards, Helen and Neil talked about it in the car. They were both shocked that she'd think of turning down treatment.

'We should phone Eklund and tell him to set it up anyway,' said Helen. 'Every day might matter. What if she's not thinking straight?'

'I'll try to talk to her tonight,' said Neil. 'I don't think the hospital will do anything without her say-so, but I'm sure I'll manage to convince her. She'd be mad just to walk away now.'

'I suppose it might be a way of feeling in control,' Helen wondered aloud. 'All that's been taken from her, she just wants to show them she can put her foot down and make decisions.'

When they reached the house, Helen planned to switch to her own car to go and pick up Barney and Alys – it would have been too much of a squash with them all in Neil's. She sent Julie a text to tell her she was (just about) on the way.

She was relieved to get the reply – *Thnks 4 lettin me know. Kids having a ball.* She hadn't been sure how they would settle with a relative stranger. Given what Julie said, Helen decided she could afford five minutes in the house to change her sandals – one of her heels was rubbing red raw – and to send another quick stalling email to her boss. Hassling Helen about when she would be back had evidently been the number one item on her Monday morning to-do list. Neil said he'd come too – he wanted to pick up a few bits from the little Tesco nearby.

As they drove to Julie's house, Helen's mind was still chewing over Barbara's comments about the chemo. She could vouch for the absence of any tree-hugging veggie loon tendencies in her mother, and, although she hadn't said anything earlier, she was worried that Barbara's ambivalence about treatment was somehow tied up with those bloody notes. She remembered Barbara saying something about cancer not being the worst way to die. Perhaps it had been more than a throwaway remark.

The estate that Julie's house was in turned out to be a bit of a maze. Helen turned the corner into her cul-de-sac, half looking at the satnav to check she'd got the right turn. When she looked up, she could see Julie on the pavement with Alys in her arms. One of her own girls was beside her, the other a few steps away on a front lawn that was presumably theirs. She couldn't see Barney. It could be a nightmare trying to get him to come home after playdates. He was probably hiding from her.

Even as Helen slowed the car, though, her mind started to register that something was wrong. Subconsciously, she began to process the anguish on Julie's features and the anxious poses of all three children. Julie hauled the door open before the car had fully come to a stop, and Helen's heart was already hammering – the hummingbird from yesterday turned into a scrabbling flock.

'It's Barney,' Julie said, her voice panicked. 'He's gone.'

'What do you mean?' There was a desperate note in her own voice now. The question rose to a screech.

'I can't find him, Helen. We've been looking for ten minutes. Barney's gone.'

*

Helen had fainted once in her life. On a visit to a pig farm with Guides. It was high summer and she was hot and dehydrated and the stench in the airless pig sheds was too much for her. She could still remember the sensation – it was almost more than a memory. When she thought about it, it was as if she was back there. If she didn't catch herself she could feel herself breaking into a sweat and her breath getting too quick and shallow.

What she remembered from fainting was that her vision went dark from the edges; she could only see through a fuzzy circle that was getting smaller and smaller all the time. The noise around her – the sounds of the pigs and happily chattering voices (nobody had realised she was unwell) – had faded too, like someone was turning down the volume control. She was terror-struck, and falling, slowly, into a deep, deep well.

That was exactly what it felt like when Julie told her Barney had gone. The darkness and the underwater noises. She didn't faint, though for a moment she thought that she might. This time she fought back the blackness and clawed her way out of the well. She had to; Barney needed her.

Helen and Neil jumped out of the car and joined Julie searching the street. Barney had been with her in the front garden not ten minutes ago, she told them. Again and again, she told them that as they called his name and looked under every car, in every bin, around every clump of shrubs.

Helen looked at her watch – 16.09 – it was more than ten minutes now, whatever Julie said. They must have pulled up at 16.04 or 16.05, and she'd said ten minutes then. It must be closer to twenty now. Twenty minutes could mean fifteen miles in a car. They were close to the motorway here. He could be almost anywhere in an hour or two.

She called and called, but it quickly felt hopeless. Barney wasn't silly in that way – if he could hear them he'd know they were worried. He'd come to them if he possibly could. He wasn't one for wandering off, either. Helen couldn't believe he'd just taken himself into another garden or away from Julie's house. She was choking down acid, fighting physical panic, clinging to Alys as she searched.

'No like!' The toddler wriggled. 'Too hard, Mummy!'

The three adults met up at the end of Julie's drive once they'd covered the length of the short street between them.

'God, I can't believe this. Do you think we should call the police?' Julie asked. Her face was ashen, her hands constantly reaching out to touch her own children.

Neil nodded his head. 'You two do that. I'll keep looking. I'm sure we'll find him soon.'

'Another part of the estate?' Julie suggested.

'Is there anywhere he could have got trapped?' asked Dad. 'Ponds, grit bins, sheds – we need to check those first.'

'Perhaps in some of the gardens. We could knock on the doors,' Julie said. 'Most of the back gardens have side access; maybe he's caught sight of something interesting and wandered in.'

Helen didn't have any words, so she let them talk. This wasn't really happening, she told herself. He'll be back in a minute.

Then a door opened across the street. The movement caught Julie and Neil's attention at the same time as Helen's. An elderly woman emerged and all three of them turned towards her, expectantly.

'Are you looking for a little boy?' she called, making her way down her own drive and towards the road.

'Have you seen him?' said Neil. But whatever she had to tell them, it seemed she wasn't for shouting it across the street.

They walked to the edge of the pavement, each second elongating as the woman picked her way towards them. Bizarrely, Helen noticed she had Hello Kitty slippers on her feet. They looked pristine; she clearly didn't make a habit of walking the streets in them. Why was she noticing slippers? Helen almost laughed. She was giddy with desperation.

'About this high?' the woman gestured as she came towards them.

'A bit smaller,' Helen said. 'He's just turned five.'

She shrugged. 'I'm not good with ages these days. Wearing a blue-striped T-shirt?'

'That's right.' The seconds seemed to slow to hours. Helen willed the woman to spit out whatever she had to say.

'I saw him get into a car,' she said. 'On the corner.'

No. No. No. No. No.

Anxiety turned to sheer panic and Helen heard a wrenching sob that could only have come from her own mouth. Once again, black clouded the edges of her vision and she had to fight just to stay standing. The old woman turned to her, her features etched with a pity that Helen didn't want. Neil and Julie were both frozen themselves, but the neighbour reached out and took Helen's hand.

'No one grabbed him,' she said softly. 'He just got in. Could it be someone you know?'

'What kind of car?' said Neil, and Helen knew that, like her, he was thinking – praying – that it might be Darren's hire car.

But suddenly she was running on rocket fuel. Her mind was whirring, and she knew they had to assume the worst, not the best.

'Wait,' she said, pulling out her mobile. 'Tell it straight to the police.'

*

The next hour was a blur. The local police took it seriously, and soon they had three patrol cars out specifically looking for Barney, and an alert on all their vehicles as well as on local news. It turned out that Mrs Tilbury, Julie's neighbour, had only the vaguest description to give. The car was pale grey, white or silver, she thought, and was a 'family car' size. She didn't recognise makes or models generally and hadn't glanced at the registration. As she had said, it didn't seem untoward until she noticed the search in the street.

'I'm so, so sorry,' she told Helen for the thousandth time, and for the thousandth time Helen had to remind herself to thank God that Mrs Tilbury *had* put two and two together because they could easily still be checking the bins around this sprawling estate as whoever had taken Barney sped off to God-knows-where to do God-knows-she-couldn't-even-think-about-it-or-she'd-be-sick. Eventually, one of the police officers guided Mrs Tilbury off and Helen watched from Julie's front window as she shuffled across the street in her Hello Kittys, still, from the looks of it, apologising.

The description she'd given might have been a match for Darren's hired Astra – amongst a zillion other cars. Helen had called him as soon as she'd hung up on the 999 call handler, but it had gone to voicemail. She'd left a message and called him back five or six times since, and also called both Chris and Adam's mobiles, and their home phone, but all to no avail. She'd not been able to give the police a registration plate for the car, but she had noticed the name of the hire company on a window sticker, so they hoped they'd be able to get the details quickly.

One of the police officers had introduced herself as Veena and had produced tea for them whilst they'd sat in the living room listening to Mrs Tilbury saying the same thing over and over again to the other two male officers.

Julie had put her cup to her lips and immediately taken it away again. 'It's sweet,' she'd said.

Veena had smiled. 'You've all had a shock. It's one of my skills, you know, finding the sugar in anyone's kitchen.'

Helen hadn't *had* a shock, she thought, she was *having* one. And what would help was the police finding Barney, not feeding her sweet tea. But she didn't say anything. After a moment, out of habit, she took a sip from her own cup. The flavour of weak, sweetened tea took Helen back to her childhood, to being in the greenhouse with Neil, or in front of the telly watching early evening sitcoms.

Veena gently suggested, after Mrs Tilbury had left, that Neil and Helen could go back home, that the police would do everything they could to find Barney as quickly as possible, but she could explain the process to them there, and they could wait for news 'more comfortably'.

Helen realised then that she was in a stranger's house, that she'd never before sat on Julie's stiff matching leather sofas or drunk from her polka dot china mugs. They took their leave awkwardly. Julie kept telling them it would be okay, reaching out to pat Helen's arm or squeeze Neil's shoulder, in between seeing to Evie and Lexie, who were buzzing about her, high on the drama. She was sniffling a little, dabbing at her nose every now and again with a tissue, but in contrast to her neighbour, she didn't apologise once.

Helen wondered if she was thinking of what people say about car accidents. Don't apologise. Don't admit liability. Why had the kids been playing in the front garden instead of the back? Helen had glimpsed patio doors from the kitchen-diner, a trampoline and sandpit. That was where they ought to have been. And what had Julie been doing when Barney was getting into the back of an unknown car?

'Did you not—' Helen started to ask her, after she'd got

Alys's shoes back on, and when Neil was holding out her handbag. But Veena put a firm hand on her shoulder.

'Not now, Helen,' she said softly. 'We'll speak to Mrs Hendricks in due course. Let us do our job. Now, do you feel okay to drive?'

Back in the car, Alys wanted to know where Barney was. Helen opened her mouth once or twice, but only a strangled noise came out. Neil came to her rescue.

'There's been a bit of a mix-up, sweetheart, about who should be looking after Barney. But don't you worry about it – us adults will get it sorted. He'll be back right as rain before you know it.'

Of course he was right, Helen told herself. He had to be.

When they arrived home, Veena made yet more tea, then she became businesslike; there were lots of questions about the family, about Barney, about why Helen was staying with her parents and who she knew in the area. Veena got her to email some photos so they could start to be circulated amongst the patrol cars looking out for him and asked her to write down as much as she could remember about every item of clothing Barney had had on.

'I don't know if he's got Rabbit,' Helen cried, suddenly stricken in the middle of describing his little cargo shorts.

'Rabbit?'

'His favourite toy – it goes with him everywhere. He took it to Julie's.'

'I'll make a note, get someone to check if it's at Julie's house, and add it to the description. Thank you.'

Helen sent up a silent prayer: *Please let him have Rabbit.*

'I have to ask you, Helen,' she said, after they'd gone through an exhaustive description and she'd relayed it back to her team. 'Do you have any inkling, any suspicion, anything you want to tell us about?'

Of course she didn't hesitate for a second over keeping Barbara's confidence now that Barney's safety was in the balance. 'My dad should hear this,' she said.

Neil had been putting Alys to bed. She still liked a song before she went to sleep and Helen paused on the stairs to listen to him finishing a chorus of 'Scarborough Fair'. His gruff voice creaked and her throat and chest tightened. A minute later he slipped out of the door.

'Asleep already,' he whispered. Helen was astonished. How could she be? But then Alys's trust in Helen, in all of the adults in her life, was so complete. Helen realised that even with Barney missing little Alys couldn't imagine that everything was anything other than okay. She hoped desperately that Alys would never have to learn how drastically they'd failed her brother.

It was almost seven p.m. now. Helen didn't know how; it was as if the clocks were against them, racing to separate her from her darling boy. Eight hours since she'd touched him, since she'd heard his voice. Three hours since he'd gone ... missing. Missing. Missing. Missing. Once she'd formed it, the word echoed round her head like a curse. She took a deep breath, trying to shut it out, then went back to the living room and Veena.

'My mum has been receiving threatening notes,' she started.

Veena took a few details about the notes, how Helen had found out about them.

'Can I see them?'

'Give me a minute, I'll get them.'

When she returned from the bedroom and handed the

notes over, Veena read them in silence. 'I see,' she said, finally, setting her pen down with a sigh.

Neil, reading over Veena's shoulder, had gone pale and still. 'The heparin, Helen – was she poisoned?'

She went towards him, looking to put an arm around his shoulders, but he shook her away.

'Was she poisoned?' Now his voice was gruff, demanding.

'I don't know, Dad, I don't know.'

'But you knew about this!' He gestured towards the green papers now stacked in an evidence bag Veena had produced from her belt.

'I promised I wouldn't tell you – she knew you'd worry.'

'Of course I'd worry, and then I'd have done something and she might not have been poisoned.' His voice cracked. 'And for all we know Barney might still be here.'

This time, he allowed her to clasp his hands, and after a moment he pulled them free and wrapped his arms around her. Neil was a broad man, with thick sinewy arms and big gardener's hands. She'd never stopped feeling like a child in his embrace. She'd never been more glad of it than now.

'What do you mean, about your wife being poisoned?' Veena asked, gently, her watchful eyes on them every moment.

Helen told her everything: her stilted conversations with Barbara, the awful night in the hospital and the move to St Aeltha's, then her tiny, clumsy steps to try to investigate her mother's past. Veena's lips grew thin when she described what Amy had done, though Helen refused to say who'd given her the information, or even what force she belonged to.

'Worrying about my friend can't help you find Barney,' she pointed out.

'No,' Veena admitted. 'But we can check who's run searches, you know.' Helen wondered if she was bluffing.

Neil had been silent through most of this, still trying to get his head around it, Helen supposed. But he was the one who asked the key question.

'Do you think there's a link? Could whoever wrote these things have taken Barney to get at Barbara?'

'We'll follow all leads, Mr Marsden,' Veena replied, suddenly all brittle professionalism. 'But what we really need to do right now, Mrs Harrison, is get hold of your husband.'

# June 1973

*Barbara*

Throughout the spring, the child grew like a knot of fear in Barbara's belly.

In the garden, Neil's flower beds were coming to life, their blooms blossoming in strict order: first the tiny snowdrops, then the crocuses, the narcissi, the tulips and finally the swollen heads of the peonies, their petals bunched tight as a punch before the extravagant frills burst out. By that time she'd left work and become too fat to move, so those blousy pink pompoms bobbing in the borders marked the limits of her world. Like the flowers, the child inside had grown steadily larger, more showy, more confident of its place in the world.

Neil had become a gardener almost from the moment they had first moved in to the little terrace, immediately beginning to fiddle around with seeds and compost and buying enough bamboo canes to build another *Kon-Tiki*. Perhaps she should have realised then that he was a nurturer and that the baby question was not going to be something she could simply ignore.

The sun beat down and the baby kicked in protest and she felt her body might melt into the cushioning of the new patterned sunbed that Neil had bought home in triumph two weekends ago. Neil's happiness, the bright optimism of the sunbed, even the intensity of the summer weather – to Barbara it felt as if it was all there to mock her. She couldn't do this, she couldn't be a mother, she couldn't be responsible for a child, and the crazy folly of it would soon come crashing in on them like a slamming cell door; she knew it.

The air was filled with the smell of her own anxious sweat, mixed with the suntan lotion she'd smoothed on earlier in the morning and the faint, grassy perfume of the garden. Tired though she was, sleep was elusive. These last few weeks, as the mercury crept higher each day, Barbara had lived her life through a haze, a gauzy wrapping that made the outside world alien and difficult and turned her in so that she became a world within herself, with the terror of the child at its heart.

The child. She thought of it as a girl; that was her instinct, although her terror about the whole thing was such that a part of her was sure she must be wrong. It would come out as a boy just to spite her.

If it was a boy, they had decided they would call him Steven, a girl would be Victoria. Nice names. Popular, and modern-sounding, but not burdensome. Neil had made a stilted little speech about not wanting to do family names, about how it was an outdated tradition that only served to cause trouble. He had tiptoed around the fact she'd never told him any of the family names on her side. She could have come from a whole clan of Stevens and Alisons.

She'd been thinking lately that she wasn't so sure about Victoria. That maybe it was a bit fusty, a little too... *Victorian*.. She was wondering about Helen instead; but then it would probably be a boy anyway. Her mind drifted to the last time she'd had to pick a name. There hadn't been nine months to think about it then, closer to nine minutes, although maybe that had made it easier. She picked up her library book and put it down again. Half-heartedly, she tried to fan herself with it instead.

They'd gone out to the Bridge Café at Moreton Chase the previous night. The two of them, plus Brian and Alison, Dave and Moira, and Alan Crookshank, who remained the eternal bachelor. The others had organised it and Neil had persuaded her they ought to go.

Barbara had been too hot and tired to talk much, besides which she had nothing to say, having spent the best part of the week marooned on the new sunbed whilst failing to read her forgettable novel. She felt brazen going for an evening out with her belly the size it was, notwithstanding the ring on her finger and Neil's arm on her waist. They'd have called it bold, when she was growing up; some things were not for public consumption. Now it was 1973 and they had free contraception and the Equal Pay Act and Germaine Greer, but sometimes it was easy to forget that.

They were Neil's friends anyway, Barbara thought to herself, stroking her belly. She had plenty of acquaintances; it was just that where Alison and Moira were intertwined, curling and twisting around each other's lives and holding each other up like a pair of Neil's pea plants, she preferred to keep a little separate. And she made that space, distinct but unobtrusive, in all of her relationships. In each case it assumed a different shape – with Alison and Moira she separated herself by choosing to work, not going shopping with them, not inviting them to use the back door. At work she ate her sandwiches at her desk and left after one drink on the rare occasions they persuaded her to go out. She didn't gossip with the hairdresser or the neighbours. She was poor at making phone calls and never sent Christmas cards to the other couples they'd met on holiday.

It was tempting to tell herself that Neil was the exception, that she didn't hold herself back from him. But she knew that she was giving herself an excuse. If she were a plant she wouldn't be entwined with Neil either. If anything, he would be the bamboo cane, keeping her upright and straight, bound to her with lovingly tied bits of twine, whilst all the time there was some force, just as invisible and irresistible as gravity, trying to pull her away from him. She wondered if he knew that, if he realised what a miracle it was that she'd found him and what a mess she'd be without him. She wondered if he had any inkling that she was having the child purely for his sake, and how much she feared it would cost her to do it. She hoped not.

It was easy now to spend hours in these musings, the weight of her middle anchoring her to the sunbed and the sky so bright she got black and white spots even with her eyes shut. She didn't notice exactly when the discomfort sharpened into a tightening and finally became pain. The realisation that this was it – that the baby was coming – stole up on her as gradually as the midsummer sun slipped down through the silhouetted leaves of the distant ash trees. What was she scared of? Not so much of the birth – it had to come out, after all. No, she was afraid of what came next.

Abe had called just the day before to say that she would definitely be allowed to keep the child, and the news terrified and thrilled her in equal measure. Social services had raised concerns, but she'd made a good impression at the interview she'd had with them, and Abe had persuaded them they didn't need to interview Neil unless there were any specific issues in future.

Now the court had endorsed their report; no one would take their baby away. If things went well, the child need never know. More importantly, Neil need never know about their narrow escape. Abe still wanted her to tell Neil everything, although when push came to shove he backed her up. Aside from that disagreement, Barbara was a model charge. Abe had more serious problems to worry about than her and Neil.

When Neil arrived home at quarter past ten, she was still on the sunbed. He'd been doing extra shifts where he could get them, to save up for the baby and in case the office had to go on short time again later in the year. He came into the garden, grimaced and glanced up to where the vapour trails from a couple of jets were reflecting the last pink afterglow of the sunset.

'It's barely cooled at all, has it?' he said. 'I suppose we won't be getting much sleep again tonight.'

'No,' she replied, blinking back the strongest twinge of the evening. 'I don't think we will.'

*

Much later, after Neil had been paraded in to be presented with his daughter, and then swiftly shepherded on by the nurses, Barbara took her daughter back and felt glad to have the baby against her skin once more. The gladness came as a surprise, a relief. 'Helen,' she cooed, drawing out the last syllable so it sounded almost French. There was a long way to go, but, just maybe, they could do it.

168

She had found it hard to watch Neil with the child in his arms, rapture written across his face and growing clearer every moment as the summer dawn flooded the ward with light. She tried to tell herself it was maternal instinct, the natural wrench of being parted from the flesh and blood that had been part of her own for all those long months. She knew, though, in her heart, that that was not the cause of her pain.

In Neil's expression she saw a reflection of another fatherly face. A man who had looked at a baby in just that way – with the same beautiful, terrible, hurricane-force love. A man who Barbara hated more than anything else in the world. A man on whom she'd sworn she would have her revenge.

Barbara sometimes wondered if she loved Neil so fiercely because he couldn't have been more different to that other man. In looks, in voice, in opinions, in everything he had been the opposite of Neil. In everything, that was, except the look in his eyes when he held his child. And, just as before, the child gazed innocently back, with never an inkling of the trouble it was going to cause.

Even now, even in this moment where she should be at her happiest, she was tainted and tarnished by the memory of *him*. He had stolen any chance of her enjoying her own child, ruined any possibility of her being a normal mother. Probably he'd all but forgotten her, but she hadn't forgotten him.

# August 2017

*Helen*

She watched the clock: 15.32, 15.47, 15.55, 15.57, 15.58, 15.59, 16.00. Twenty-four hours. Barney had been gone for twenty-four hours. She didn't know where he was, who he was with or if he was okay. She didn't know if he had Rabbit or if he was crying for her. She didn't even know the exact moment when that twenty-four-hour milestone had been reached, and she didn't know why that bothered her as much as it did.

Neil said she should sleep. Veena said the same. How was she meant to sleep without her son? How was she meant to exist at all? She had no tears left. She had no words left.

She had nothing.

*Barbara*

You knew you were old, Barbara realised, when you stopped caring about what happened to you. Her ambivalence towards this cancer – trivial, tiresome, terminal (possibly? probably? She sensed, rather than knew the answer) – threw the point into stark relief. She felt a crushing tiredness and a general disengagement from life. What a gift it would be to start her sixty-nine years again, she thought, and what a curse to have another sixty-nine to go from here.

She told herself she should shake off such morbid thoughts and accompanied the resolution with a determined little twitch of her shoulders, which then set off a pounding in her head. She'd take another ten years and be grateful – twenty even – if she had her health. There was no point in wishing it away. But the cancer wouldn't kill her quickly, not from what Eklund said. And she needed a few days, perhaps weeks, of clarity and energy and purpose (as much as she could muster at any rate) more than she needed a few more months or years of twilit, fading life.

She might take the chemo in the end, but she wouldn't take it now. She needed to be sharp and there was too much risk it would blunt her. Plus, there was still a chance that she would need an exit route, and there was no point in giving up the most obvious one. For now though, her mind was fogged enough, and she needed to keep it as clear as possible. She'd started this game and she needed her wits about her to finish it.

Anyway, not *all* that she had once been had crumbled. Barbara knew about being hunted and being trapped. She knew about it in her veins and her sinews, just as a fox or a hare knows about it. The worst she had to say about the bloody cancer was that it stopped her from running. Barbara had always kept shoes by the door, cash tucked in the bureau. She had always been ready to run away; now it was time that was running away from her.

Eventually, she focused on the clock. It wasn't enough just to look at it, *looking* did not penetrate the miasma, *looking* left her swimming in these drugged and indolent thoughts.

With effort, she interrogated the clock; she drilled into its mysteries to read the time: almost half past four. Her brow furrowed, the action was slow and deliberate, almost as mechanical as if she'd had to lift a hand to pull a thread that would concertina the skin. The curtains were open and the sun was shining, so it must be afternoon. This thought was confirmed when she turned to the tray by her bedside, which showed evidence of lunch. Yes, she thought, asparagus soup. And no one had come.

Slowly, she turned to the unit beside her bed and fumbled for her washbag. She had to pause for several breaths before she was able to lift it to her lap and draw the zip. Inside, there was another zipped bag, a little needlecord purse that she'd bought at a Christmas fair. The pattern of holly berries danced before her eyes. Inside that, a cheap plastic phone, a text message waiting for her: *IT'S DONE.*

An uneasy wave of excitement flooded through her. Then she carefully replaced the phone and rang the bell.

'Everything okay, Mrs Marsden?'

The nurses came quickly here. There was a smiling head poking round the door frame almost before her finger had left the buzzer.

'Yes, I just wondered ... is it half past four?'

'That's right.'

'Where are ... I mean, have I had any visitors today?'

'No, Mrs Marsden, don't worry, you're not going mad! Your husband called to say there was a problem at home. Nothing for you to worry about, but it means they can't get in today. We would have told you, but you were dozing earlier.'

Barbara nodded and the nurse bustled out. She considered phoning, even going so far as to pick up the hospital handset from beside the bed. It was a proper phone – the handset was made of chunky moulded plastic and attached to the base with a spiral cord. At home they had a sleek dinky cordless model that was always getting itself lost. Should she phone Neil or Helen? She cradled the handset on her chest, never quite able to bring herself to dial either of their numbers.

'Mrs Marsden? What's wrong? Do you need something?'

It was the same nurse as before. Barbara was puzzled. 'I'm fine. You've just been in.'

The nurse sighed and pointed to the handset. 'Your phone's been off the hook for three minutes,' she said. 'It alerts us in case you're trying to get help.'

Barbara looked down at the handset, surprised she'd been holding it for so long. There was a faint buzzing coming from it.

'Sorry, my fault.'

'Don't worry, Mrs Marsden, it's what we're here for. Do you want to call home? I could do it for you if you like?'

But Barbara shook her head.

'What about some television then?'

'It's all right, I'll just doze I think.'

'Good idea. Get some rest.'

The nurse left for the second time. Barbara used the remote control to shut the curtains, closed her eyes and tried to empty her mind of the worry. It might have worked, it might not, but the same nurse opened the door again before she had a chance to get close to sleep.

'I'm sorry to disturb you.' She looked pale and worried, her cheery, bustling competence suddenly deserting her. All of Barbara's senses pricked to attention as the woman continued to speak. 'I'm afraid the police are here to talk to you.'

The policeman took off his hat as he came into the room, followed by a young female officer who did the same. 'Mrs Marsden?' he said, waiting for her confirmation. 'Mrs Marsden?' the officer tried again, awkward, as he moved towards her in his clumsy boots and stiff vest.

'Yes. Sorry.'

'I'm PC Hurran. This is my colleague PC Merrick. Do you mind if we sit down?'

'What are you here for?'

He took a seat anyway. 'I have some bad news for you, I'm afraid.'

'What's wrong? What's happened?'

His stomach bulged as he sat and there was a glisten of sweat on his brow. He didn't look tall enough or fit enough to be a policeman, she thought. He wouldn't have got through in the old days. She felt a flicker of contempt.

'Barney, your grandson. Unfortunately, he's gone missing. A member of the public saw him getting into an unknown vehicle yesterday afternoon. He's not been seen since.'

His tone was flat, his eyes searching. Barbara's heart lurched and it took her by surprise. She had felt only half-alive since the operation; she almost wouldn't have believed she still had it in her to react like that.

'No!' It came out as a sob. 'Why are you here? Surely you should be looking for him?'

'We're doing all we can, Mrs Marsden, believe me. Your husband wanted to come and visit – in fact I'm sure he'll be along this evening – but I wanted to speak to you first.'

'Why? I don't understand.'

'Yesterday your daughter told one of my colleagues about some letters, Mrs Marsden, anonymous letters addressed to you.'

Barbara nodded slowly. 'That's right, I've been so stupid ... Sorry ... what did you say you were called?'

'PC Hurran. Ned Hurran.'

'Do you think, PC Hurran, do you think Jennifer has taken Barney? I couldn't live with myself if I've put him in danger.'

'I don't know, Mrs Marsden, but I'd certainly like to know more about Jennifer.'

'Of course,' said Barbara. 'Of course. I'm sorry. Of course I should have told someone before now.' Her throat was dry, she realised. She wasn't used to making long speeches to her visitors. She coughed. 'PC Hurran, would you mind pouring me some water?'

He nodded to the female PC, who lifted the sinuous carafe by the bedside and handed a glass to Barbara. PC Hurran, meanwhile, settled himself in the deep cushions of the velvet armchair, and took out an electronic notepad.

'So ...' he looked expectantly at her, '... tell me about it.'

# June 1970

*Neil*

He'd been a nervous groom. It wasn't a question of cold feet – he'd wanted to marry Barbara within a fortnight of meeting her. No, it had been the wedding itself that made Neil nervous. He felt like a dancing bear in a circus, or a turkey at Christmas. He couldn't wait for it to be over, for the wedding and all that went with it to be done with, and for him and Barbara finally to be heading off together, husband and wife.

A touch on his shoulder made him jump. He hadn't noticed his mum slip round the bedroom door. Now, Beryl was standing on her tiptoes to peer over his shoulder and into the little rectangle of the mirror.

'You look lovely, Neil. I'm right proud of you.'

'Thanks, Mum.'

'So's your father. You know that, don't you?'

Neil sighed. 'If he is, he does a grand job of keeping it to himself.'

Ten minutes later the family were walking together up the lane that led to the church, Frank Marsden's medals clanking against his chest as he reminisced about his own wedding.

For once, Neil was pleased that his father was chuntering on – he could just say 'hmm' occasionally. His sister Vicky, as bridesmaid, was with Barbara. In her place, kicking his heels and failing to make small talk with Beryl was Alan Crookshank, Neil's best man.

Neil glanced at his watch. In an hour they'd be married. In four hours or so the worst of the public humiliation would be over. This time tomorrow ... He felt himself blush.

'And you're sure that you know what to do, lad?'

The change in his father's tone caught Neil's attention; the familiar lecturing voice had suddenly become hushed and gruff, but he no idea what the lead-up to the question had been.

'In the church, you mean ...'

'*No.*' Frank had put on a little spurt of pace, and he glanced behind him before continuing in hushed tones. 'Tonight. With Barbara.'

*Bloody hell.* This was not a conversation Neil wanted to be having at all. 'S'awright, Dad,' he blurted out.

Frank nodded. 'Good lad.'

Neil was convinced that Alan Crookshank was killing himself with silent laughter a few steps behind.

*

They spent their honeymoon in a hotel on Loch Lomond. Friends had suggested Spain or even North Africa, but Barbara had been firm that she didn't want to go abroad.

It turned out that a dodgy tummy wasn't the only thing she didn't want to risk on honeymoon. Neil discovered that there had been a trip to the GP a few weeks before the wedding and a small dial-pack dispenser had appeared in their shared toilet bag. His face had flushed when he saw it, almost as red as that walk to the church with his dad.

He had picked up the pack with a trembling hand, and turned back into the bedroom, holding them out to her. 'Did you ask the doctor for these?'

'What do you think? I didn't buy them on the street, Neil.'

'But, weren't you ...' He faltered.

'Mortified?' she'd prompted, as she smoothed the felt of her good hat and reached up to put it safely on top of the wardrobe.

'Well, *shy?*'

'No. I'm a married woman, Neil. And it's 1970, not the Middle Ages.' She flashed a smile towards the doorway of the en suite, where he still stood, awkwardly, holding the edge of the pill pack. 'Hurry up, Neil, or we'll miss breakfast.'

Despite his hesitation over the pill, those nights on the shores of the loch would stick in Neil's memory as some of the best times of his life. The pair of them had spent three years not doing it; Neil had been brought up to believe that good girls didn't. In their early days he'd cajoled her a bit for the sake of good form, but in truth he desperately wanted Barbara to turn out to be a good girl. Something told him that if he pushed too hard he might get what he had asked for and regret it.

That first night in the hotel had been a little awkward. Barbara had been solemn before, and a little tearful afterwards, but wasn't that what girls were supposed to be like? Up in Scotland they both relaxed into it more. Barbara still seemed to need to retreat a little, to find some hiding place within herself just as he got close to her. But when he asked her about it she claimed she was enjoying sleeping with him and couldn't explain the shadow that seemed to creep over her.

The image of the little pack of pills kept floating into his mind, though, intruding on his contentment. Should it bother him, he wondered, that she'd not talked to him about it first? Nah, he decided. A couple of years in their own place before the kids came along didn't seem like such a bad idea.

Neil liked the misty mountains well enough, but his favourite time was the rainy day when they drove down to Glasgow. In Lewis's, Barbara tried on frocks and bought a kohl pencil to do her eyes like the girls on TV. Whilst she took her time in the ladies', Neil sneaked to the cashier's desk with a swooshy baby-doll dress in a vivid blue that had set her eyes off perfectly.

At his insistence, Barbara opened the tissue-wrapped package in the street outside.

'My God, Neil, it's beautiful. I only meant to try them on as a joke.'

'Hey.' He lifted her chin and could see the tears threatening to spill onto the kohl. 'You deserve it, Mrs Marsden. Now, why don't you nip back in there and put it on?'

'Shall I?'

'Yes! But I'll do my waiting in the pub this time.'

Neil headed down the street to the bar he'd pointed out as Barbara disappeared back into Lewis's. As he waited, he thought back to when they first met, on a Friday night over an ice cream float in the Bridge Café at Moreton Chase services.

Barbara and the other waitresses wore stiff new caps and the lights of the cars on the motorway streaked beneath them in the September gloom. The stretches of bypasses and relief roads were gradually linking up just as Macmillan had promised. Up to Cumbria; down to Birmingham; onwards to the future. The ice cream floats they served in the restaurant seemed more American than the dull pints of heavy that they sometimes drank in the same pubs and clubs as their weary fathers. But a little way down his float, Neil had found his teeth ached with the cold and sugar.

'Frozen teeth?'

It had taken him a moment to register that the young waitress was talking to him, and then another to realise that she must have spotted him wincing as he sipped at the float. She wasn't mocking though; she looked sweet, with wide brown eyes and a slight blush on her cheeks that he couldn't help but smile at.

'Yeah.' He'd shrugged. 'I should just have had a cup of tea.'

'Oh, I wouldn't do that now. The heat'll make it worse, see? I could get you a plain Coca-Cola if you like.'

Her pen had hovered efficiently over the pad, and her efforts could simply have been in aid of another order, but Neil hadn't thought so. A canine had pressed into her pink frosted lips and it had dawned on Neil that she was nervous.

'I'll persevere, thanks,' he had said. Then, taking a gamble: 'Are you new here, love?'

She had nodded quickly. 'I just moved here, started the job last week. Someone else let them down. It's hard to get in here, you know! But I won't stay for long. I'm going to be a journalist.'

She had shaken her hair back, looking even younger suddenly.

'I can believe it,' he'd said. 'You're doing great. And maybe I will have that Coke.' He'd paused while she wrote carefully on her pad, then he'd taken a deep breath. 'What time will you get off at then?'

The chatter between Brian and Alan had died away beside him. The waitress hadn't answered immediately. Instead, her bottom lip had disappeared further behind her teeth and Neil had let himself imagine kissing the tiny pink marks off the slick enamel.

'Not till ten,' she'd said, tucking a wisp of dark hair back under her cap. The clock over her shoulder had said ten to nine.

He'd waited, though, and it had paid off. She'd been grateful for the lift and directed him to a large Victorian villa in a part of the town he didn't know very well. He still remembered his first sight of the hostel, how the street lamps outside made a spiky jungle of the blackberries that had taken over the garden. Inside, two windows had been lit on the upper floors, one covered with newspaper and the other partially obscured by a sweep of brightly striped cloth. Neil had seen a woman with a baby in her arms peer out at the car and then quickly turn away from the window. The light in that room had gone off and the colours of the stripes had disappeared in the darkness.

'This is your ... home?'

Barbara had nodded, and again he'd seen the flash of her teeth as they scraped her bottom lip. The pink lipstick was all gone. Her hair had flattened and she looked younger still.

'I'd really like to take you out for a drink sometime, Barbara.'

'I'll have to think about it.'

'Do you have a telephone number then?'

She'd glanced towards the house. 'That wouldn't really work.'

So she'd only been being polite when she said she'd think about the drink.

'I see. Okay,' he'd said, turning away to mask his embarrassment. He'd waited for her to open the door and get out, but instead she'd put a hand on his sleeve. Her touch had been light, but enough to make him turn.

'You could give me yours. I'll call you. I promise.'

Thank God she'd kept her word.

*

She finally appeared, walking with an uncharacteristic air of self-consciousness down that dour Glasgow street in the blue dress. He caught sight of her just as a flash of evening sun cut through the city skyline. She looked like a girl from a fashion plate, with the swing of the dress and the kohl drawing out her figure and sparkling eyes. Her brow was set in the slightest frown of concentration as she scanned the shopfronts, looking for the pub.

She was blind to her own beauty, he realised, completely unaware of the way she drew admiring eyes from men – and women – as she walked past. Neil's heart could have burst with pride, and he knew that would be the way he'd always remember her. Not as the nervous bride, drowned in white and standing in front of the empty half of the church, but walking down Argyle Street in a burst of sunshine, her face breaking into a sudden, wonderful grin when she saw him wave through the window.

# August 2017

*Barbara*

'I gave them my name.'

Tears were seeping slowly onto her cheeks, but she ignored them. These days, her tears were sparse and lethargic, like everything else about her. She could afford to let them fall. She spoke hesitantly, coaxing out the story that had haunted the forgotten, dusty corners of her mind for decades. With every word, the past took on a form and substance she'd tried to deny it for years. Bit by bit, word by word, she was resurrecting Katy.

'My name was Katy Clery. I went to prison when I was fourteen. They called it a secure unit. It was meant to be a children's home, but it was prison really. I went to a real prison after, so I should know.'

PC Hurran passed her a tissue from the box that was closer to her than to him. She dabbed vaguely at her jawline.

'They let me out at twenty and gave me a new name, a new life.'

'You said a minute ago you gave them your name. You mean your old name? Who did you give it to?'

'I'm telling you ... Let me get there ... It was with the breast cancer diagnosis. They told me ... they told me genes were important. My mother died of cancer at about my age. I think it was breast cancer – I'm still not completely sure. When they asked about family history, I told them ...' She could feel some strength returning to her voice, the frustration surging into it. 'I undid almost fifty years of being careful and I gave them the names and asked them to look up the medical records.'

'Your mum's records?'

'Yes, and my sister, Sonia. I'm in touch with her – secretly. I can trust her. She had a breast cancer scare a couple of years ago.' She paused, motioning to Hurran to hand her another tissue. 'And then the notes started. I got the first one only a few days later, and another two before I came into hospital. They were hand-delivered to the house – just horrible. I wanted to throw them away, but I couldn't make myself do it.'

'It must have been very disturbing for you, Mrs Marsden.'

'Of course.'

She let her eyelids slip down. Sleep was lurking in the corners of the room, ever-ready to embrace her worn-out body.

PC Hurran wouldn't be able to understand how she could let herself give way to it, given the things they were talking about. Barbara wouldn't have understood herself, a few months ago, before this illness taught her what tiredness really meant. Who would have known that tiredness could be so physical, so extreme, that even this couldn't stand in its way? This tiredness was death's handmaiden, numbing her to go gently. How could this young policeman be expected to understand that?

He coughed. 'Helen told us there had been an incident in

the General. She was concerned that the threats might have turned into action, and that the author of these notes might have been responsible?'

Barbara opened her eyes with some effort.

'I didn't tell her about the notes initially – my family were worried enough with all of this – but she found one.' Barbara felt a flicker of pride for her clever girl, refusing to be fobbed off. She loved Helen, in her own way. She hoped that Helen would be able to see things from her point of view.

'So, this "Jennifer" was connected to the crime you went to gaol for? You'll have to tell me about that. And also about why you kept this from your husband and daughter when it was clear it was getting dangerous. Why did you let the senior medics at the General think it was some sort of accident?'

'Well, that was what the doctors wanted to think.' Her speech was slowing now, and slurred. She could hear the faults in the cadence well enough but could do nothing to fix it. 'Of course I will tell you. I'll do whatever I can to help Barney. But you have to understand.' She paused, unsure for a moment what she was trying to say. It was all such an effort now. 'You have to understand I'm very tired.'

Through her sinking eyelids, she saw PC Hurran nodding, earnestly. And then sleep took her.

*Helen*

Twenty-eight hours. It would be his bedtime soon. The second one without her. If only they could bring him home before bed.

Operation Denim had taken over their lives. Veena, or rather DS Sawhney, was officially appointed as their family liaison

185

officer and they were – briefly – introduced to the senior investigating officer, one DI Nelson. He had a faint Caribbean accent and weary, bloodshot eyes. The street and the house buzzed with officers. Helen sat in the middle, useless and terrified. She hadn't slept; she had barely eaten. Time had lost all meaning except as a way to keep track of the growing number of hours that her boy had been missing.

Darren had called in to the police just before seven a.m. and spoken to her as soon as they'd finished the call. His phone had been out of battery. He'd been staying with 'a friend'. He had no idea what had happened to Barney and was frantic with worry. He would set off to drive back from London as soon as he could. Helen crumpled after the call. The thought that Barney had gone with Darren had been the last straw of hope she'd been clinging to. Yes, it would have been appalling, but so much better than the alternatives. Whatever else she thought about Darren, she knew he would never hurt either of the children.

She spent the day drifting around the house like a spectre, weeping over Alys – however hard she tried not to – folding and smelling Barney's clothes, obsessively checking her phone even though Veena was downstairs and any news would most likely come through her.

When they asked her to come and sit in the living room, her heart raced giddily and she was forced to pause, holding the headboard of Barney's bed for a second or two to steady herself before she felt able to make her way down the stairs. Neil was already sitting on one sofa, opposite Veena on the other, and he patted the cushion, hurrying her to take her own place. Of course she was desperate for any news, but at the same time her fear held her back, dulling her movements as if she was wading through treacle. She sat heavily, blinking up at Veena and waiting to hear something, anything, about her boy.

'We have some news, but not about Barney directly.' She stressed the 'not' and looked at them in turn, checking they'd taken it in. Helen exhaled deeply. 'About your mother,' Veena continued.

'What's happened?' Neil gasped and groped for Helen's hand.

'Two police officers have visited her this afternoon. Basically, she told them that she's been living under a false identity. She underwent gene testing at the hospital and there's a chance this could have compromised her, that persons from her past could have been alerted to her new identity.'

Veena seemed to be reading from a script. Helen couldn't take it in. She was so exhausted that thinking hurt. She could barely form the questions in her own mind, never mind work out what to ask Veena.

'So, as I said, Barbara Kipling is a pseudonym.' Veena rattled on briskly, as if that would keep the wholesale unravelling of Barbara's life – and theirs – somehow on track. 'She was born as Katherine Clery – known as Katy. She was gaoled at fourteen. When she was released, she was given the chance to change her identity.'

Slowly, the bare facts settled in Helen's whirling mind. Her mother, Barbara, wasn't 'Barbara' at all. She'd always known her mother had a secret, but this was more than she could ever have conjured in any flight of imagination. Far from the daydream of her glamorous mother stepping down in the world to marry for love, she had been a criminal on the run from a murky past. Helen was convinced that this secret changed everything – but how, exactly? Her scrambled brain struggled to keep up and to join the dots between this news and poor Barney.

'But why was she in prison? What had she done?' asked Neil.

Helen could tell they were thinking the same thing, that it must have been serious for her to need a new identity. Veena wasn't talking about a spot of shoplifting. Helen was caught off-guard by a spasm of fury. It was all about Barbara; it always had been. She'd led her husband, then her daughter, through a merry dance of lies and deceit, letting them think she was the victim, when it sounded as if she was nothing of the sort. And now Barney was somehow caught up in this dark web, and Helen hadn't been able to protect him because Barbara had kept it all from her. She thought of the years of trying to be close to her mother and feeling shut out, of all the hours of worry about her cancer. When had Barbara ever done anything to earn her daughter's concern?

Veena glanced downwards, her voice dropping. 'Manslaughter.'

'What!' Neil slammed his hand on the table. 'This is crazy, it's just ...'

'Dad, wait. We need to hear her.'

'I'm not sure of the details. I don't want to tell you anything that turns out to be not quite right.' Veena looked tired suddenly. 'It's an old, old case, as you can imagine. We've got people looking for records but ...' She shrugged.

'So what do you know?' Helen said, fighting to keep her voice even.

'The victim was a young child, a girl called Mary Gardiner. The families lived a few streets away from each other.'

'So Barbara knew this child, or what?' Neil asked, frowning.

Veena hesitated. When she spoke again, her tone was cautious. 'Like I said, we've not got the full picture yet. We've called up the papers from archive, but stuff that old isn't scanned in. I don't know what they'll be able to find.'

'Is there anything else you can tell us? You said something about gene testing, and this new identity being compromised?' Helen made a conscious effort to fight back her own emotions and placed a soothing hand over Neil's, which was turning white with the force of his grip on the arm of the sofa.

'This is coming from your mother. She stressed repeatedly to our officers that she'd kept this secret for fifty years. After all that time, she'd thought it would be safe to give the hospital details of her family so they could carry out these tests – to do with her cancer.'

Helen was still puzzled. 'Okay. But what makes her think that's caused a problem? What links Barney – or even what happened to Mum at the General – with all this stuff from her past?'

'Good question. Your mother had told us that Mary had a twin. A twin called Jennifer.'

Veena then swung into interrogatory mode, wanting to go over again every bit of information about the Jennifer notes. Helen found herself reeling too much to protest. Could her mother really be a murderer? The bit of her that should have screamed no was oddly silent. After the initial shock, she felt only numbness and the hard, hard ache for her own missing child.

Helen and Neil sat together long after Veena had retreated to the kitchen to call in to her supervisors. As far as Helen was aware, Veena would have gleaned nothing new about the notes from their conversation, which had largely gone round in circles. That was exactly what Helen's mind continued to do, as she half listened to Neil making his own attempts to make sense of any of it.

The thing she kept coming back to was the gene testing. As far as Helen understood, the point of identifying a family history was to help women who didn't yet have the disease. Barbara already had cancer – it had been found through a mammogram and confirmed by the hospital. What use were the records of her mother and sister? Barbara had managed to keep this secret all her life, as her daughter knew only too well. It seemed odd that she'd let it crumble so unnecessarily. And with such terrible consequences.

But Neil didn't share her surprise.

'You didn't see how the diagnosis hit her, Hels,' he told her. 'She was always sharp as a tack, but it was as if she suddenly lost all her sharpness, her confidence. She didn't know what to do with herself. It makes sense that there was breast cancer in the family. She suddenly felt there was a connection with them, realised she couldn't sever it completely, however hard she'd tried in the past.'

'Perhaps,' said Helen, vaguely. But her mother had been switched on enough to spin a story about the notes coming from a woman who had harassed her for years. If they had started as a result of the cancer diagnosis then they were recent. What possible reason had she had for deliberately encouraging Helen down the wrong track? And if she'd already done that once, then who was to say she wouldn't do it again?

Her thoughts were interrupted by her father's voice. Every so often, Neil would say the name aloud, wonderingly – 'Katherine Clery'; 'Katy, Katherine'; 'Katy Clery' – as if he was trying to make it fit the woman he'd lived with for most of his days. Helen opened her mouth but found she had no words for him. It was all she could do to squeeze his hand.

*Neil*

Eventually, they let Neil go to the hospital. As he drove, his mind raced, kicking and stumbling over the unfamiliar name that supposedly applied to his wife of over forty-five years. She wasn't Katy; she was Barbara – a name that in his mind spun elegantly like a ballerina in pirouette or the handworked spindle of a crafted chair. Katy, on the other hand, lurched like a seesaw, unremarkable before today, but now horrific and alien.

*What Katy Did.* Word association – the title of the book jumped into his mind, along with an image of the paperback cover that Helen had as a kid, a girl in pigtails on a swing. He didn't know what it had been about; she was old enough to do her own bedtime reading by that time.

Neil didn't know *What Katy Did*.

Neil didn't know what Katy had done.

Barbara wasn't a killer. Barbara was prickly and opinion-ated and didn't suffer fools gladly. Barbara was quick-witted, thoughtful and generous in word in deed. But then the shadows started to crowd in. Barbara had never wanted children. Barbara had never fallen in love with Helen in quite the way that Neil had. Barbara had had to cut herself the day she met her baby grandson. But he fought back his doubts: Barbara wouldn't hurt a hair on any child's head. Barbara, whatever her faults, wasn't a child-killer. But was Katy?

Of course he'd been curious over the years about his wife's mysterious silence. He'd imagined some sort of scandal – probably a pregnancy, perhaps a married man. When they were married, Neil was hardly 'experienced' himself, but even back then he sensed something off-kilter in Barbara's sexuality, an underlying fear, or perhaps shame, that didn't sit easily. It turned out that, for Neil, his instinct to heal, to protect, was stronger than his need to know.

In fact, what he'd told Helen was largely true – he'd learned to live with the silence like people learned to live with a bereavement, or a missing limb – after a time, it becomes normality. Plenty of men would have struggled more than him, he supposed, plenty couldn't have married her without finding out the truth. It wasn't only women who felt the need to look in Bluebeard's cupboard. But not everyone. Not Neil.

Once, he recalled, he'd dropped a hint that he knew about the phone calls to Liverpool. It wasn't even that long ago, sometime after Barney was born. Barbara didn't take him up on it, her lips pursed, clam-tight. That night she had brushed past the dresser, knocking off a vase that had been a wedding present from his parents. It smashed beyond repair. An accident. A coincidence.

When he arrived at St Aeltha's, Barbara was alone, and asleep. He allowed himself to gaze at her. With her sculpted cheekbones and dark hair spread across the pillow, she was still beautiful, in his eyes at least. He touched her arm, then her hair. He felt the need to reassure himself that she remained the same person, that Katy Clery *was* Barbara Marsden and not some new creature that had emerged, leaving only the shed skin of his wife behind.

Eventually, her eyes flickered open and the question in them was unmistakable.

'Yes. They told me,' he whispered. His voice shook as he tried to control the emotion rising in him. 'You let me think you were the victim, Barbara. You let me think that for fifty years. How could you?'

His voice was rising and he heard the clack of heels in the corridor. He exhaled a slow, shaky breath.

A fat tear welled beneath Barbara's eye.

'I'm sorry it had to be like this, Neil. I'm so, so sorry ...'

'Then tell me what happened. It's time, surely?' He leaned forward, a drowning man grasping for a lifeline. He stared at her, desperate to turn back the clock, to go back to the before, when she'd just been Barbara, his wife, the love of his life.

'I didn't kill her.' Her eyes pleaded with him, tears glistening as she struggled to keep her voice even. 'No one's ever believed me, but you have to.'

She inched her hand forward and grasped his own and relief flooded him. His anger withered instantly. Something told him she was telling the truth. He knew her better than anyone; even though he'd never known about Katy, he'd known Barbara. And Barbara wouldn't lie to him now.

'Thank God. I knew it!'

It was only when he saw the pain flicker across her face that Neil realised he was crushing her hand in his grip.

He tried to press her for more, but she could only tell him how tired she was.

'It was a long time ago,' she said, unknowingly echoing Veena's words to him. 'Things were very different back then.'

Before long, sleep took her again; she murmured as she slipped away. He picked out the name Gardiner, and another that sounded like Stephenson. The rest was incoherent, so much so that he wasn't sure if it was speech at all. Eventually she slept peacefully, and Neil wept fierce tears all over the bedcover.

# March 1968

*Katy*

The deal was this: she would get a new birth certificate, National Insurance, all the documents. There would be a reference for work, and a place in a hostel paid up for the first six months. Katy's return home had gone so badly wrong so quickly that she actually moved into the hostel before all the paperwork was sorted out. Before that there had been two nights on the sofa of an old school friend, and three nights in police cells for her own protection.

'It's all arse about tit,' said Abe, the probation officer, who was a fan of plain speaking. Katy smiled to herself to think what Eric Robertson would have made of his language. 'I said we should set up a new identity before you were released, but those at the top said it could only be done for a witness, not an offender. Well, here we are, worse things happen at sea. I'm sure you're not the first, not that they would tell me one way or another.'

It was easy for him to say, thought Katy. He wasn't being bundled into a new life drawn up for him in five minutes on the back of a fag packet.

'So, what do you think?' He gestured vaguely around the long narrow attic room she was now to call home.

'Does it matter what I think?' Katy picked at a thread in the Indian throw draped over the bed. There was only one chair in the room, and Abe was sitting in it. She had her legs drawn up under her to one side because otherwise they would be in danger of touching his. Stephenson liked to call it her ballerina pose.

'Well, you could always turn me down,' he said, calmly, 'but I think we both understand that wouldn't end well.'

'So it doesn't matter.' She was smiling at him, enjoying his discomfort.

He shrugged. 'Well, you do get to pick your own name, not many people can say that.'

She'd had a couple of days to mull it over, when the talk of this plan first started over at Canning Place station. But she still wasn't quite sure.

'Do I have to decide today?'

Abe sighed. 'Preferably. We need to get things moving. And the fewer people round here who ever knew you were Katy Clery, the more likely things are to work out well for you.'

'Barbara, then – I'll be Barbara.' She'd spent the last twenty-four hours trying to decide. Until the name left her lips she'd still not been totally sure it was the one she would go for.

'Surname?'

'What?'

'Have you picked a surname?' His voice was slow and patient, like a nursery teacher.

Katy – Barbara – hesitated. She hadn't expected to have to change her surname too, but now she felt stupid not to have realised. She didn't want to admit it to Abe.

'Stanwyck,' she blurted.

He smiled. 'Are you a fan? She's one of my mum's favourites.'

'It was my dad who liked her,' Katy admitted. 'He used to take me to the pictures on a Saturday.'

'I know it'll be hard,' said Abe, suddenly serious, 'to have to cut them all off.'

Katy shook her head. 'He's dead. He died before ... well, before any of this.'

Was she glad about that? She knew about the whispers, about how Hugh Clery was lucky to have passed on without having to witness the shame brought on his family by his daughter. They never paused to wonder whether the shame might not have landed if he'd still been around. Katy still talked to him; in fact, if she prayed to anyone, it was to him, careless of the heresy of praying *to* the dead, rather than *for* them. Even if she couldn't keep in contact with Ma, or Sonia or the others, she could speak to her dad just as well if she was Barbara Stanwyck, and that brought a little unexpected comfort.

Abe's scratchy cough intruded into her thoughts.

'I'm afraid it can't be Stanwyck,' he said gently. 'It's too noticeable. People will comment. Any other ideas?'

She was tired now, tired of this surreal conversation, tired of Abe and of holding herself so carefully in this confined space. Her eyes cast around the room, landing on the two books leaning against the side of the small shelf. One, perhaps inevitably, was a Bible, the other an old children's book with its cover torn off. The lettering on the spine was clear, though: *Just So Stories.*

'Kipling,' she said. 'Will that do?'

'Barbara Kipling it is,' Abe confirmed, making a note. 'Now, last thing, I'll get the job references made up in a day or two. The firm's name will be Hewlitts, and any telephone enquiries will come through to my secretary. Do you have any skills? What do you want to be?'

'A journalist,' she said, shyly.

'You'll have to work that out for yourself, I'm afraid.'

'I've got shorthand.'

'Can you type?'

'A bit.'

'Secretary it is then. Don't worry, I'll tell them you've got an imaginative mind and the potential to go far.' He riffled through the papers and waved one with the reform school name emblazoned across the top. 'I'm not even lying – your man Robertson himself said it. You made an impression on him, Barbara.'

Katy looked at him blankly for a heartbeat, then nodded.

# August 2017

*Helen*

He wasn't back for bedtime. She watched the hands of the clock slip treacherously onwards: 20.00, 20.30, 21.00. Without a CCTV sighting, Julie's guestimate of the abduction as taking place just before four p.m. was the best they had to go on. Barney should be asleep by now. Another tear slid through her fingers as she stood staring at his empty bed, hoping against hope that he was warm and safe with Rabbit.

Veena, back on shift following an afternoon break, had gently discouraged any idea of Helen leaving the house, not barring her as such, but insinuating that it would be easier for them all if she didn't. Actually, much of Helen's interaction with Veena had a similar feel. It wasn't so much a silk glove concealing an iron first as a consoling hug concealing a forced restraint. Short breaks aside, the detective sergeant had now been camped out at the house for more than twenty-four hours. With every cup of tea she made, every time she picked up the phone, every little job she got the hidebound uniformed PCs to do, she seemed to be putting up bars around the house, around their lives. Helen knew as well as Veena did that those bars could protect her or imprison her. The decision was still in the balance.

So when the doorbell went, Veena rose smoothly to answer it. They'd already stopped the pantomime of Helen or Neil standing up and Veena ushering them back to their seats and reminding them that they didn't want to be doorstepped by a reporter who had managed to blag his way past the uniforms. Now, with Neil still at the hospital, Helen just let Veena go and waited meekly to see what came of it.

This time was different, however. This wasn't a muttered consultation on the doorstep.

'I've had more than enough questions from your lot, thanks, and I don't care if you're Stella-sodding-Rimington,' came Darren's raised tones from the hallway. 'I'm coming in and I'm going to see my wife.'

He marched into the room, trailing Veena, startled, in his wake. Helen rose to greet him, thinking wryly that it was the first time she'd seen Veena's composure slip and that perhaps it was no surprise that Darren would be the one to achieve that. Before she could worry about how to greet him, particularly in front of spectators, he'd pulled her into his arms. Her head turned automatically to rest against his collarbone and she closed her eyes, feeling a little of the tension flow out of her. In spite of herself, she let her shoulders drop and clung to him.

'Darling, darling, Hels,' he was muttering into her hair, 'Barney's out there. We'll find him, I promise.'

Guilt needled her. She'd been absolutely ready to believe it was him. Some stunt put on to get his own way or else to pay her back for not agreeing to let him take the kids back to London when he'd first asked. But then, she could hardly be blamed for looking for reasons why he might have taken Barney – not when the alternative was the hell she was going through now. Darren had turned back to Veena, now, still with one arm wrapped tight around Helen's shoulders. She breathed the spice of his cologne, underscored with a tang of anxiety.

'There's been no public appeal yet,' he said. 'We should have filmed one. We should be out there ...'

'There's been a missing child alert. It's on all the media channels.' If anything, Veena's tone was dismissive.

'But that's you, not us. Not his family.'

'What does it matter?' said Helen. 'If anyone's seen anything they'll come forward either way. Barney's not a runaway; he's too young to respond to an appeal.'

But Darren was shaking his head. 'It matters because they think it's us.' He emphasised the last word, almost spitting it back to her. 'That's the read-between-the-lines. That's why she's got you holed up here and not in make-up at the BBC.' He took a shaky breath, making a visible effort to keep calm. 'Don't get me wrong, I don't give a monkey's if the *Daily Mail* thinks this is some sort of screwed-up custody battle. But while that's the cops' working hypothesis, whoever took our son has still got him and is getting clean away with it.'

Helen turned to Veena, hoping she'd deny it.

'We have to be open to all possibilities.' There was an edge to her voice, a tilt of the chin that gave the truth to Darren's accusations.

'God,' was all Helen could bring herself to say. The word was drowned, anyway, under the smack of Darren's palm hitting the table beside him. A china candlestick on the mantelpiece jumped forward a fraction and all three of them turned to statues for a moment, watching to see if it would fall. As if it mattered.

Darren took another step towards Veena. 'You know it

wasn't me. You've wasted the best part of a day checking that to the nth degree. Hels and I may have our problems, but I'll tell you for free *she* wouldn't harm a hair on those kids' heads. They mean more to her than anything.' He turned his gaze to her for a moment. 'And I should damn well know.'

'Listen—' Veena tried to interrupt.

'I've not finished yet. There's no side to Helen, no funny business, no shady mates or kinky sex or whatever else it is that you lot think you might be trying to sniff out. Nada. End of. You can be as open to all possibilities as you want, but if ... if some fucking ...' He was shaking his head now, struggling again to hold it together.

'Come on, Darren,' Helen said, gently pulling him down to sit with her on the sofa. For a while, he sobbed and she held him. She wondered if her arms still held any comfort for him, as – in spite of every fibre of her will – his arms still did for her.

'It's late,' said Veena, carefully neutral.

'You should see Alys,' Helen told Darren. 'She's asleep upstairs. Take as long as you want.'

'Do you want him to stay here?' Veena asked, quietly, once Darren had left the room.

Helen turned to her, finding some of Darren's acid had seeped into her tone. 'Why? Is he allowed to leave? Or is he on lockdown too?'

Veena shrugged. 'Nobody's under arrest. I'm going to make some tea. I'll give you two a chance to talk about it.'

Darren decided he would go to his parents. They were expecting him, he said. They were frantic. They'd gone to Clitheroe yesterday for the market and Chris was beside herself that she'd missed Helen's calls because she'd had her phone in her jacket pocket and decided at the last moment to take a raincoat instead, forgetting to swap the phone back.

When Darren closed the front door behind him, it was as though he'd taken the breath out of her. She hadn't told him her mother was a murderer, she realised. It hadn't come up in the conversation. A giddy laugh, a laugh that belonged to someone else, slipped out of Helen's mouth.

She was wired but exhausted, tortured with the knowledge that someone out there knew how Barney was. Whether he was asleep. Whether he was crying. Whether he was dead. All his life she'd carried the knowing of him with her. Even on odd nights away she'd get babysitters to text when the kids had gone off: what they'd been doing, what they'd eaten. Now the craving to know was like a black hole inside her, expanding with each minute she was away from him.

In these last few weeks, she'd come to know herself in a different way – come to know how her mind and body worked and felt when pushed to the brink. This was different. This was a not-knowing, and it was quite literally driving her mad.

# February 1968

*Katy*

Katy sat perfectly still on one of the hard wooden chairs outside the governor's office. The slats at the back of the chair pressed into her spine in two different places, but she didn't slump. She had been sitting for so long that she was able to note the creep of the shadows from the window bars across the floor. She wasn't bothered; she was good at sitting still.

The clock opposite told her she'd been waiting for one hour and forty-three minutes. The countdown in her heart, on the other hand, measured in a different scale. Five years, three months and sixteen days. More than a quarter of her life. That was how long she'd been waiting. Her arse could put up with a hard chair for a while longer. Today was her release date. Today, before those clock hands reached midnight, they had to let her go.

She let her gaze drift back down to the chequerboard of sun and shadow on the tiled floor. It must be a good omen, she decided, for it to be such a sunny day. New beginnings, she thought, imagining the sensation of the sun on her shoulders and the sight of the new growth in the hedgerows as she walked down the drive and through the gates. She savoured the image, though it was silly. This was hardly Spandau.

Once her release date had been decided, she'd been moved to an open prison to prepare for life beyond the walls. The women could wander the grounds – still referred to as the Park, as it had been when the place was a landed estate – as much as they liked. For Katy, who had spent years in a mixed Secure Unit because there weren't enough girls in the system, a women's prison felt soft in a way, almost homely.

Sunshine *and* freedom though, that would feel different. It would feel like roses and perfume and honey and a great big 'fuck you' to all the idiots still stuck here.

The mahogany door at the end of the room swung open, and Miss Price, the governor's secretary, stood in the doorway.

'Mr Wilde will see you now, Clery,' Miss Price announced, and stood back a fraction to allow her to come through.

Katy jumped up smartly. The stiffness and numbness instantly dissipated.

'Yes, Miss,' she said, but Miss Price had already turned on her heel and disappeared.

Mr Wilde was a middling-sized man of about forty, with a waxed moustache and a jacket sleeve pinned neatly flat where his left arm should have been. He was leaning back in his chair, and he gestured that she should sit across from him. The chair set out at her side of the desk was a match for the ones in the hallway and her spine knuckled against the slats in the same tender spots as before. Katy gritted her teeth and pulled her back even straighter.

'So, your time has come, Miss Clery?'

His voice was oddly nasal, almost strangulated. The women speculated on whether, like the lost arm, it was a war wound of some sort, or whether it was just to do with him being a toff. Either way, Katy had to give herself a moment to tune in to him, like a radio. She nodded, carefully, noting the 'Miss' that no one had ever before appended to 'Clery' in this place. Probably not anywhere.

'Our loss, I fear.' He picked up a fountain pen and began to unscrew its barrel.

'Thank you,' she said. Sure, there were bastards enough around here, but she'd never counted the governor among them. She decided she could afford a little courtesy.

'Some people leave, Clery, and I worry about what they'll do when they get to the outside.' He paused, scrabbling about in a desk drawer and eventually producing a bottle of ink, before looking up again. 'In this case, I worry more about what the outside will do to you.'

Katy didn't say anything, and he didn't seem to expect her to.

'There's a curious thing I've learnt since I came to this job, and it's this. Very often, it's not the worst people who do the worst things. People will try to drag you down, Clery, try to turn you into the person they already think you are.' He drew the ink carefully into the barrel. She watched the operation closely, transfixed by the dexterity of his single hand. 'I believe you have the character to rise above it. Eric Robertson at Ashdown certainly thought so.' Finally, he looked her in the eye. 'And Mr Robertson's good opinion is not won lightly.'

In a moment of sudden realisation, it dawned on her that the governor had prepared this speech. It shocked her, that he should consider her worth the effort.

'I hope we've given you something? I mean, us here and at Ashdown?' he said, looking at her in expectation of a reply. But she'd not caught the lead-up to the question.

'Shorthand,' she hazarded. 'I'm good at shorthand now. I like it.'

He gave a quick laugh. 'That's not quite what I meant, Clery, but fair enough. It'll stand you in good stead.'

The governor pushed back his chair to stand. It seemed the interview was over, and Katy rose to stand too. After a moment's hesitation, she took his outstretched hand.

'I understand your sister is coming to get you,' he said. 'She'll have had a drive. I've told Miss Price to give you both tea. Make sure you get it.'

'Yes, sir.'

'Off you go then.' And with that, the governor looked down at his papers and Katy walked away from the place she'd been forced to call home. She walked to freedom.

\*

'Bloody hell, Sonia, what the fuck have you got on your head?'

'Katy!'

Katy's sister turned, her mouth a taut 'O' of shock. The car nearly swerved into the boggy verge, but then her driving hadn't been particularly smooth even before Katy's question, not least because of the amount of time she spent patting the weird structure rising up from her hairline.

'Keep your eyes on the road. It was only a question.'

'Well, if you must know, it's called a beehive.' Sonia patted the back of it, gingerly.

'Smells like a leak at the fucking Elnett factory.'

'I'll tell you something for free, Katy Clery, you'd better not try that effing and blinding with Mum. She'll string you up before you know what you've got coming.'

Katy allowed herself a studiedly bitter laugh.

'I think I've learnt how to cope with worse than our Ma with her knickers in a twist, Sonia.'

'It's nothing to be proud of, you know,' sniffed Sonia, patting her hair again and swinging the car a good three foot into the opposite carriageway in the process. 'Just because you've been away for the best part of six years – and it was nothing more than you deserved – doesn't make you better than the rest of us. Opposite, in fact.'

'Never said it fucking did.'

'Just stop it, Katy! I've got a job, and I can drive, and I'm walking out, and you've got flat hair and hands like a Land Girl and a criminal record. You always used to swank around like you were the cool one, but you needn't think nothing's changed since we were schoolkids. And that's true, however much you try to show off with your swearing.'

Katy shrugged, suddenly bored of winding her sister up. 'All right, Sis.'

'*And* I've driven the best part of a hundred miles – two hundred by the time we get back – to come and pick you up. The least I should get is a "thank you".'

Sonia turned to face her younger sister again, and Katy could see the mousy roots at her hairline and the ghosts of freckles under the panstick. She still had the deep brown eyes with long lashes that Katy had called 'cow's eyes' as a child, trying to conceal her envy of them. Sonia was almost twenty-one now – the neighbours used to call them Irish twins. Katy couldn't stop drinking in her sister with her eyes; it felt surreal, tracking the changes in the face she knew so well.

Sonia had written to her over the years; she was the only one who had. Katy knew that she ought to show that she was grateful, perhaps even that she should be trying to make Sonia understand the truth. But just now she couldn't cope with that. The only way she could manage was by acting as if everything was the same as when they were love-hate eleven-year-olds, ready to scratch each other's eyes out over the biggest bit of jam pudding.

'Sonia – the road!'

'Shit!'

They'd strayed over the line again and a Transit van was bearing down on them, horn blasting. Sonia hauled the Anglia across and battled with the steering whilst the Transit driver passed them making a finger-looping mental sign, which Katy answered by flicking him the Vs. The near miss was over in an instant, and both girls began to giggle, the laughter of each of them fuelling the other's hysteria as it had done since they were kids.

'Thought you didn't swear, Miss Goody-Two-Shoes?'

'Aw, piss off, Katy.' Sonia scrabbled at her feet and threw a clutch bag into her sister's lap. 'Get me a ciggie out, will you? And take one yourself if you want it.'

'Ta, Sis, that's more like it.'

They wound their way through the countryside, Sonia rabbiting on endlessly about her man, who was called Johnnie Maguire, and his lovely mum and dad (who had leant her the car for the day, a fact Katy couldn't help but be impressed by) and her job at a salon on Bold Street.

Katy only half listened; it was hard to draw her eyes away from the scenes outside the window. After years of having only crumbling walls and dun fields to watch, week in and week out, season after season, everything she saw from the car took on a technicolour novelty. The hedgerows, at their springtime best and still laden with a heavy dew, bristled with life and energy. The villages were fascinating little worlds and the people – old and young, pretty and plain – all endlessly intriguing. Katy noted that two or three of the younger women they passed seemed to have 'beehive' hairdos too, although none were as exaggerated as Sonia's.

They'd been in the car for getting on for three hours when Katy began to recognise the names on the road signs and to have a sense that they were getting into familiar territory. The outskirts of the city looked different from how she remembered them: glossier, bigger, with adverts everywhere. She noticed new buildings and fewer of the long-standing bomb-sites bounded by their semi-permanent hoardings. It wasn't that she recognised these streets as such – but she sensed she was getting closer to home.

'Do you know … is Simon Gardiner still living here?'

'Nah.' Sonia shook her head vigorously. 'The bastard moved after the trial. You don't need to worry about bumping into him. Or his wife.'

Sonia's chatter died away after that. Katy wondered if it was true, or if Sonia would say it anyway to protect her – or keep her out of trouble. She'd find out soon enough, she supposed.

The roads became smaller and more residential. A couple of times, Sonia took wrong turnings and swore gently under her breath, but she never asked Katy for help, and the Shell road atlas that had been floating around on the dashboard earlier ('Careful with that, it belongs to Mr Maguire!') had now been firmly relegated to the back seat.

Eventually, Katy felt compelled to break the silence again.

'Sonia?'

'Yes?'

She paused, still unsure how to phrase what she needed to know.

'Will they – I mean Mum and everyone – will they be pleased to see me?'

'Course,' said Sonia, a heartbeat too late.

Neither sister said any more for another ten minutes or so, not until they closed into the warren of terraces surrounding St James's church. Katy felt her weight swing in the seat as they rounded each familiar corner and the rhythm of it felt like a well-known hymn or lullaby, even though, in truth, she'd rarely been in a car all the years she had lived here.

But then there was a wrong note. Sonia took a left that should have been a right. Katy looked sharply towards her, but her eyes were fixed on the road.

'Why're we going this way?'

'Our Terry lives along here. We're going there first.'

'Why?'

'You'll find out. Look, we're here now. There's Mum at the window.'

And so she was. Katy's eyes met her mother's, but the older woman turned away quickly. Even at a glance, she was instantly recognisable: the petite, erect frame, the thin mouth and big eyes, topped with her carefully curled dyed-blonde hair. Joyce Clery had the quiet air of a hand grenade or a coiled cobra – always ready.

Five of them sat drinking tea in the kitchen. Katy, Sonia, Joyce, Terry, and his wife, Bernice. There had been a child jiggling in Bernice's arms when they first came through the door, but it had been quickly taken into the bedroom. No one asked Katy if she would like to see her baby nephew.

As it turned out, no one asked Katy much at all. Terry talked about her in the third person – 'There ain't room for her to stay here more than a night or two,' and 'How's she going to get a job with her record?' Joyce asked her questions – 'You must be shattered from your journey, love?' – but rarely seemed to wait for a reply. Sonia and Bernice said nothing.

Eventually, Katy learnt there'd been some 'nonsense' at her mum's house. Burning newspaper or dog shit shoved through the letter box. Once a burning newspaper *and* dog shit.

'We're worried you won't be safe there,' said Joyce, not looking at Katy.

'The police are worried *you* won't be safe with *her* there,' Terry corrected his mother.

Katy looked around the table; there was nothing but numbness and she stared harder at the faces, willing her mother's gold locket on its thin chain, or the scar on Terry's chin, to make her feel something. Nothing came. It had been too long, she realised. The last time she sat round a table with them all, she'd just been a kid.

They were embarking on a desultory pudding when the brick came through the window. It was at the front of the house, the little empty parlour, and no one would have been harmed had Bernice not been pouring a round of tea. She dropped the pot, slightly scalded both her own hands, as well as Sonia's, when she jumped to help.

Terry crashed out of the door and came back with the offending article held aloft.

'See!' He waved it towards Katy, but he spoke to Joyce. 'The baby could have been asleep in there. I told you we can't have her.'

When Bernice and Sonia had wrapped their burns in soaking dishcloths and the tea had been mopped up, Katy stood up. 'I'll go,' she said quietly.

'No,' said Joyce, without looking at her. 'Not tonight. Tomorrow.'

Katy felt a stab of hurt that her mother hadn't protested more, but she sat down nonetheless. 'Tomorrow,' she agreed.

# August 2017

*Helen*

The next morning – forty-one hours and approximately fifteen minutes after her son went missing – they came to tell her they'd found Jennifer.

'She doesn't work at the hospital,' said DI Nelson, who'd come in person to update Helen and Neil. A thick file of papers lay where he'd slapped them down on the coffee table and he periodically drummed them with his fingers. 'She's a fifty-five-year-old primary school teacher with three kids and a dachshund. And she lives in Queensland.'

'Australia?'

He nodded. 'Proper Australia: petrol generators, dingoes, bush-tucker trials, the works. Apart from an annual holiday to the coast, she's not left home these last ten years. We've had her phone and her email checked. She doesn't do social media. Whoever sent these notes to your mum, it isn't her.'

'How do you know this is the right Jennifer? I mean, who *is* she?' asked Darren. He'd returned to the house at eight that morning, to the utter delight of Alys, who'd had to be physically detached from his legs and placated with *Toy Story* when DI Nelson turned up.

'It is her.' The DI turned from Darren and glanced warily towards Helen. 'Her family have good reason to hold a grudge against Mrs Marsden. Your wife can fill you in on the details.'

'So,' cut in Veena, a little too brightly, 'we'd like you both to do a press conference.'

It would be at two o'clock in the main police station in town. Veena would help them to prepare a statement; she checked if Darren had a suit with him. Nelson's expression seemed to sour further. Helen wasn't sure if his distaste was for a man who travelled with a suit or for the whole circus of the press conference. He picked up his files and made his excuses.

They spent a macabre couple of hours drafting their lines, rehearsing and ironing their outfits. Helen finally managed to corner Neil in the kitchen for a few moments whilst Veena was caught up with Darren. He was rinsing yet more teacups. Her mouth was sour from tea, but she still nodded when he lifted the kettle.

'Did Mum tell you much, when you went to see her yesterday?'

'She said she didn't do it.'

'So, who ...'

He shrugged. 'They'd given her sedatives, I think. That was about all she managed to say.'

'What about Jennifer?'

'I don't know, love, I really don't. And who is the Jennifer who wrote the notes, anyway? The police seem pretty certain this woman in Queensland couldn't have anything to do with those notes.'

'I suppose so, but someone wrote them, didn't they? Whether or not it's got anything to do with Barney. Someone still wrote them, and if it wasn't Jennifer, then it was someone who knew all about her. All about her and her poor dead sister too.'

*

The press conference was horrendous. Helen and Darren were kept waiting in a stuffy first-floor office while Veena went backwards and forwards to the conference suite, looking increasingly irritated.

'One of the reporter's cars has broken down,' she told them, 'and it's the ITN guy, so we don't want to lose him. I'll get them to bring you up some drinks.'

'Mine's a vodka,' said Darren. Helen managed a weak smile. Veena didn't.

Darren had insisted that Helen take the only armchair. It was one of those dinky upright things, and she was shuffling around in it, conscious of the feel of the scratchy, stain-retardant material through her thin silk top. Darren paced, alighting on one or other of the office chairs for only a few moments at a time.

Ten minutes after promising drinks, there was still no sign of Veena's return.

'I'll go downstairs, shall I?' suggested Darren. 'They must have a vending machine at least. I might be able to get a Red Bull.'

'All right. I'll have a bottle of water if they've got one. Don't worry if not.'

She didn't know how he could think about having a caffeine boost – the adrenaline was making her far too jittery as it was.

He was back a couple of minutes later, calling 'Room service!' as he came through the door. She smiled for a moment in spite of herself. Instead of plastic bottles, though, he was carrying two paper cups filled with water.

'I'm afraid it's not exactly Babington House, is it?' He gave a wry grin.

She shrugged. She didn't want to think of Babington House, where they'd gone for a few birthdays and anniversaries since the business took off. They'd ordered champagne on room service, Darren might watch a film while Helen slathered herself in the posh toiletries and then they'd have the sort of lazy, sprawling sex that toddlers made infeasible at home.

Suddenly she wished to God they'd never had any of those conversations about how lovely it was to be without the kids. She wanted to grab them all back as if they were a sin through which she'd brought this horror upon herself – upon Barney.

She gulped at her water – she'd been more thirsty than she realised – whilst watching Darren out of the corner of her eye. He leant heavily on the windowsill, staring down to the street. She wondered if he'd been back to Babington House, if that was why it popped into his mind like that. As soon as the thought occurred to her, she was sure that he had. Did the nice receptionist or the joking Aussie waiter remember them? Did they realise that he was now with a different woman? Had he taken Lauren there before they split up? Perhaps the waiter and the receptionist were so friendly because they felt sorry for her.

Her water sloshed over the side of the cup. She resented him for putting her in this position – for making her think about that stuff for even a minute, when all that really mattered was Barney. She imagined for a moment refusing to speak to him – demanding that they put her in a separate room. But something stopped her; Darren was the only person who could share this hell she found herself in, the only person who could feel even a tenth of her agony.

Veena bustled back in just as Helen had mopped up the spill with a pack of tissues.

'Sorry, guys ... Shit, I totally forgot your drinks, didn't I? I am so sorry. Anyway, this is Philip. He's in charge of the techie end of things; he's going to chat to you about speaking into the mics. The ITN guy is here now, so that's good news, but they've got some sort of hitch with one of the links. Anyway, Philip's going to talk you through stuff, like I said, and there's a girl coming in to do just a tiny bit of make-up so you don't pale out on screen, and hopefully we're going in five ...'

When it started, Helen read the statement they'd prepared that morning, while Darren held her hand and glared around at the reporters as though challenging them to a fistfight. She felt like an actress as she read out the words on the page. Even when her voice broke and she had to repeat things, it was as if someone else was struggling, someone else was drowning in the lights.

There was a backdrop behind them with Barney's first – and please not last, she prayed – school photo emblazoned across it. Her eyes kept straying off to one side, to the laptop screen that was projecting the image, of Barney with his dimples and the bit of his hair sticking up at the back. She'd been so annoyed that the photographer hadn't sorted it out. If she could just brush his hair down, she thought, if she could just brush it down one more time and bury her face in the biscuity, little-boy smell of him.

As arranged, Darren read the final couple of lines of the statement. He let go of her hand to grip the paper with both of his. His hands were steady, as was his voice, but she could see his fingers turning white from the pressure of his grip.

'We won't be taking questions, ladies and gentlemen,' said Veena. 'We'd like to thank you all for your support in helping to get Barney Harrison home as quickly as possible.'

There was an eruption of sound as the journalists ignored Veena's statement and called out their questions, trying to get a reaction from Helen and Darren as they collected themselves and followed Veena out. She wanted to spit back how did they think they'd be 'bearing up' in the circumstances, but, terrified that making enemies could somehow hamper the search, she kept her eyes down and followed Veena meekly from the room.

'Aren't we going back to the car?' asked Darren, when Veena turned onto the staircase that led back to the room they'd been waiting in.

'Not yet.' She shook her head. 'We'll let them clear the room first. It might be uncomfortable for you to bump into someone on the way out.'

They frittered a few minutes. Darren went down the corridor to the toilet and Helen sat awkwardly with Veena. The adrenaline that had built up for the press conference seeped from her system, leaving her feeling exhausted and broken. The exhaustion was such that even her fingers felt heavy and clumsy as she reached for her phone. She had nothing worthwhile to give to the search for Barney in this state; but she knew she couldn't pull herself out until there was news. Was there something she was missing? She'd been wrung out for days. Was there some obvious clue that her frazzled brain wasn't letting her see?

She texted Neil to tell him that they'd be back soon. At Veena's suggestion, he'd taken Alys for McDonald's and to the cinema, so she was a little surprised when he responded straight away. Of course, she realised, feeling even more stupid, he was almost as desperate for news as she was.

Eventually, they made their way out, the three of them returning to the same unmarked BMW that had brought them to the station a good three hours earlier.

*

The two big police vans were obvious as soon as they pulled into the street. Veena had to nudge the BMW through because the tacitly negotiated parking conventions of Neil's neighbours had been cast into turmoil by the vans. Helen's heart started to thud; had they brought Barney back to her?

Darren leaned forward at the same time she did, a hard frown on his face.

'What's going on?' he said, repeating himself when Veena didn't answer straight away.

'Let's get inside,' she replied, tucking the car neatly behind the van closest to the house. 'There are more photographers,' she warned.

Helen hadn't been aware of any before, but sure enough, when she strained round to look past the van, there was a little encampment along the low wall of the next-door neighbour's front garden. It didn't occur to her to try to hide her face; after all, they'd just been giving a press conference, but when they started calling her name, shouting out questions, she panicked and stood rooted to the spot. Darren gently pulled her arm to urge her forward. Veena was ahead of them and the door was already opening from the inside.

They stepped through the front door and into a disaster movie. It looked like a hurricane had ripped through the place. Carpets and floor coverings were peeled away, cupboard contents were disgorged onto the floor, walls were denuded of pictures. As she took it in, Helen realised this was no natural disaster. Hurricanes didn't stack paintings neatly in a corner. Floods didn't make chalk markings in code on cupboard doors.

'We've done a search,' said Veena, before Helen or Darren could say anything.

'You searched before,' Helen said, and of course they had, in the attic, in the shed, anywhere a small boy could hide or be hidden.

Darren had gone pale. 'That whole press conference was a set-up. You wanted to get everyone out with no chance of us realising what you were up to. This is all just ... just gone to fuck ... Barney's out there.' His voice rose and he was trembling. 'When are you going to stop pissing around with us and actually do something about finding him?'

Veena fixed him with a hard look, but said nothing. Instead she turned her head and called into the kitchen.

'PC Andrews?'

'Yes?'

'Have you found anything?'

A young man with a shock of ginger hair stepped out of the kitchen. In his latex-gloved hands he carried a thick stack of paper. At a glance, it looked to be a mixture of cuttings – both from newspapers and colour magazines – and computer printouts. The papers packed tightly together were neatly bundled with elastic bands. Whoever had hoarded them was organised and pressed for space.

PC Andrews looked less comfortable with his role in this little performance than Veena did. He shuffled his feet and held the papers up a little, as if they might have missed them.

'These, Sergeant, under the floorboards in the study. They're all about missing children.'

*Barney*

The lady had pictures of flowers on her neck. Barney had noticed them even from the back of the car. They were blurry and wrinkled. Dead flowers. Yuck.

The lady had said she was taking him to see Nana Barbara in hospital, but they hadn't gone to the hospital at all. He thought he was in a hotel. There was a big bed and a telly and a desk and a bathroom. It smelt bad, though, not like the hotels he'd been to with Mummy and Daddy.

'Where's my mummy?' he asked the lady.

'She wants me to look after you for a bit.'

'While Nana's ill?'

'That's right, while Nana's ill.'

'But I didn't say goodbye.'

'Oh, big boys don't worry about things like that, do they? Let's put on some telly.'

At first, the lady tried to be nice and she brought him McDonald's to eat and a new toothbrush and she asked him all about Rabbit. But she didn't know that he was only meant to watch a bit of telly and not all day. She gave him medicine that made him sleepy and the programmes all fudged together.

Once or twice, she let him draw pictures for a bit at the desk, but there was only one biro, no pencils or crayons, and mostly he was too sleepy or too sad to draw.

The lady also didn't know that adults weren't meant to leave children by themselves. And she didn't like it when he kept on saying things about missing Mummy and Daddy and Alys and Nana Barbara and Granddad Neil and Nana Chris and Granddad Adam and his friend Leo from nursery and she told him to shut up and then once she hit him when he didn't.

Soon she stopped getting McDonald's and just got him cheese strings and crisps and things. She kept talking about what the fucking police were going to do and getting angry. Barney didn't like cheese strings and he didn't like the lady and he didn't like being here. This place wasn't a safe place.

# August 1964

*Katy*

It was hot. Airless in the baking fields, scorching in the sticky kitchens, sweltering in the dormitories. But hotter than anywhere else was the foetid cellar they called chokey. It didn't make sense. It had been colder than death any other time she'd been stuck here, but this time she felt as though she had been entombed in a brick kiln – the damp, the mould, the very air; all dried to nothing by a three-week heatwave. Katy fought in the dark to stay calm, to drag some of the thin air into her lungs and out again.

It was all she could do to keep going – pull the air in, drive the air out. She forced herself not to think of the outside. If pictures came to mind of her family, her home, or even just the kids she used to run around with in the park, she pushed them away quickly before the tears came; before it all became too much. Instead, she focused on *his* face. If she concentrated on him, there wasn't space for the others. Anger, she'd learned, was better than sadness or fear. You could control anger, and it could be useful. *Breathe in. Breathe out. Breathe in. Simon Gardiner. Breathe out. Simon Gardiner. Breathe in. Revenge.*

It was Stephenson's fault that she'd landed in here – it

usually was. They were the only two girls in for long stints. They'd become friends, and they looked out for each other, but Katy was subtle where Maureen Stephenson was brutal; Katy relied on cunning, where her friend was happy to stick to simple terror. The kid Stephenson had beaten up this time had felt her arse in the dinner queue or something equally misguided. His punishment should have been a straightforward mishap, a shove down the stairs, or a crack of his stubby nose against the hard stone laundry room sinks. Of course, the staff would guess what had really gone on, but who was going to bother getting to the bottom of it?

He'd crumpled too easily, though, the boy. Katy wasn't even sure of his name. As soon as Stephenson dragged him aside and started whispering about what he'd let himself in for, he'd started wailing. Wet his Y-fronts, Stephenson said. The weakness of him riled her – it was like an extra insult after he'd thought he was man enough to paw her over. Stephenson had gone for him, right in the middle of a corridor. Broken jawbone, very messy. There was a fair chance he'd lose the sight in one eye, apparently.

Katy had had to pull her friend off in the end. All the kids who had been there were too shit-scared to try, but one of them had at least had the nous to come and grab her. She'd hauled Stephenson back, still spitting and yelling, and got a black eye herself for her trouble. Then she'd carried the can for her.

Stephenson had a release date. She was due out in two months, a few weeks shy of her eighteenth. If she was disciplined for this, then she'd get at least another couple of years, and that would mean a transfer to prison. There was no talk of a release date for Katy. She was sure that when *she* left Ashdown, she wouldn't be headed for home. This fracas would be water under the bridge by then. The screws hadn't really believed it was her, which was probably why she'd got two nights instead of the five she'd been threatened with. With her, Stephenson, the boy and all the witnesses sticking to the same story, there wasn't much the staff could do about it.

Two nights would be a walk in the park, if only it wasn't for this heat, and the lack of air that went with it. She tried again to focus on her breathing. Tried to shake off the injured face of the boy, his eye already swelling up, gibbering for his mother. She wondered if Stephenson was thinking about him. Maybe they'd talk about it someday, in the future. She'd make sure to keep in touch with Maureen Stephenson, despite the rules. After all, Stephenson owed her.

*Breathe in. Breathe out. Revenge.*

Katy fiddled with the waistband of her work apron. At least they'd not bothered to take that off her. When she found the row of unravelled stitches and slipped her finger inside, the breathing became easier. Her nail glanced against metal. It only took her a little while to wriggle her blade out. It was the prong of a buckle. She'd managed to get it in the laundry room, from one of the staff aprons. The pupils' aprons had buttons – no metal, no sharp edges. She'd tried to sharpen it over the weeks, on the brick walls of the dorm, on various tools in the gardening shed. When she got the chance, she stuck it in boiling water. That wasn't often, though.

But needs must. She rolled up her sleeve, found a good spot on her upper arm. There was one way to stop the faces from haunting her.

Katy squeezed her eyes shut and dug into her skin.

\*

The first time she had a chance to talk to Stephenson properly after getting out of the chokey was in an art lesson. They had amazing stuff at Ashdown – oils, pastels, even these new Cryla paints – and that was just in the painting room. The two of them were working on a swirly mural. Stephenson had done the outline. She had a much surer hand than Katy, and the two of them were now blocking out the main sections in purples, oranges and greens.

'So I'm definitely getting out,' Stephenson murmured. 'Three weeks' time. Robertson told me himself.'

Katy felt a pang of remorse at the idea of losing the closest thing she had to a friend in here. 'That's good,' she managed. 'I mean, it's not like they could keep you anyway.'

'Yeah, thanks to you.' Stephenson paused, working some paint into a corner of the design. 'We'll keep in touch, yeah?'

Katy shrugged. 'They won't let us write while I'm still in. You know the rules.'

'Don't matter. I'm not going to forget you, Katy Clery. And you'd best not think you can forget me neither.'

'Course not.'

Katy stared hard at the painting. Stephenson's slim frame still imposed itself in the corner of her eye: her freckles, auburn hair and that creepily fascinating tattoo. Katy's eyes pricked with the thought of how much she would miss her. She stepped away slightly, tightening her grip on the paintbrush and pursing her lips. Katy Clery was a survivor.

Stephenson's hand on her arm made her jump. She turned to the other girl and could see the shine of tears in her eyes.

'You should do it, you know.' Stephenson's voice was an urgent whisper. 'Get the bastard that put you in here. You're smart enough, God knows. And whatever I can do to help, you only need to say.'

Katy nodded, a thin smile on her lips and an ache in the back of her throat. Had she said or done something that had let slip to Stephenson that she planned to do exactly that? She didn't think so. Stephenson wasn't bright enough for subtle clues. It was just natural justice – that was all; even Maureen Stephenson could see that, by rights, Simon Gardiner had it coming.

# August 2017

*Neil*

Neil had never been a brave man. Not like his father, who, for all his bigotry and bile, had undeniably staked his claim as a member of the greatest generation. Now, Neil found himself here, not facing a landing ground or a machine gun installation or anything like it, yet the cold sweat was sopping at the bottom of his shirt. He was all eye-twitching and finger-trembling and, like the coward that he was, he didn't think he could trust himself to speak.

'Like looking at pictures of kiddies, do you?'

He didn't know this copper. He'd seen Nelson, the stony-faced inspector, as he was led through the station, but this was a sergeant, who introduced himself as DS Addison and his younger female colleague as DC Hemmings. Addison must have been in his fifties, with greying hair and a world-weary attitude. Hemmings' role seemed to be confined to fiddling with the tape recorder. Neil found it hard to believe they still used tapes, but had been told at the outset there was a digital video recording too. Still, it was the tape machine, familiar from countless TV dramas, that filled him with anxiety.

'Whatever you're insinuating, you've got it wrong.' Neil's

protest sounded weak, even to himself. For the first time in his life, he found himself envious of his son-in-law's bluster.

'Then how do you explain what was found under the floorboards of your home?'

Neil hadn't put anything there, and from the glance that he'd had, the papers hadn't looked like anything indecent. The words jumbled in his mind. If he argued on one point, would they take it as an admission on another? The tongue in his mouth was thick and useless.

'Water, Mr Marsden?' DC Hemmings finally spoke and pushed a plastic cup towards him. Her tone was solicitous, but a smirk threatened at the corner of her lips and Neil sensed a taunting undertone.

'I didn't put anything under the floorboards,' Neil stated, making an effort to be plain and clear. 'I don't know what you found, because I didn't put it there, and never saw it. You've not shown me any of it.'

'You're not telling us your wife likes looking at pictures of kiddies?' It was back to Addison now.

'Should you be asking these questions without a lawyer?'

The copper shrugged. 'You tell me, Mr Marsden, do you need one?'

'No,' he said, praying that was the right answer.

He picked up the water. The kid had overfilled it, probably deliberately, and a few drips rolled down Neil's chin. He swiped them away, a little shocked to feel the prickle of stubble on the back of his hand.

'We've got guys checking your computers,' Addison continued, 'home and work, that old laptop from the attic, your phone. They get to every little thing you've ever looked at, you know. If you had a peek at some vintage postcards of seaside lovelies on eBay three years ago they'll know about it.' He leant closer and Neil caught a whiff of banana. He thought, distractedly, that he wouldn't have pegged Addison as a healthy eater. 'They're all half our age, those techies, Neil, and fuck knows how they manage it, because most of the time they don't seem to know their arse from their elbow. But they do manage it. So if there's any little whisper of a guilty secret; any little peccadillo that's weighing on your mind, you'll be well advised to tell me now. It'll give us a reason to go easy on you if you help us out. Get me?'

Before Neil could answer there was a sharp rap on the door and Addison was called out of the room, looking none too pleased about the summons. Neil and the young detective eyed each other silently, until eventually she muttered something about going to check her emails.

'Look, love, before you go, could you point me to the gents'?'

The woman looked dubious.

'Come on, I'm not under arrest. Even if I was, I'm not a likely candidate for a breakout, am I? The prostate's buggered is all.'

'Right. DI Nelson's the same,' she said, her frown lifting and then clouding again as she realised the senior investigating officer might not be too happy about the revelation. 'Come with me.'

By the time they returned, Addison was back in his seat, looking none to happy about being kept waiting. Neil only wished he could be confident that the urgency came from a desire to find Barney, rather than a desire to go home for his tea.

'First sweep of your tech stuff was clean, so I'm told,' he said, almost before Neil had had chance to sit down.

'Surprisingly clean, in fact. Are you in the habit of using any specialist deletion software?'

'You'd have to ask Barbara – she's the techie. But I could have told you at the outset there was nothing to find,' said Neil, truthfully, although that didn't explain the giddy relief he felt at having it confirmed. If his precious, wonderful wife was apparently a child-killer, who was to say he couldn't be a paedophile? The world had gone mad.

Addison now pulled a cardboard file from a bag by his feet and shoved it across the table. 'But that leaves us no closer to understanding what the hell all this is about.'

'This is what you found at the house?'

'Yes, well almost. Those papers are being kept securely in our evidence room. These are copies, but all the little sticky tabs and cross-references have been reproduced too. It's quite a little research project.'

Neil smiled in spite of himself. 'That'll be Barbara,' he said. 'She's a journalist. Old-school. If a thing's worth knowing, it's worth its own index card.'

It was DS Addison's turn to smile, although Neil couldn't tell if it was genuine this time, or more of his self-serving camaraderie. 'Sounds like a woman after me own heart,' he said. 'But this should have been more my bag than hers, don't you think?'

Neil pulled the papers forward, slipped off the elastic band and opened the top flap of cardboard. The papers inside were separated neatly into bundles. Once he'd got through more elastic bands, he was able to read the first document. It was a report from a Sunday broadsheet supplement – fairly recent – about the trial of a white-van driver who'd been convicted of abducting, raping and killing a thirteen-year-old. The disappearance and then the trial had had huge publicity, and behind that report Neil found many more, as well as close-typed notes, full of acronyms, about the case. Beneath that, in other bundles of varying thicknesses, the familiar names continued. Child victims; child-killers; children who had been found and those who had been killed and those who remained missing. The names and the articles went back further: careful annotated notes of cases from the 1970s and 1980s, the dated hairstyles and pre-digital photography lending the pictures now giving those forgotten children a sense of the ageing that they had been tragically denied in real life.

At the very bottom, tucked into the expanding file, were a couple of true crime books. One was on a famous case of a staged kidnapping, where a family had grimly sought to capitalise on the exposure and money that a missing child case could generate. The second looked to be a 'Greatest Hits' of twentieth-century missing children cases. It had a pale cover, across which the word 'bollocks' stood out in black marker pen, clearly in Barbara's hand.

'She's been collecting this stuff for years,' said Neil, almost to himself.

'Looks like it,' agreed Addison, 'although it's pretty selective. You can imagine if you kept even a tenth of the guff that's been printed about just one of these cases over the years, you'd have filled your entire house up, never mind the gap under the floorboards.'

Neil nodded. 'It's investigations, isn't it? If you look at the focus of the articles, they're all written in the aftermath, years later some of them. And the stuff she's highlighted and annotated, it's mainly about the police.'

It was Addison's turn to nod. 'Seems to be. Budding Patricia Cornwell is she, your wife?'

Neil felt a flare of exasperation. 'No, she isn't, no more than I'm a paedophile, even though you were quite happy to suggest it to my face fifteen minutes ago.'

Addison's face tightened, his mateyness suddenly vanishing. 'As my colleague has already stated, we've got to exhaust all possibilities.'

There were more sheets at the back of the pile, separated from the main chunk by a loose file divider. Neil pinged off the elastic bands and began to look through these too. There were a few press clippings, again, but more handwritten stuff this time. Addresses, dates, two black and white pictures: stiff, glossy prints, clearly of some quality. The same name kept appearing – Simon Gardiner, Simon Gardiner.

'There's no more kiddie stuff,' said Addison, sliding the file back across the table out of Neil's reach.

'Yeah, well,' said Neil. 'I don't think it'll take long to exhaust this one. Barbara's a journalist. No doubt she was doing a series of articles on this stuff. Or perhaps she planned it and it never got anywhere. That happens a lot. She probably stuck it out of the way when we had the kids visiting – it's not exactly family-friendly, is it?'

'You seem to forget that your wife has something in common with some of the people that feature in these articles.'

'What do you mean?'

'Well, as you now know, Barbara Kipling, or rather Katherine Clery, is a convicted child-killer too, isn't she?'

Neil was taken aback by his bluntness. Barbara had told him she hadn't done it. He supposed the police couldn't simply take her word for it, but what could it amount to, really? A child judged harshly in a harsh time over what, he was sure, could have been nothing more than a tragic accident. It hardly bore comparison with the child molesters or serial killers of this world.

'It was nothing like this stuff, though,' he protested. Again, Neil cursed his own meekness, Darren would have ripped into Addison by now, but that just wasn't Neil's way.

'Of course not,' agreed Addison. 'But it's strange all the same. She pleaded not guilty, didn't she? Her lawyers spun some story about it being someone else?'

'I wasn't there at the time, as you well know,' said Neil, stiffly. 'But I'm sure whatever evidence Barbara gave it would have been the truth. I was told you were getting the papers out of archive, but exhausting *that* avenue doesn't seem to have been anyone's priority.'

'Hmmm,' said Addison, leafing through the papers, 'maybe it's us she was trying to get a story on. *Dumb coppers mess it up again*. Can't deny it's a classic.'

'Well, as I said, I only found out about these when they were waved in front of my face earlier. If you want to know what Barbara was doing with these, then you'll have to ask her, but I don't see that it'll be any help to you in finding my grandson.'

The interview fizzled out like a Bank Holiday barbecue when the rain starts. Addison had clearly been expecting something to show up on the computers – perhaps he worked on the premise that everybody had some dodgy internet history. But even if there had been anything, it was a big jump to make Neil responsible for whatever had happened to Barney. As if he'd do anything to his own grandson; as if he'd have time to hatch some sort of plan with his wife in hospital fighting for her life.

Addison's handshake in the reception area was cursory, his mind already seemingly turning to other avenues. It was left to Hemmings to confirm that Neil intended to return to his home address, that he could be contacted and would return if requested.

He'd been told to hand his phone in when he arrived, and only just remembered to collect it from the unsmiling female constable on reception. He hurried outside before checking the screen, keen to be free of the place as quickly as he could be. It was a warm afternoon and he slowed his pace walking across to the pay and display where he'd left his car. Town seemed busier than usual. There were lots of kids and mums around with it being the holidays. The rush-hour traffic was just starting to pick up. Neil felt relief at being free of the police station, relief that whilst he seemed to have teetered on the edge of some Kafkaesque abyss, he had managed to emerge intact.

Perhaps nothing was worse, nowadays, for a man of his age, than the suggestion of paedophilia. For one hour, Neil had seen the web of his whole life – his standing and reputation, his job and his relationships – for the gossamer structure that it was. How easy, it seemed, to destroy it all in an instant. For a moment, the world sang with the cleansing, life-giving freshness of relief. But, like a spring rain on dry ground, it faded almost at once, leaving behind the stony ache in Neil's chest that was his fear for Barney.

Town had never seemed bigger. Neil recognised none of the faces that bustled past him. Any one of them could know who had taken his grandson, but the likelihood was that none of them did. They'd see the appeals and the headlines, shake their heads and pull their loved ones closer, and that would be all.

When he did look at his phone, there was just one message, from his old mate Alan Crookshank, expressing his shock at the local news report about Barney and the offer of a quiet pint if Neil needed it.

His first thought was to refuse, but he realised he'd no desire to see Veena, or any of her like, and the idea of escaping for even an hour or so was appealing. He called Helen quickly to check there was no news and let her know where he was going, then he set off.

*Helen*

16.00. Forty-eight hours. Two whole days. Eternity.

Helen wasn't prepared to wait any longer to see Barbara. Although a clique of sullen reporters still huddled outside, the phone calls and knocks on the door seemed to have died down. Life, if you could call it that, was settling into a surreal routine of yet more tea, wearying bouts of verbal jousting with Veena and trying to keep things normal for Alys.

After the press conference debacle, Darren had stormed off to Chris and Adam's, but he'd returned quickly with a couple of bags and his iPad, installing himself in Barbara and Neil's back room, where he swung like a weathervane from scowling thunder at the police, to doting sunshine on Alys. Towards Helen, he was solicitous but careful. They stood close together to talk privately (out of a sense of intrusion, rather than because they had anything private to say) and his breath across her neck or shoulder was like the whisper of a sweet and longed-for breeze.

She was happy to leave him with Alys for the evening, especially when Neil called to say he was going out to meet

Alan Crookshank. She could still remember her feelings from a few days ago, when she hadn't wanted Darren near the children, when she thought he was trying to poison their minds and take them away from her, but she found that she couldn't connect with those fears any more. It was as if she'd been afraid of the bathwater and now found herself adrift on the ocean.

When she got to the hospital, a nurse, one she recognised, ushered her through the corridors, despite Helen's assurances that she knew her way by now.

'I was so, so sorry to hear about your son,' she said, in an undertone, 'I hope they find him very soon.'

'Thank you,' Helen replied automatically.

The nurse glanced over, and Helen had a sinking feeling that she was about to try to take the conversation further. Instead, though, she was talking about Barbara. Mr Eklund had been in today, she said, and Barbara was still wavering about starting chemotherapy. They hadn't wanted to call the family, what with them having so much else on their plates ...

'What do you mean? Is she in danger?'

'No, no, of course we'd have contacted you. She's getting stronger following the operation, but it's important to have a treatment plan decided. Mr Eklund is a little concerned about her. I can't go into the detail – you understand – but he asked me to mention, if anyone visited, that he'd like to discuss it with the family in the next day or two.'

'I see. What about Mum? Has she said anything else about it?' Helen thought about Barbara's comments from a few days earlier and remembered her own surprise at her mother's hesitation. It was like remembering something from years ago – her mother's treatment hadn't crossed her mind for a moment since Barney had gone.

The nurse hesitated. 'We've not discussed it with her directly. She's seemed a little ...' she paused again, looking for the right word, '... a bit less lucid. Some of the time. She's running a temperature. There may be some infection some-where, but that along with ... well, I understand there's been some old personal history dug up, so to speak. She's a little confused sometimes. We're not finding it all that easy to engage her.'

The conversation took longer than the walk to Barbara's room. They were huddled in the corridor, outside her door, speaking in whispers.

Helen half expected to go in and find her raving. Instead, she was asleep. Her skin looked grey and wan against the warm rose colours of her room, and her body seemed even smaller than Helen remembered it; creating a bare wrinkle, rather than a lump, in the blankets. Her breath was too shallow to shift them at all. Helen hadn't seen her looking so bad since the night of the heparin overdose.

The nurse withdrew tactfully, and Helen slipped into the chair at the head of the bed.

'Helen,' Barbara whispered, her eyes blinking open and closing a few seconds later.

'Yes. I thought you were asleep.'

She turned her head carefully from side to side. 'Just resting my eyes.'

Helen expected she would ask about Barney, but perhaps she didn't have the energy. Perhaps she was too confused to understand that he was missing.

'How are you feeling, Mum?'

'Old.' A smile flickered on her lips.

Helen thought about what Veena had said. She looked at

Barbara and tried to see the girl who had supposedly killed a child all those years ago. She imagined the crime occurring in a black and white film, a different age, a different world. Helen had always known, without fully realising, not until now, that Barbara's love for her wasn't straightforward, not like Neil's was, and that her mother was frightened of her – or frightened of something she represented. It must have been *her*, Helen thought, not Jennifer after all, but Jennifer's sister, Mary. The girl who would never be a woman, because of Barbara.

'Well, your secrets are all out now,' Helen said, and Barbara's ghostly smile appeared again, somewhere between a smirk and a grimace of pain.

'They are.' She spoke slowly. 'It's good that your dad knows. Poor Neil's put up with my woman-of-mystery act all these years. He deserves to have his questions answered.'

Helen felt a stab of jealousy. What about *her* questions? What about *her* son who might have been taken purely to make Barbara suffer, when Barbara, it appeared, wasn't suffering at all?

'Barney's still gone,' she said, hating her mother for making her say it like that. It was the way Helen might drop into conversation the fact that one of the kids' birthdays was coming up, knowing Barbara might well forget otherwise, and wanting to remind her for their sake rather than hers.

She nodded. 'I know. You'd have told me sooner if there was news. I didn't want to rake it up for you.'

Helen let her anger flare a little. 'You make it sound like he's dead already!'

'No, love, I didn't mean that.'

She waited, wanting to make Barbara work harder, but her

mother's eyes were closed again. Her breathing slackened and Helen sensed she would lose her to sleep if she was too stubborn to keep the conversation going herself.

'Do you think it's her – Jennifer, I mean, or someone connected to her? Do you think ...' Her voice broke. 'Mum, do you think they've got my boy?'

'I know he's somewhere safe, darling, I know it.'

'What do you mean? What do you know?'

But Barbara's eyes were closing, and a sage and saintly smile formed on her lips.

'He's not dead!' Helen's voice rose to a shriek. 'Barney's not dead, how bloody dare you!' Her rage died back as quickly as it had flared and her cries petered out to sobs.

Barbara lay there, unmoving, unreached by any of it, as far as Helen could tell. The smile was still in place, but her lips were slightly parted now. There was a tiny shred of dried skin that fluttered as she exhaled.

'You get your strength from me, Helen.' The words were so quiet that Helen felt almost as if it was a voice in her head. 'I wasn't able to give you what I wanted to give you – what you deserved. I was too angry, and too scared, after everything he did to me.'

Her breath came in wheezy, unhurried lengths. Helen inched to the edge of her seat, forcing herself not to speak, grasping every word like a treasure.

'But we're strong, you and I. You might not forgive me, but I know you'll be all right in the end.'

Helen couldn't say how long she sat there, waiting and waiting for more words that didn't come. She watched Barbara, and her mother disassembled in front of her. She was no longer a mother, no longer a person, just an array of dissected, desiccated human matter. Helen watched the wiry hair that sprung from Barbara's head to follow the path that almost seventy years' worth of her hair had followed: twisting into the cow's lick set down by a random stutter of DNA all that time ago. Then she turned to Barbara's papery skin, the origami complexity around her eyes and her neck and the peeling layers on her still-pink lips. Helen looked at her nails, her freckles, her nostrils, her eyebrows.

The fabric of Barbara was utterly familiar, both from those early intimate years and from the echoes Helen saw every day in her own, ageing features. Yet now, Helen took in the ailing – perhaps even dying? – body with the cold eyes that we turn on famine victims or refugees, people so removed from us that empathy comes at too high a price.

She didn't know how long she had sat there before the nurse came to change the water jug; before she had to reply to a text from Darren about Alys; before there was a tap at the door and Veena walked in, accompanied by a nurse.

'There's been a development,' she said, gently, but without preamble. 'I think you should come home.'

'You've found him?' There was fear rather than hope in Helen's voice, as Veena's manner was all wrong for good news.

She shook her head.

# October 1962

*Katy*

The jury returned its verdict on Tuesday 23rd October – the same day that the British public had woken up to the news that Khrushchev had put missiles on Cuba. As the grand court room at St George's hall filled, Katy gazed upwards, at the distant ceiling and windowless courtroom walls, imagining thick clouds cantering past on a stiff autumn breeze and wondering how the ponderous lawyers would react to the four-minute warning.

They talked about it at school sometimes, as they talked about every subject that they couldn't mention to their parents. Mary Elton had said she'd let her boyfriend go all the way if the four-minute warning came because she didn't want to die a virgin. The other Katy – Katy Flannagan – had said God would still see and Mary would be in hell as soon as The Bomb went off. Mary had laughed and said she didn't expect Kenneth would last very long, so she could probably squeeze a few Hail Marys in before the four minutes was up. Katy Clery had crossed her legs and hoped no one asked her about dying a virgin.

She wondered if Mary and Katy and the other girls at

school had been following the trial. Would they believe her version of events, or Simon Gardiner's? Would they be thinking about her today, or would they be too busy worrying about Cuba? In a way, it didn't matter. Whatever the verdict, Katy knew she'd never be one of them again.

At last, the foreman was invited to stand. His large, rheumy eyes kept flicking to the piece of paper in his hand, as though he was scared of saying the wrong thing.

The judge's questions came quickly, almost impatiently.

'Do you find the defendant, Simon Gardiner, guilty or not guilty of the murder of Mary Gardiner?'

'Not guilty.'

'Do you find the defendant, Katy Clery, guilty or not guilty of the murder of Mary Gardiner?'

'Not guilty.'

'Do you find the defendant, Katy Clery, guilty or not guilty of the manslaughter of Mary Gardiner?'

'Guilty, on the grounds of diminished responsibility.'

Katy heard no more. For her, the awesome, terrible nuclear starburst bloomed there and then. Not in the October sky outside, not over the Mersey shipyards, but across the vaulted courtroom ceiling. They thought she had lied. Those seven men and four women. They had all fallen for Simon's smooth story like a pack of dockyard apprentices sent out to buy a plimsoll line.

The sentencing was a blur; she was still reeling from the verdict, from the horrible realisation that telling the truth hadn't been enough. In her heart, she'd never believed it would come to this. She couldn't blame her lawyers – they'd painted it black from the start – and her mother had had scarcely a word to offer beyond 'oh, Katy', repeated endlessly. No, she'd been the one who had kidded herself that somehow everything would be okay if she only stuck to the truth. Now it was far from okay, and she only had herself to blame for the shock of it.

Whatever her fate was, the judge pronounced it with a nasal growl and an air of retribution, his fingers seemingly itchy for the black cap. Simon wept tears of relief and his wife Etta howled so loudly she had to be led out by an usher. Joyce Clery dabbed her good handkerchief – the one with the Bruges lace edging – against her eyes and took herself out quietly when the clerk got everyone to stand. Katy wasn't sure if Joyce would come down to the holding cell or not, but she was there when the policeman led Katy in a few minutes later.

'He said eight years, but that's the absolute maximum,' explained Mr Browning, the solicitor. 'It could have been a life sentence. This way, it might be as little as four years if you keep your chin up and tow the line, and once the eight years is up they can't call you back like they could if you were a lifer. Plus, Katy, you must remember you're not going to gaol. It'll be more like a boarding school really.' He smiled weakly. 'Yes, I think we've had rather a good innings there, all things considered.'

'It could've been a whole lot better if they'd believed me.'

'That's true,' he admitted. 'But we always knew that Mr Gardiner would make a good fist of it, didn't we?'

Katy wondered if *he* believed her version of events. She had asked him once, earlier on, before the trial had even started, and he told her it didn't help to think about whether his clients were guilty, so he didn't. He certainly seemed untroubled by the verdict, judging from his slightly impatient manner and the occasional, gentle rumbling of his stomach.

244

Joyce didn't say much initially, just a few muttered 'oh, Katy's whilst she was still dabbing with the handkerchief. As Mr Browning made to leave, though, she became more animated, pestering him for details of how often she could write to her daughter and when she could visit. Despite all her fuss, Joyce couldn't seem to bring herself to actually speak to her daughter. Katy knew her mother believed her story; she didn't have any doubt on that score. The problem was, Joyce would probably have been less devastated on the whole if Katy *had* killed the girl.

Eventually, the policeman on the door stepped in to draw matters to a close. The prisoner had had enough time, he said. There was a van waiting for her.

'One thing about ruddy Khrushchev's antics,' said Mr Browning, as a parting shot to Joyce whilst he did the buckles on his leather briefcase, 'at least it'll knock little Missy here off the front pages.' He stood in the corner, making a show of busying himself cleaning his glasses, whilst mother and daughter said their farewells.

'I'll be fine, Mum,' said Katy, hesitating a moment before throwing her arms around her mother's waist, pushing her cheek into that familiar shoulder. It seemed that Joyce couldn't bring herself to say anything, but at least she hugged back. The relief hit Katy like a wave and she clung all the harder for fear that if she didn't, she might drown. Her sobs came silently, building in force until she was shaking with it.

The policeman stepped in and pulled her back, but gently. She tried to watch her mother leave; she wanted to imprint a last image of her in her mind. But her eyes were too blurred by tears to see her, and, with the policeman's arms pinning her own to her sides, she couldn't even wipe them away.

*

The exit from the back door of the court building under a blanket; the long, bumpy journey in the police van; the bewildering induction procedure at Ashdown – all these, too, passed in a haze of confusion and unreality.

At last, though, Katy lay alone and silent between the scratchy sheets of a metal bed that was bolted to the floor. The blackness outside gave no clue as to the time, but she guessed it couldn't be earlier than two a.m. Never before in her life, she realised, had she been awake for so many consecutive hours. If Khrushchev decided this *was* to be the Last Day, then, on one view, she'd made the most of it.

As she lay there, and her thumping heart gradually managed to quiet itself, the tears came again. Running rivers of salt water marched down her cheeks and on to soak the thin, dead pillow beneath.

*Perhaps it will be better in the morning*, she told herself, trying to rally a little. Sleep would give her some strength back, and everything would seem less daunting in the daylight. With some effort she closed her eyes and began to will her adrenaline-wretched body to slow down, to succumb to the forgetfulness that sleep offered. Gradually, her breath deepened, a heaviness settled on eyelids, so that finally keeping them shut was no longer a struggle. The low bed was soft and its faint human stench was oddly comforting.

She was only a whisper away from oblivion when the voices started.

*Murderer.*

It could have been the breath of the wind in the branches outside, or the rattle of water through an ancient pipe.

*Child-killer. Freak. Murdering bitch.*

The voices rose, swirling like floodwater, seeping through the walls and under the doors. The vicious chorus was backed by the creak of springs and banging of metal bed frames. Her eyes wide again, Katy pushed herself upright on the bed. The taunts rushed towards her, stinging at her like needles.

'Quiet!' It took only a few harsh words for the voices of authority to quell the noise, but the threat echoed in the air, lingering around her like smoke. There would be no sleep that night.

*

There were always staff around in the Unit. The routine of locking, unlocking, staff escorts and timed checks was ever-present. After a few days, she started to get used to it. Occasionally, however, the hostility slipped through the cracks. A boy in a classroom, pushing a sharpened pencil into her arm; another boy detailed to clean a corridor with Katy, refusing to speak or to look at her. They were virtually all boys here. They were like the bad boys she knew from school – the very worst of them.

It came to a head one teatime, when she'd been there for four or five days. Of course, there were staff in the lunch hall, but they couldn't be everywhere at once. This was a prime opportunity for insults to be exchanged, secrets to be whispered and, occasionally, for blows to be traded. Katy was in the queue, alone as usual, when a sharp shove to her back caused her to lurch forward.

'Child-murdering bitch!' The taunt was whispered just loudly enough for those around to hear.

Heart pounding, Katy turned around. She sensed that this was a test that could define the time she spent here, but she was far from sure she'd pass it.

She faced a huddle of smirking boys, jostling each other and leering at her with unconcealed fascination.

'Well, it's true, ain't it?' She recognised the voice from the earlier taunt. He was a meaty kid, probably about her own age, with livid acne flaming on his neck, and fleshy lips that sprayed spittle as he talked. 'We don't like people who mess with kids in here,' the boy sneered. 'We might need to teach you a lesson.'

Katy's tongue felt thick in her mouth. He was disgusting. But he had friends here and she didn't. They pressed in on her and, almost imperceptibly, she felt herself shrink back. Panic began to rise in her chest.

'You'd better believe it, Carter, she's queen of the fucking child-murdering bitches, and if I were you, I'd think twice and think again before I decided to say anything about it.'

Another girl had materialised at Katy's shoulder, hissing venom towards her tormentor. Katy had been told there were only three of them in the forty-strong unit. This one was slim, with a scabby, hard-bitten face and big green eyes that might have been pretty elsewhere. As she glanced sideways to take in her possible rescuer, Katy couldn't help but gasp. The girl had a tattoo of a climbing rose twining down her neck and across her shoulders. Katy had never seen a tattoo on a girl of that age before – rarely on any woman at all, for that matter.

Carter's paper-white face turned a shade paler, even the angry red on his throat seemed to fade a little, and it was his turn to edge back. The boys outside his immediate little gang were smirking with delight, but alert enough to shuffle

248

carefully inwards, tacitly arranging themselves to best conceal Carter and the girls from the duty staff's view.

From somewhere, Katy found the nerve to curl her lip to a sneer, although her heart was still battering against her ribs. You didn't grow up where she had without getting some idea of how to handle yourself if it came to a fight, even if in Katy's case the knowledge was largely theoretical. She wasn't stupid enough to think that this girl, whoever she was, would put herself in harm's way for Katy without expecting something in return and she realised it was best to try to minimise her indebtedness.

The world stopped for a moment. Then Carter's hand flashed forward. His knuckles dragged across Katy's neck, missing her face only by dint of her speed and instinct. Blood rushing in her ears, Katy bunched her fists and flailed out, spitting and stamping. The room roared its appreciation, the boys' attempt at secrecy abandoned. Katy reeled from a blow to her kidneys from one of Carter's gang, but she kept lashing out. Green-Eyes, though, was on a different level. She whirled around, gouging and shrieking like she was possessed. Carter rolled on the floor clutching his groin. Another of the lads was spurting blood from his nose, whilst the noise in the dining room had risen to a roar.

The two nearest staff members might have loitered for a second or so, or it might just have been Katy's imagination. Either way, she felt nothing but relief when a rough pair of arms finally jerked her away from her opponents.

'Maureen Stephenson, no surprise to find you in a ruckus. And the new girl, Clery. Well, you'll both be down in the cellar for the rest of the night. And you, Jonathan Carter. Anderson, go and get some extra hands and we'll shift these idiots downstairs.'

The cellar was split into separate isolation cells, so Katy had no chance to find out more about her new ally. Her head was spinning, but she saw little opportunity for comfort or rest when she took in the damp cubicle with the wooden bench against the wall, too short to lie down on.

In fact, sleep took her immediately, almost as her limbs were still curling up to fit the cramped space. It might only have been early evening, but Katy had barely slept in days, and her body simply had nothing more to give.

When she woke, every part of her ached stiffly from the cold and the odd sleeping position and most of all from the beating she'd taken upstairs. But there was daylight seeping in through the murky slit of a window at the top of the wall and, as far as she could judge, the sun was well up in the sky.

Katy didn't have to wait long before the thump of boots on the flags and the clang of metal announced the arrival of the wardens. Apparently she'd missed breakfast; a sanction – or a blessing, depending on how you looked at it – that was part and parcel of spending the night in chokey.

The warders who came to get them – day shift this time, new faces to Katy – marched the pair of them off with little fanfare. Katy was to join a group weeding in the smallholding. Green-Eyes was going elsewhere.

'Maureen Stephenson,' Green-Eyes whispered to Katy as they walked, then she winked. 'Carter's a knob. You're all right, though, you are.'

'Katy Clery,' Katy replied. 'Yes, I think I will be.'

# August 2017

*Helen*

When Helen and Veena got back, Alys was sleeping, so the police were able to speak to Helen, Darren and Neil together. DI Nelson was there, along with DS Addison.

'The first thing is, we've got the papers out of archive on Katy Clery's trial.' Nelson was speaking, but it was Addison who placed a slim bundle of photocopies on the table.

'A homicide trial would be twenty-odd lever-arches' worth these days, thanks to bloomin' email. But the gist of it's there. The headlines are that Katy was in a sexual relationship with a married man. He'd been her teacher at primary school, and it seems to have started shortly afterwards.' Here Nelson paused, looking uncomfortable, and Helen wondered if he was deliberately calling her Katy, trying to make it all seem a bit more distant. 'Looking at it now, she was clearly a victim of grooming and sexual exploitation. I'm afraid they didn't quite see things like that in the early sixties.'

Helen glanced anxiously at her father, but he didn't meet her eye. 'Go on,' he said gruffly, nodding to the DI.

'The man was called Simon Gardiner. He and his wife had young twins, just about nine months, Jennifer and Mary. One night, after the wife had been away from home, Mary was reported missing. It didn't take the police long to establish that Katy had been there that night – some of her school friends had twigged roughly what was going on and it came out in the door-to-doors. Once the investigation was onto that, Katy quickly confessed to taking and hiding Mary's body.'

'But she hadn't killed the girl?' asked Neil.

Nelson tapped the documents. 'She said not. Her version was that Gardiner got frustrated and shook her. The death was an accident.'

'He said otherwise?'

'He claimed to know nothing about it. He said that Katy had been pressuring him to leave his wife and kids. He tried to end the affair; she broke in with the keys he'd given her and killed the girl in cold blood out of spite or jealousy.'

'And a jury believed him?' Helen felt her stomach heave.

Nelson shrugged. 'She'd already pleaded guilty to the Coroner's Act offences – hiding the body and so forth – and she'd gone to some lengths to do it. His defence made a lot of that – why would she involve herself if it had had nothing to do with her? He was an upstanding pillar of the community, big noise in the church, all that stuff. They paint her as quite the Lolita. It makes a pretty hairy read to modern eyes, I'll be frank with you.'

'If they'd found the body, and been able to tell the cause of death, that might have backed up her case,' put in Addison. 'If she was telling the truth, then the irony was she carried out her part too well. Without any evidence of cause of death, it could well have been murder, but the jury went for diminished responsibility, so the conviction was manslaughter instead.' He paused to flick through the pages. '"An underde-veloped mind crazed by infatuation for her lover" – that's how it was put in court.'

Neil swiped his eyes with the back of his hand and Helen felt a catch in her own throat watching him. He'd been living with Barbara's demons almost his whole life, she suddenly realised, and only now was he finally getting to see them for what they really were.

She thought back to what Barbara had said in the hospital. It was clear she blamed this Gardiner character for how her whole life had turned out. For not being the mother to Helen that she thought she should have been. Did her mother even love her at all, or was it all just a twisted act? Was that why so much of their relationship felt 'almost there', why there was always that slightly off note? The doubt opened up in Helen's heart like a sinkhole.

But then what about Barbara herself? What about that fourteen-year-old kid abused and tormented and hung out to dry? Amidst the hurt and self-pity, here was anger, too, on her mother's behalf. Where had *her* family been? Where was the protection that *she* was entitled to expect?

'Anyway, that's not the only news.' Veena was speaking now, in her bright, moving-things-along voice that gave little quarter to the seismic aftershocks of what they'd just been told. 'We continued to pursue the "Jennifer" line of enquiry whilst the archive search was ongoing. As you know, Jennifer Rutherford – Gardiner as was – has been ruled out of any direct involvement in Barney's disappearance, but we looked into other members of the family.'

'Okay,' said Darren, the only one of the three of them able to speak.

Here, DI Nelson took the lead again. 'Simon Gardiner himself is still alive. He's old now, going on eighty, but he's still with it.'

'Right,' said Darren.

'It was him that Barbara was keeping that file on, wasn't it?' said Neil, quietly.

Nelson nodded and filled Helen and Darren in that there had been information about Gardiner in the papers found under the floorboards. 'Gardiner separated from the twins' mother, Etta, and married again in the 1980s. Younger woman, you know how it is.'

Helen felt Darren bristle, but this was too important to worry about whether there was any side to the DI's remarks.

'Go on,' she urged.

'Well, Etta moved to Scotland, nursing her broken heart and, most nights, a whisky bottle, from what we can tell. But Simon Gardiner's current wife, she's called Sue, works in one of the labs at the General.' He paused. 'The lab where they carry out the breast cancer gene testing.'

'Gene testing,' Helen echoed. 'She would have had access to Mum's identity details when she supplied them to the hospital?'

Nelson nodded. 'That's the theory we're working on. We brought Gardiner in for a bit of a chat, and he acted perfectly innocent, all ancient history, he said. Very sad and difficult at the time, but life moves on and all that. The second wife said she knew he'd lost a child from his previous marriage but claims she wasn't told the details at all.'

'Right,' said Darren.

'Well,' continued Nelson, 'I got the lads to look over his computers.' Here he glanced at Neil, who remained impassive, although Helen noticed the young DC coloured slightly. 'As soon as we told him we had a warrant to seize his equipment, he coughed to possessing a large number of illegal images of children.'

'You mean kiddie porn?' said Darren.

Nelson nodded.

Helen found her heart was hammering. She groped for Darren's hand and he squeezed hers hard.

'We've charged him on several counts. He seemed to be singing like the proverbial canary.'

'Seemed to be?' Darren's voice was a whisper. Helen didn't think she'd have been able to speak at all.

'The boys have found something new, just an hour ago – we came straight here. There's a cache of emails Gardiner didn't mention in his interview, from an email address set up a couple of months ago.'

'Yes?'

'It looks like—'

'Although we can't be sure of anything yet,' put in Veena.

'No. But it looks like Gardiner was very recently in touch with certain known criminals to procure a young boy.' He took a deep breath. 'The emails are written in quite veiled terms, presumably to stop any triggers appearing if they were digitally scanned, but reading them as a human being it's quite easy to interpret what's going on. They seem to say that the boy was found and arrangements are being made for Gardiner to make a payment and receive the child. The message, which we interpret as saying that Gardiner's contacts have got the child, was sent at 16.35 on the 6th of August from an IP address within half a mile of Julie Hendricks' address.'

'Barney!' Helen felt herself begin to shake almost immediately.

'That's our fear.' Nelson looked more awkward than ever. 'I'm afraid that's not the end of it.'

'What do you mean?'

'Well, from references in the emails, it looks possible that your son was specifically targeted. That Gardiner identified and, um, requested that it should be him.'

'You mean this bastard *ordered* my son, like a fucking takeaway?' Darren's voice was a whisper no longer.

Nelson, Veena and Addison nodded like a trio of gormless dashboard toys. The living room that Helen had known all her life, that she'd grown up in, was suddenly unreal and insubstantial. She wanted to push down the walls like a stage set and find Barney waiting in the wings.

Her little flight of fantasy was shattered by Darren smashing his fist through the glass of the coffee table.

# June 1962

It wasn't hard for Katy to sneak some clothes into her school bag and then skive off as the others headed their separate ways to registration. Remembering the brambles, she'd packed jeans as well as thick gloves, the kitchen scissors and a rusty old trowel that was kicking around at home.

She saw a few people searching the edges of the wood. Her stomach fluttered with nerves, but she'd just say she was searching herself if anyone asked. The kids had been told they couldn't miss school to help to look for Mary, but she'd spotted some of the older ones – fourth- and fifth-formers and a few third years like herself – doing it anyway.

It was easy enough to find the place – the patch of toadstools that she'd destroyed the night before gave it away – although the area seemed even more trampled. When she examined them closely, the brambles had a battered look about them from her efforts, but they'd held their secret well enough. With the scissors and the gloves, she was able to deal with the thorny, twisting stems much more efficiently. After only a few seconds, she glimpsed the white of the sheet and felt a powerful mix of relief and horror. But she could hear the call of voices and the crunch of feet on the ground; she knew there was no time to waste.

Quickly, more easily than she expected, she extracted the bundle from the thicket. She could still sense how stiff and cold the body was even through the fabric. The feel of it made her shiver.

Trying to be gentle, she eased the body into her backpack. She was proud of the army-style bag that she'd got for her fourteenth birthday a few weeks before. After today, she realised, she'd never want to look at it again. She'd always feel the weight of Mary when she carried it. Carefully, she exited the woods onto a ginnel, and then out into one of the streets.

Simon had told her to go to Lime Street station. She had money for the bus, but she decided it would be safer to walk and stick to the quieter streets. After she'd gone about half a mile or so, the tension started to drop out of her shoulders. Now she was reaching less familiar, busier roads, where an unknown face wouldn't seem out of the ordinary.

Despite her meandering route, she was at Lime Street before ten o'clock. The station was quiet. The commuters would have cleared out and only a few well-dressed women, probably coming into town for a day's shopping, strolled through the ticket hall.

Katy had only been here once or twice. The grandness of the building awed her a little, but she knew she had to keep focused and finish what she'd started. There was a stopping train to Blackpool leaving in fifteen minutes. She looked at the list of stations on the timetable and jabbed a finger at the middle of the list, rehearsing the unfamiliar name with a quick whisper. It sounded like a small place, probably rural.

Hopefully there would be a peaceful hedgerow or copse that she could find and do what she had to do, decently, before it was time to get the train back home.

She made her way to platform 3, almost retching when the smell of cooked meat caught her off-guard passing the station cafeteria. She thought of the times they'd gone to Blackpool as kids. It seemed so long ago; how had her life become so lonely, so burdened, in a few years? The Blackpool of her memories was a happy place, and for a moment she thought of going there. But the journey would take too long. Besides, it wasn't as if Mary could appreciate the lights or the beach or the trams.

In the end, Katy got off exactly where she'd planned. It was a small station, just one platform on each side of the tracks, as she had imagined. She was the only passenger to alight, and the lady in the ticket office had her nose stuck in a *Woman's Weekly* and didn't seem to have noticed Katy slip by at all.

There was a little signpost indicating which way passengers should head for the town centre. Katy turned the opposite way, and within moments the gaps between the buildings had stuttered wider. She found herself striding down a street of big detached and semi-detached houses, their long front gardens neatly separated by beech hedges and dotted with mature trees of all kinds. After two or three minutes, she came to a junction where a smaller lane met the main road she was on. Down the lane she could see rolling fields; it looked like a promising place to find a ditch or a hedgerow.

It went well at first; she walked out of sight of the road she'd been on and found a spot that looked promising behind a small copse of trees. But as soon as she unpacked her trowel and started to try to dig, she realised she was doing little more than scratching at the earth. The soil was dry and packed, with tree roots crowded together below the surface.

It was hopeless. She threw the trowel down and it clanked off a tree stump. The only thing for it was to walk further and see if she could find a better spot. A doubting voice in her mind niggled that all the soil would be hard-packed after a dry spell, that a fourteen-year-old girl with a garden trowel was never going to be able to adequately bury a body, even a small one like Mary. She was smart enough to realise that she was in this up to her neck now, and she'd better do it right, for her sake as well as Simon's. Fighting to keep it together, she walked on.

Then she noticed a change in the landscape across the fields. There was a farm gate off the lane that led onto a large field, which then dipped away into a shallow valley. Beyond the second rise of the land, she could see the brown of fresh earth. It wasn't a ploughed field. There were a couple of cabins and some vehicles, although they all looked stationary. It was some sort of building site.

*Genius.* Her heart leapt. That was the solution. If she couldn't dig, she would take advantage of someone else to do it for her. If she was careful, and lucky, they might build over the body and that would be the end of any worry about being found out. She swiftly climbed the gate.

As she got closer, she heard the hum of traffic, and on the lip of the first rise she could see the road, with two lanes in each direction, bisecting the countryside about half a mile ahead of her. It was one of the new motorways, she realised, the first time she'd seen one. From here she could see the building site more clearly too. It was right against the motorway. They must be building a new access road, or perhaps a petrol station.

It took longer than she thought to get there. She'd had to find a place to cross the little stream at the bottom of the valley, and then fight through a wooded section on the other side. Nervously, she skirted a field with cows in it. Then, quite suddenly, she was at the perimeter of the site. There was a little wire fence – nothing more than a marker really – and beyond it the ground was churned and levelled and cut through with the tracks of the machines. She could see some men working, but they were still quite distant. The part of the side she was approaching seemed deserted. Pushing back tendrils of honeysuckle draping down in the shadow of a tree, she entered the site.

She could see access roads, already sketched out with marker poles and, judging from the compacted state of the ground, already in use by the construction vehicles. The sweep of road nearest had a bend, and around the edges of it was a rough bank of loose earth and stones, presumably kicked up by the passing traffic. That was her answer.

Once again, she took out the trowel. With a final rueful thought at how far this was from the peaceful resting place she'd imagined for the child, she started to dig. This time, the earth did her bidding. The soil was crumbly and loose; the only problem was stopping more loose clumps from tumbling into the hole as she dug it. After a short while she found a way of using the slope of the banking to her advantage, and soon she was making quick progress.

Only when she was absolutely sure that she'd done enough did she stop to open the main part of the bag. Easier though the digging was, she'd still been working for a good fifteen or twenty minutes and she could feel her T-shirt damp with sweat up and down the length of her back. Her upper arms ached, and her fingers too, and when she rocked back on her heels, she found she had to pause for a moment to recover her breathing.

The smell that seeped from the bag as she worked open its drawstring top took her by surprise. She hadn't noticed any smell this morning, hadn't expected any now. But the body was two days old, and in a confined space, warm against her back, nature had begun to take its course. It was an earthy smell, pungent, though not yet particularly strong, and it caught her in the gut. As she lifted the thing from the bag, she couldn't stop her hands from shaking, and in her haste to be rid of it, she dropped it and it rolled a couple of turns to come to rest where she'd intended.

Working as quickly as she could, she scooped the loose earth and rubble back into the cavity she'd made. Gradually, the reddish soil obliterated each trace of the white sheet. She took a few moments to arrange the final layer of clods and stones, to try to make the disturbance as inconspicuous as possible, before roughly wiping the trowel on her jeans and putting it back in the backpack.

She'd done it, and there was a sense of relief, even a grim satisfaction. But she knew too that this wasn't how it should have been for Mary. Her mind flashed to her dad's funeral, the impatient horses snorting steam into the morning air and the black-clad huddles round the open grave. There was dignity there, certainly, but that wasn't what was right for Mary either. Mary ought still to be pink and warm, sticky and gurgling. Mary deserved her life.

# August 2017

*Helen*

Helen was woken abruptly from a sleep she'd thought would never come. There was a dull ache in her head, probably courtesy of the tablets Veena had produced from her handbag after Nelson had dropped his bombshell last night. The blood in her temples was throbbing in time with the ringing on her phone, and she answered the call just to make it stop, without thinking who could be ringing.

It was Kelly Edwards, an old uni friend. She'd just seen the papers and was horrified to learn Barney was missing. She wanted to let Helen know she was there for her. If there was anything she could do ...

Helen muttered something incoherent and killed the call. Her phone screen was crammed with missed calls and messages – a dozen or more colleagues and friends. People she'd never been able to make time for since the move to Chiswick, all now wanting to help her. Or, more cynically, wanting a piece of the action.

Helen glanced at her bedside alarm clock. It was almost half past ten in the morning. She was shocked at how Veena's pills must have knocked her out. Blearily, she reached for her tablet to check what was online. It was the headline story on the BBC website. *Man suspected in Harrison abduction case.* Below the careful headline, breathless text explained that Simon Gardiner was now the prime suspect in the mysterious disappearance of Barney Harrison. There were links to further articles about the death of Mary Gardiner and the trial of Katherine Clery, about the family that abandoned Clery when she had served her sentence, and about her decades of living under an alias as Barbara Kipling.

Helen flicked between the different sites for a few moments, too dazed to take it in properly, then, almost blindly, she fumbled her way to the stairs. One of the junior officers, DC Hemmings, was stationed by the door. She was in uniform today, presumably for the benefit of the press, and she gave Helen an embarrassed half-smile.

Darren, Neil and Veena were sitting around the kitchen table. They had newspapers spread out in front of them and Helen winced as she caught sight of the front pages. Many of the papers were not as careful in their headlines as the BBC.

'What's happened?' she asked, but they all looked as bewildered as she felt.

'We're trying to work out where they've got it all from,' said Veena, with a sigh. 'It's not the sort of detail that can be pulled together overnight.'

'Amy?' Helen said it almost to herself. 'But why would she?'

Veena shrugged. 'We worked out who your friend was, yes. We're looking into it.'

'And what about Barney?' Helen snapped back. 'Are you any further forward with working out where he is?'

Veena shook her head. 'I spoke to DI Nelson this morning. The interviewers aren't getting anything out of Gardiner at all. The DI's got people searching his house, of course, and looking into any other locations he might have had access to, but so far we've come up blank.'

'Same old story,' said Darren, bitterly.

'We're doing *everything*, Mr Harrison,' said Veena. Neil put a hand on Darren's arm. To Helen's surprise, he didn't explode. Even Darren was being worn down.

The doorbell rang. Helen looked at Veena, expectantly.

'There's been press all morning,' she said, not making any movement to get up. 'We've got a couple of extra uniforms in to deal with them.'

But a moment later the young woman from the hallway stuck her head nervously round the door.

'There's a Sonia Maguire here, Sergeant – says she's Mrs Marsden's sister.'

'Tell her to wait,' said Veena. 'I'll speak to her in the dining room, find out if it's a blagger.'

'No,' said Neil, speaking for the first time. 'I want to see her. Tell her to come in here.'

The young officer turned to Veena for approval, and after a pause she nodded her assent. They all waited with eyes on the door for a long few moments.

It was uncanny. Sonia Maguire was Barbara in a different life. The same height and proud, almost stiff, bearing; the same dark eyes and high, rounded cheeks. Although visibly anxious, she also looked healthy, and seeing her standing there was a sharp reminder of how much Barbara had deteriorated over the last few weeks – probably even months, if Helen thought back. She realised she'd been too preoccupied with her unravelling marriage to really notice.

Despite the similarities between the sisters, though, there

would have been no chance of confusing them, even when Barbara had been well. This woman's hair, though dark like Barbara's, was cut short. She wore tight jeans, bright lipstick and a top that pushed out her chest.

Neil stood up, pushing his chair back noisily, but then was unable to move any further. The woman stepped towards him.

'You must be Neil?' she said, her words wavered slightly, but even those few words were enough to show that warm, confident voice was something else she shared with Barbara.

He nodded, and somehow, they were in each other's arms, tears streaming down both of their faces.

'I can't tell you how much I've wanted to meet you.' Sonia sniffed the words out, hugging, and patting and gazing at Neil as if trying to convince herself he wasn't an illusion. 'You meant everything to her, you know, right from the moment she first told me that she'd met someone. You saved her, Neil, you ... you ...' She couldn't finish. He helped her to the table, pulling over another seat.

Gently he introduced Helen and Darren without asking any of the questions that must have been gnawing at him. Darren brought Alys in from where she had been doing jigsaws in the sitting room and Sonia cooed over how pretty she was and brought out her phone to show a picture of one of her own granddaughters who was the same age. Helen felt the ache of Barney's absence like a knife wound.

'I had to come,' she said, eventually. 'When I read today that the little boy who's gone missing is her grandson, and it said in the papers she might be dying. They gave the street name too and I suddenly realised I could find you. Katy never told me her address.' She glanced up at Neil. 'She never even told me her married name.'

266

'I'm not sure that I can blame her.' Veena stood up from the table as she spoke. 'From what I've heard she came in for some pretty shabby treatment when she came home.'

Sonia's temper flared dramatically. 'Well if you lot hadn't decided to charge her instead of the paedo then she wouldn't have been in gaol in the first place!'

'Mr Gardiner *was* charged, as I understand.' Veena's voice remained cool. 'And when it got to trial, the jury decided that Katy Clery – not Mary's father – killed Mary Gardiner. I'm sure you'll appreciate it was well before my time in any event.' Veena tactfully withdrew to go and check on the officers at the door.

'We've all been trashed in the papers ...' Sonia was telling Neil. 'I was scared if I didn't come quickly you wouldn't let me over the doorstep at all. I do hope they find the little lad, but I suppose if they've got Gardiner it's only a matter of time. We've had the little boy in our prayers anyway, before we even knew it was ... well, you know ...'

She gestured around the table occasionally, or glanced at Helen or Darren in a token of inclusion, but really it was only Neil she was talking to. *Why not?* Helen thought. They'd lived with each other's ghosts for decades.

The pictures of Gardiner stared out at her from the front pages. Wild-eyed, with his mouth set either in a snarl or a thin pressed line depending on which shot the editor had chosen, he looked exactly like the monster the press wanted to portray. It didn't mean anything, she tried to tell herself. It was just about selling papers. Still, she couldn't bring herself to imagine her son in his hands. She simply couldn't let herself go there. Not yet.

The talk between Neil and Sonia had turned to going to

see Barbara. Neil had planned to visit that morning – would have been there already if Veena hadn't stopped him to brief him on the press stuff. Sonia wanted to go but was uneasy about how Barbara would react. Neil, with a confidence Helen didn't share, was trying to persuade her it would be fine.

Helen got up to get a glass of water and some paracetamol and Simon Gardiner's eyes followed her around the room. On impulse, she turned to Darren.

'How about taking Alys to the park?' she asked him.

'You want some space?'

'No, no.' He'd misunderstood her. 'I mean both of us – go for a walk, try to clear our heads a bit.'

He nodded slowly. 'What about the cameras?'

'I'm not sure, but I can't stay cooped up in here forever. Could you have a word with Veena while I have a quick shower?'

# June 1962

*Katy*

The body in the cot was lifeless and unmoving.

There was no injury to see, but she looked horribly wrong nonetheless. It was her stillness, and a cold tinge just creeping onto the surface of the translucent baby skin at her temples. Perhaps you could have thought she was just sleeping, were it not for the second child lying next to her – *her* breath catarrh-filled and grunty, *her* face hot and sweaty in sleep. The contrast of the pair of them together was like the fork in the road; if Simon had only seen sense, if he'd only been able to stop, if only ... if only Mary could still be as warm and real as her sister. There had been two twins and now there was one. Mary Gardiner was no more.

'My God, my God, my God.' Simon's hands gripped the cot railing in terror. Katy looked at him, but he couldn't seem to take his eyes from his child. He was always so controlled, so certain. It frightened her to see him like this.

'We have to do something,' she said. 'Shall I phone for an ambulance?'

'No!' Finally he turned to her. 'Don't you know what this

means? They'll say it's murder. I'll get life for it. God help me, Katy, I might even hang.'

She'd never seen his eyes so wide, his face so panicked.

'It was an accident. I'll tell them – the police, anyone!'

He laughed, but it was a bitter sound. 'And that'll make it better, will it? That I was here with a little underage tart at the time? I don't think so!'

'Simon!'

'I'm sorry, love, I'm not thinking straight.' He paused to pull her towards him, but the embrace lasted only an instant before he took her by the shoulders and bent to speak. 'This is what we have to do. No one at home knows you've come here, right?'

Mutely, she nodded.

'You take Mary. I'll push the sash open as far as it goes. It's a warm night; it won't seem strange. Anyone could have got in, a ... a burglar ... even a dog or a fox, for God's sake. Take her and hide her. I'll go to bed and Etta will wake me when she gets in and realises something is wrong. I'll find somewhere to bury her.' His voice started to crumble. 'I'll find somewhere peaceful ... and good ... Oh, my darling Mary.'

He was already rummaging in a chest in the corner of the room. Eventually he produced a thread-worn sheet, laid it on the top of the chest and lifted Mary from the cot, his hands stroking – almost pawing – at her hair and face as he carried her over. Katy hung back a little, uncertain, and watched from the doorway as the father deftly wrapped his daughter's small body, like a bag of chips being wrapped in newspaper. Fat tears dripped from his face as he worked, soaking into the thin, soft fabric. He gabbled about the woods; not really a woodland but a bit of waste ground by the canal with a few trees where the kids played. She could hide the child there, he said. It would be just until tomorrow, until he could come and bury her.

Katy recoiled when he finally held the thing out towards her. Her heart was thumping and she could taste bile in the back of her throat.

'Take her,' Simon urged, thrusting the bundle towards her with outstretched arms. 'Katy, please, I need you.'

Perhaps that was what made her do it. He'd never needed her before. Wanted her: yes, desperately. Loved her: perhaps, in a way. But now a giddy surge of power rushed through her, propelling her to take the chance – to *make* him need her, perhaps forever.

She stepped forward and held out her arms.

Almost before she'd got the measure of it – the stone-weight heft of the child and the slipperiness of the fabric – Simon was hurrying her downstairs and towards the kitchen door. The weight of the bundle was surprising. Katy shifted it in her arms again, worrying that she would trip on the stairs, the way Simon was harrying her. A sweat broke across her forehead.

She would go out the back way, as usual, Simon gabbled. He opened the door, but she paused. A look of exasperation crossed his face and for a moment she was back at junior school and he was her teacher again, professionally irritated by a messy composition or a simple error in a page of sums. But the expression was gone as soon as it had appeared. He bent and kissed the bundle, the sheet where Mary's head was, and then turned to kiss Katy too.

'Thank you, love, thank you. You'll be at practice tomorrow?'

She nodded.

'We'll speak then. Stay safe, Katy, and not a word, remember. If they hang me it'll be on your head.'

She crept out and did what he'd asked – stumbling in the dark to get to the middle of the woods and pushing the bundle into the thorny undergrowth. Even when she pushed it as deep into the bushes as she could, she could still see the white of the sheet in the gaps between the bramble stems, and it would be worse come daylight. She tried again, rolling up her cardigan sleeves to stop the thorns catching on the wool and getting long scratches to her arms for her trouble.

Eventually she turned, sitting on her bottom on the dank mossy ground and edging her feet forward towards the brambles. Her left hand skidded slickly through a patch of fungus as she pushed forward, and she let out a cry, wiping the slime furiously on her skirt. Stretching her legs forward into the undergrowth, she was able to kick with her feet to move it further in, all the time willing herself not to think of what she was actually doing.

Something screeched in the darkness, startling her, and she was disgusted to feel the warm wetness of her pee spreading down the insides of her legs. She was crying properly now, frustration and despair coming out of her in great sobs.

She gave one last kick and felt her sturdy school boots connect with the child in a sickening thud. *It can't hurt her now*, Katy tried to reassure herself, scrabbling to her feet and rubbing her wrists and calves where the scratches were the deepest.

Finally, thankfully, the thing was done.

*

The next day, the news that one of the Gardiners' twins had vanished swirled round Katy like rising floodwater. With every new voice that added itself to the gossip, she felt a little closer to drowning. When she turned up at the church hall, the practice was fuller than it had been in weeks. Miss Tilley, who normally did the accompaniment on the piano, announced, in her flustered and slightly timid way, that she would be taking the session due to Mr Gardiner being 'indisposed'. It was clear that there wasn't going to be much singing going on.

Ten minutes before they were due to finish, after a few slapdash numbers, and a tea break where Katy's cup rattled so much in its saucer she was getting funny looks, Simon blustered in through the main doorway. He held his hands aloft to silence the clamour, looking not unlike the image of Jesus in the picture above his right shoulder.

'There's no news,' he said, pausing to give his brow an anguished wipe. 'We're going to be organising search parties for tomorrow. If any of you can help, we'll be meeting at the primary school. Children, do ask your parents if they could consider helping us, please. And make sure you all have someone to walk home with tonight.'

Only she knew that it was a performance – that he was really there to see her. When she had the chance, she slipped off unnoticed into the dusty room where the hymnals were kept. He'd know to find her there, assuming he could get away.

Sure enough, about twenty minutes later, the door opened.

'Katy?' came his voice. She'd left the lights off in case anyone else came to investigate.

'Here,' she said, stepping towards him.

'Oh God.' He held her tight, but only for a moment.

'Did you do it?'

'Yes. But she'll be found soon …'

'I know, I know, we have to move her.'

'But if she's found you can bury her properly. Nobody need know she wasn't stolen.'

'Keep your voice down, for Christ's sake, Katy! No, it's too risky. It wouldn't work.' He paused again. 'You understand I can't do it, don't you? They're practically going with me to the lavatory. It has to be you.'

Katy's tongue felt thick and dry in her mouth. She didn't want this. She wished with all her heart she'd never had anything to do with him. But then who could have known it would come to this?

Simon was pushing paper money into her hands. 'Thirty shillings,' he told her. 'It has to be tomorrow, as early as possible. Bunk off school and get her out. Get to Lime Street and take a train somewhere. Not somewhere you know – somewhere random. Find some proper woods or a farmer's field and bury her as well as you can. Don't even tell me where it is. Try not to remember it yourself.'

'You won't be going to get her?'

He shook his head. 'I can't. It has to be you, Katy.'

# August 2017

*Helen*

An hour later – over sixty-seven hours since Barney had been taken – Helen, Darren and Alys had left the house. They were tramping along a footpath towards a local picnic spot with a duck pond. Veena had negotiated that they would give the photographers the chance to take a posed shot of the three of them leaving the house, and then the press would leave them alone. She'd recommended that they stick to the footpath rather than the road, and that was why they'd ended up coming here rather than the play park Helen usually visited with the kids.

She remembered the path from when she was a child herself. Neil would bring her blackberrying here in the autumn. In her memory it had been wilder then, more overgrown, and she couldn't decide if it was true, or if she'd just got taller.

Alys ran on ahead a little and Helen managed to convince herself that she was happy to let her go. The ground was still too bumpy and rough for her little legs to get up much speed, and Helen was conscious that Alys had had very little chance of fresh air and exercise since the day that Barney was taken. There was no sign of anyone else around, but Helen still kept her eyes locked on to her daughter.

'Do you think we'll get him back, Darren?'

She whispered it. The words had been jostling on her lips for minutes and she didn't know whether she'd be able to say them at all until, suddenly, they were out. She knew that Darren would tell her the truth.

'I don't know. I just don't know.' There was an intake of breath. He had more to say but was trying to work out the best way of saying it. 'It being ... it being ... someone like Gardiner – I would have said that was the worst thing that could happen. But now they've got Gardiner in custody, well, we've just got to hope I suppose.'

'But if he was keeping him somewhere, why not tell? Better even for him than letting Barney ...' She couldn't say it. The thought that he was still alive but languishing somewhere, that Gardiner would allow Barney to die alone in order to protect himself, was torture.

'There's just this part of me that feels like it's different ...' Darren was speaking slowly now, working out his thoughts even as he shared them. 'He suddenly manages to find Katy Clery because of her health records – okay. He sends her threatening notes – fine. He poisons her in hospital – fine. Then, at the same time as he's up to all that, he's also arranging for a child to be kidnapped, when there's no evidence he's ever done that before.'

'There's no evidence he hasn't. People do horrendous things and stay under the radar for decades.'

'Yep, I'll give you that, but the child who ends up being taken isn't any child. It's Barbara – Katy's – grandson.'

'Because it's about revenge – she killed his daughter; he goes after her grandson.'

'But her story is she didn't kill his child. And if that's right,

276

then he would be the only person in the world to know that apart from her.' He paused, as if trying to decide whether to share his thoughts.

'Go on,' she prompted.

'All right. I heard Nelson on the phone, you know, talking about what they found on Simon Gardiner's computer. The pictures were all girls – not boys. *Young* girls, but not infants. Nelson seemed to think it might not stand up in court. He said a lot of them could be sixteen or seventeen, picked out and dressed up to make them look younger. Having a thing for teenage girls is a bit different to having a thing for five-year-old boys, don't you think?'

'So you're saying he's *not* a paedophile now?'

Darren shrugged. 'I just wonder if this is more about Gardiner and your mum than about Barney, but maybe that's just because that's what I want to think.' His voice rose as his anger returned. 'Because I'm praying that some fucking pervert isn't doing God-knows-what to our boy.'

She reached out for his hand. He let her take it, then squeezed hers tight enough to hurt. For a minute or so, they walked in silence, apart from the occasional word of encouragement to Alys. The sun was warm and there was a slight breeze rummaging through the hedgerow. Even the birdsong sounded lazy. There was an idea, skittering just out of her reach, like the daddy-long-legs in the grass at their feet. Then Darren's phone rang.

'Probably work,' he said, but she saw Lauren's name flash up on the screen as he pulled it from his pocket.

'Take it if you want,' she said. 'I'll go on ahead with Alys.'

'I won't be long.'

They'd pretty much arrived at the duck pond. She called

Alys over and pulled the bag of crusts from her handbag. Darren hung back, speaking in a brusque undertone, and ending the call quickly, as he'd predicted.

Helen didn't ask about Lauren, but handed him some bread, which he began to break up and pass on in bits to Alys. Left to her own devices, she'd throw it a slice at a time and then complain when there was none left ten seconds later. Helen threw some crumbs from the bottom of the bag, tossing them over the heads of the ducks to encourage them to back off a little. The other typical conclusion to duck feeding was the ducks getting closer and closer until the children ended up running away.

'I've told Lauren we need to put a pause on things.' Darren's eyes were fixed straight ahead.

'Oh?'

'I just couldn't ... and it wasn't fair to her ... not with everything that's going on.'

'I see.' Though Helen didn't see, not entirely, but nor did she have the energy to pursue it. A bit like him, she supposed. As they stood together, throwing the bread, laughing with Alys, her daddy-long-legs of a thought fluttered closer. She began to have glimpses of it, to make out its shape and its substance. She glanced at Darren. 'I want to ask you something.'

He shot an anxious look back. 'Not about Lauren ...'

'No, not that. I just think I might be going crazy. No one else would get it.'

'Fire away,' he said, but then, picking up on her hesitation, he showed Alys that the bread bag was empty and sent her off to pick some dandelions growing by a fence post, safely back from the water's edge. 'Go on then, what is it?'

'Could Mum be setting Simon Gardiner up?'

He frowned. 'What do you mean?'

'All the stuff you said, about why it doesn't fit for him to have taken him. What if it's not his revenge on her; what if it's *her* revenge on *him*?'

'So she's arranged for Barney to be spirited off somewhere, entrapped Gardiner into sending those emails ...'

'Or even planted them on his computer. Remember all those OU courses? I bet she'd be good enough to do that.'

'But what about the notes you said she was getting that were supposed to be from Gardiner's daughter? In fact, never mind those, what about the overdose in the hospital?'

Helen's mind was whirling faster than she could get the words out now. It all fitted. The whole cancer gene testing thing had never sat right with her, not when she knew the lengths Barbara had gone to, to keep her identity secret for all those years. Helen couldn't imagine for a moment that she'd accidently give up those details, that she would *encourage* NHS bureaucracy to link her with her estranged family.

'That was her way of leading them to Gardiner.' Helen flung the few crumbs that she still had in her fingers onto the path. 'Don't you see? That was the trail of breadcrumbs leading straight to the witch's cottage. She *knew* all this would happen.' She slapped her palm against her forehead. 'Of course *Amy* didn't leak anything to the press, it was all Mum. She's been setting this up for years. It's probably all part of the plan that her family get dragged through the papers into the bargain. That's their just deserts for turning their backs on her all those years ago.'

He whistled. 'You really think she'd do that to you?'

'I wouldn't have thought it before – because who would,

right? That's why it's so good; it's just too much to believe. When I visited her, she was making this big deal about me being strong. I think she's spent decades plotting her revenge. She's so obsessed with making him suffer, she'd blinded herself to the suffering she has to put others through to get there.'

Darren let out a long sigh. 'Well, you're right about one thing – it does sound crazy.'

'But crazy-right or just crazy-crazy?'

She needed him to back her up. Darren knew them all better than anyone else outside the family. If it didn't fit into place for him, then she knew it couldn't be the truth. Her heart was in her mouth waiting for his verdict, but before he spoke she remembered something else. The tears came before she could get it out. Alys wandered back with a floppy bouquet of dandelions. Helen wasn't able to say thank you as Alys pushed it into her hands.

'Mummy's a bit sad, sweetie,' said Darren, scooping her up into his arms.

Alys gave a solemn nod. 'Mummy sad you go and Barney go. Now you're back, so Barney come back soon and make Mummy all happy.'

He kissed her forehead.

'She told me he's safe, like she really knew for a fact.' Helen got it out in a whisper. 'When I was at the hospital, she told me Barney was in a safe place.'

'I don't know what the hell she thinks she's playing at dragging our son into this, but I think I actually believe you,' said Darren. He bent down to meet her gaze as he said it and Helen had never seen him look so earnest. 'We need to get back.'

In a cramped office, Haldor Eklund loosened his tie and rubbed his eyes, looking at the MRI results for the twentieth time. Given Barbara Marsden's presentation, he'd feared the worst – rapidly advancing metastases, perhaps even affecting her brain. But there was nothing here to explain her confusion, or her vagueness. Not the slightest indication of any cancerous spread. Of course, she would have been tired following the surgery, but all the physical signs were that she was recovering well. The constant, leaden fatigue that she seemed to be experiencing was a familiar hallmark amongst his patients, but not for someone whose surgery seemed to have been so comprehensively successful. Particularly a patient who was fairly young and otherwise in good health.

He had to acknowledge the unwelcome possibility that there were other reasons for this patient's presentation. Were tiredness and confusion convenient cloaks for Mrs Marsden to pull on just at the moment? Was his patient an actress as well as a victim? And should he share his suspicions with the police?

He decided he was overdramatising things. Making a mountain out of a molehill, as the English would have it. No, even the thought of breaking patient confidentiality turned him cold. He would keep a close eye on her and continue to try to persuade her to begin chemotherapy. She was an elderly lady in hospital, after all – what harm could she pose to anyone?

# June 1962

*Katy*

She slipped down the hallway, taking care to avoid the places where the boards creaked. The voices from the telly were murmuring. If there was snooker on then Ma would be up till all hours.

It was late June. The darkening street was full of evidence of the kids who had whiled away the evening there. There were hopscotch squares chalked on the pavement; burnt-out squibs and strips from cap guns; pop bottles stacked neatly inside gates that would go back to the shop tomorrow for sixpence. A home-knitted cardigan cast a shadow from a gatepost.

She didn't bother to keep to the shadows herself. If Ma had really wanted to, she'd have twigged what was going on long before this. It'd been three years since Mr Gardiner had called her back on the day before she left St Gregory's to offer her singing lessons. Back then she'd been eleven and ready for high school. Mr Gardiner was young and new, with slick dark hair and a smart tweed jacket.

At first, the lessons were a secret because the Clerys couldn't afford to pay and the money was a struggle for almost all his students. He said he made an exception because she was special and, back then, she never thought to question it.

Given that he was teaching her for free, though, it seemed rude to complain that they did more talking than singing. Truth be told, Katy quite liked the chance to talk about herself; it didn't come along often in a family of four kids with a four-month-dead Dad. She could talk about Dad with Mr Gardiner, when they'd all learnt it was a mistake to mention him to Ma.

When talking turned into touching, Katy wouldn't have known what to tell, even if she had someone to tell it to, which she didn't. When Simon told her she was beautiful, she didn't believe him, but the fact he said it was good enough.

He'd leave Etta for her, he said – damn the Church and the school and the neighbourhood – they could move to the seaside, or even to France. He'd play piano in a bar for money and they'd live on bread and cheese and she could try oysters. They weren't so prudish in France – the pair of them could stroll along holding hands and kiss on the beach. She could try French cigarettes.

It never happened.

A year or so after Katy first started going to Mr Gardiner's house, his wife had fallen pregnant. Katy hadn't known about it straight away; she heard from her Ma, who picked it up at the grocer's. Soon after that, though, Etta swelled up big as the side of a house, and no wonder, because it was twins. Jennifer and Mary.

They came early and Katy first knew they were born when she was in the little front parlour Simon used for the singing lessons and their cries started up from above. 'It was last week,' he'd said.

'You should have told me,' she replied. 'I'd not have come today.'

But he had simply shaken his head, turned the key in the lock and moved quickly to undo his trousers.

That first year, Katy wondered if Simon had invented the things they did together, if she was the first girl in the world to seethe like a witch's cauldron with the pleasure and pain and love and hate and shame of it all bubbling around together. Later, when she finally started to piece together her bits of whispered knowledge about 'women's business', with the things that happened in her singing lessons, she was hit by the fear that what had happened to Etta might happen to her too. Luckily, Sonia, who was almost fourteen by then, was able to enlighten her.

'You only get pregnant if a boy puts his thing in you,' she whispered as they lay side by side under Katy's blankets. Although it was dark, Katy imagined she could feel the heat radiating out from her sister's red cheeks. 'Even then, it's okay as long as nothing comes out of it.'

They both giggled, but Katy's fingers prickled with her own knowledge. Her mouth ached with it. Perhaps she could tell Sonia; they could keep it between them, in the cocoon of the blankets. This secret that Katy feared would otherwise overwhelm her.

'Don't you let any of them dirty lads near you, though, Katy. Our Terry would batter them. You wait till you're older, yeah?'

'Yeah.'

Now the twins were getting on for one, and she knew he'd never leave Etta. She daydreamed of France sometimes, of oysters and café bars. Simon's face in the scene was becoming blurred, changing slowly into one that was closer to her own age, a broodingly handsome French teen, with a leather jacket and an attitude, rather than a music teacher who was getting paunchy, with a tweed jacket that was now old and shiny at the elbows.

But Katy still went. Part of her was still drawn to him, to the chance to be listened to like an adult, the chance to feel loved. But she was also a little afraid of his reaction if she said she wanted to break it off. He'd told her once before, with tears in his eyes and a knife in his hand, that if he couldn't see her he would die. It was easier just to carry on.

Tonight Etta was out at her sister's over in Birkenhead. She went most weeks, to play gin rummy and catch up with her family. She took the bus over there, and a brother-in-law would run her home well after midnight.

By the time Katy arrived it was about half nine. She was more careful on the last part of the walk, mindful of Simon's paranoia. As usual, she gave the back door a faint tap and, as usual, Simon opened it almost immediately, pulling her into the kitchen and into his arms in one smooth movement. He kissed her on the head, then released her quickly, and she immediately noticed he looked agitated.

'Mary's ill,' he said. 'She's hardly stopped howling for two days. It's driving me mental.'

Sure enough, Katy could hear noises from upstairs, more a whimper just then than a howl.

'Mrs G's not here is she?' she asked, suddenly worried, but Simon shook his head and laughed ruefully. 'She was going to stay, but I told her that a break from it would do her good.'

Taking in the room, her gaze fell on a bottle of Johnnie Walker open on the table. It had one of those sticky gift bows attached to the side.

'School Christmas raffle,' he said, by way of explanation. 'Want some?'

'I've never seen you drink before.'

She hadn't answered his question but he poured her a glass anyway and refilled his own to clink against it. A third of the bottle was gone.

'Whatever you do, don't have twins, Katy,' he said, darkly. 'In fact, don't have bloody kids at all.'

'Well, I wouldn't have the chance, would I?' she said, with a forced brightness. 'You're the one who always says I'm lucky you're so careful.'

It was too clumsy. She had intended, in some unformed, awkward way, to steer the subject away from the twins and onto herself. To flirt or tease him out of his black mood. But flirting was new to her, despite all her experience of what should come after. Plus (she realised years later), knowingness was the very opposite of what he wanted from her.

'Is that right?' he said, in a low voice. 'Because it doesn't have to be like that, you know.' He eyed her coldly for a long moment, and then downed his glass before quickly pouring another. 'It's not like anyone would believe it was mine, anyway,' he muttered, speaking more to the bottle than to her. 'If you're anything like the tales I hear of that sister of yours, then it probably wouldn't be mine anyway.' He jerked a thumb towards the stairs. 'C'mon.'

She was scared now. Uneasiness slid and slopped in her stomach like iced water. Almost without thinking, she gulped back the whisky in her own glass, blinking back the fire of it.

In the bedroom, amidst Etta's silver-framed wedding pictures and ruched pink curtains, he watched her strip, his eyes hard and critical, his mouth set in a frown. Mary's cries had become more insistent, but Simon had led her past the girls' closed door without so much as a pause. Now, though, he kept casting irritable glances towards the wall that adjoined their bedroom. Katy tried to reassure herself; after all, what could he do to her, really, that they'd not done before? For all her efforts, she couldn't quite settle, and she couldn't switch off the way she'd taught herself to do when it had been frightening or painful in the past. Tonight, something was different. There was a dark charge crackling in the air.

When the cry of a second child joined the first, even Katy winced. Simon swore and marched out of the door to go and see to them. Left alone in the bedroom, she took off her socks, the only clothes she had left on, and slipped between the pink sheets, listening to the sounds from next door. It seemed that Simon managed to settle Jennifer, for her cries died away quite quickly. But she could still hear the low murmur of his voice, as he tried wearily to placate Mary.

He returned to her about ten minutes later, and the fire had gone out of him.

'Poor mite's red raw about her mouth. I don't know if it's teeth or what,' he said, as he pulled off his clothes, not bothering with the socks himself. 'You can't help but love them, though. When they make such a big noise, you forget how tiny and helpless they are.'

Suddenly it was Katy who was filled with anger at his dopey grin and bad breath and the way he scratched his balls and thought it was okay to make her wait shivering in his wife's bedroom and then tell her how much he loved his baby daughters.

'You really love them, don't you?' she said, coldly.

'Of course I do. I've told you, if it wasn't for them we'd be off, Katy. We'd have been nothing but red tail lights on the highway a long time back.'

His fake American accent made her cringe. How could she ever have thought he was glamorous, when he was just ... just pathetic. Malice and mischief sparked inside her. Why should she tread on eggshells? Why not make him share some of her anger?

'Bet you love them so much that you won't be able to keep your hands off them. When you start ...' She looked for the word. 'When you start *interfering* with them that's what you'll tell them, I bet.'

The slap stung her and left her ears ringing. She must have cried out because the noise in the next room started again. He'd never hit her before. Unbidden, she felt tears slide out from under her eyelids.

'Now listen to them! Happy with that are you?' He didn't wait for an answer to his own question. He was climbing on top of her, pushing roughly at her knees. 'You were never a child when you came here, Katy Clery, not for all the white ankle socks and the pigtails in the world. You wanted this; you asked for it. Don't try to kid yourself about that.'

His words whirled in her mind like dust or smoke. Was it true? Had she brought all this on herself? She'd enjoyed bits of it, at times, but had she *wanted* it all along? She'd had no idea at the time, of course, but what if he was right? What if she hadn't known her own mind? She remembered the terror she'd felt the first time he kissed her; the dry, clenched horror when he touched her there.

But there wasn't time to try to work it out now, as he talked he was still looming over her. The smell of whisky hung around her face and he was pawing at her nipples and between her legs. She realised that something was wrong. The crying from the next room was louder and his thing wasn't getting hard. He was cursing and kneeling back, trying to use his hands.

*Let him stew*, she thought, closing her eyes like she'd done so often in the old days.

'Shut up!' he shouted, and she knew it was directed towards the wall. 'How am I meant to ...' The weight on the bed shifted and for a moment his hands were behind her head, twining in her hair and pulling her mouth onto him. Nothing made a difference, though.

Finally, she felt him roll off and his weight left the bed completely. She opened her eyes to see his naked body framed, briefly, in the doorway, before he slammed it behind him, leaving her in darkness.

'Shut up!' The scream was on the other side of wall now, but louder than it had been when he was beside her. *Jesus*. She sent a half-muttered prayer towards the shadowing shape of the fringed lightshade above her. It sounded like he'd really lost it this time.

Of course, his anger only served to stoke the child's upset, and Mary's voice rose to match his, till they were roaring together like the wind and the waves of a stupendous thunderstorm.

'For Christ's sake, I told you to shut up!'

Each word was dragged out, pleading and commanding in the same breath. Behind it, the shrill cries carried on. Katy began to wonder if she should get up, get dressed perhaps, when, quite suddenly, the noise stopped.

She lay still. Simon would be back in a moment. She strained her ears to listen for him, but there was nothing. After a while she sat up. Then she became aware that there *was* a sound, so soft she could barely hear it. An odd, keening, cry; it came in waves, slowing getting louder. The night chill had settled round her bare shoulders and she shivered. It was the prompt she needed to finally reach for the switch on the bedside lamp, swing her legs from under the eiderdown and start gathering her things from the floor. Her mouth felt fuggy from the whisky and the taste of his breath, but that didn't explain the sick feeling in her stomach.

In the few moments it took her to dress, the keening sound became unmistakable. Simon was crying. Mother of God, what horrendous thing must have happened to make him sound like that? She tried to move more quickly, but her shaking fingers were fumbling the last buttons of her blouse. Finally, she walked the few steps into the hall to stand in the doorway of the twins' room.

In the corner nearest the door was a nursing chair, and it was here that Simon was sitting, his daughter held up at his shoulder as if he was winding her. At first glance, they could be taken for a picture of familial bliss; but he was naked and that awful sound still spilt out from his lips like poison.

'Simon?' She kept her voice low and gentle, holding back the panic. 'What's wrong? What's happened?'

For a moment, it was as though he hadn't heard her. Then, slowly, he lifted his face towards her and held out the child in his arms, awkward, and still as stone.

'I couldn't stand it any more, Katy. I had to make her stop.'

# August 2017

*Nelson*

The DI's upper lip twisted involuntarily as he stood, arms crossed, feet planted, observing DS Addison's second interview with Simon Gardiner. Nelson didn't like a nonce any better than the next man did. He'd met plenty of Gardiner's type in his time, too, not so much meaning the kiddie-fiddling, but rather the attitude. He'd been supercilious as fuck when the uniforms had brought him in, all righteous indignation and 'we'll see what your gaffer makes of this'. Then he'd tried to get matey with Addison, right down to the funny handshake. Addison had had none of it and Nelson allowed himself a thin smile of pride.

Gardiner was composed as the interview got underway. He'd recognised quickly that he wasn't going to be able to grease his way out of it and he'd settled in for the long haul; all 'I only hope I can help', and only accepting DC Hemmings' offer of tea, 'if it's not too much for you, Miss.' That got Hemmings' back up and Nelson smiled again, although the girl was smart enough not to let it show to the interviewee. She'd turn out to be a good 'un too, he reckoned.

When Addison got out the log of evidence from Gardiner's

PC, the patrician pillar of the community was shaken for a moment, but quickly found the right note of contrition. Yes, Gardiner readily accepted, it was foolish and looked bad. He had a taste for saucy schoolgirls that was an embarrassment, all the more so given his now advanced years.

'But what man doesn't have a weakness?' Gardiner cast his question around the room, almost as if he knew he was taking in Nelson behind the mirrored glass. 'Let him without sin cast the first stone and all that, yes, DS Addison?'

'There's sin and there's crime, Mr Gardiner; it's the latter that we're interested in.'

'Quite,' said Gardiner, punctuating the air with a finger. 'And, as I said the last time we met, I hope that the websites that I visit are legal. Nothing illegal about photographing a sixteen-year-old who happens to look like she's twelve, is there? I'm not very computer-savvy, I admit, and if I've followed a few links that I shouldn't have, then I'll take it on the chin, but this isn't the hard stuff.'

'That's for us to judge.'

Addison was keeping his composure well, but behind the glass Nelson shifted from one foot to the other.

'Like I said ...' Gardiner was warming to his theme, '... I'm not into computers – too old, aren't I – I wouldn't know how to get my hands on the really dodgy stuff, even if I did want to.'

'Is that right, Mr Gardiner?'

'It is. And I don't want to, believe me. Wide-eyed innocence and everything tight and tidy, that's what does it for me – if you don't mind my frankness, Miss.' Gardiner's aside to Hemmings had a flavour of his earlier patronising tone.

'Let's leave the pictures for now, Mr Gardiner,' said Addison.

'We are working to verify the sources and to establish whether any criminal activity is indicated. If there is anything for you to 'take on the chin', as you put it, we'll make sure that happens.'

Gardiner pursed his lips but waited for Addison to continue.

'I want to move on to something new, though. Emails.'

Now Gardiner looked puzzled, and Nelson couldn't tell if the appearance was genuine or artifice. Again, he said nothing and waited to hear the policeman finish his piece.

Addison pushed a piece of paper across the table.

'Is that your email address?'

'It is.'

DC Hemmings read the address for the tape.

'And whose is this address?'

Gardiner squinted at the paper. 'eltel69@mailthing.com? I have no idea.'

'Well, that surprises me, given that you and El Tel have exchanged a good few emails recently. Emails that you have been very assiduous in moving to your deleted items folder.'

'Let me see them.'

Addison did as he was requested and slid the thin sheaf of paper across the table.

Nelson scrutinised Gardiner as he took his time to read through them. The only sign of emotion was a slight tremor in his hand as he shuffled the pages. Finally, he put them down.

'I didn't send these. I didn't receive anything from that address.'

'It's your account.'

'My account's been hacked.'

Addison tutted. 'That's what they all say. Hackers steal bank details; they don't write little coded messages about kidnappings.'

'Well this one does. Because it sure as hell wasn't me.'

'A child *has* been kidnapped, Mr Gardiner.' Addison raised his voice, slamming his hand on the email printouts. 'The child referred to in these emails – Barney Harrison. Barbara Marsden's grandson.'

That was when Gardiner lost it. Nelson rocked back on his heels and let a slow smile of satisfaction creep across his face as he watched it slip away. The bonhomie was gone; the ingratiating, weak-willed fallibility was gone. Simon Gardiner clutched at the edge of the interview room table with veiny, desperate fingers but was helpless to stop each element of his controlled persona slipping from his grasp.

'It's *her*, isn't it? I saw a picture of the boy's mother in the newspaper. She's the spit of her,' he said, his voice coming out as a hiss. 'It's that bitch, after fifty fucking years.'

'Who?'

'Katy Fucking Clery.'

Addison laughed out loud.

*Helen*

She wanted to speak to Barbara before she spoke to the police. It would be too easy for DI Nelson to dismiss her theory as hysterical ranting. More than that, though, if it was Barbara who held the key to Barney's disappearance then she also held the key to getting him back, and Helen had no time to waste.

They rushed back to the house, hurrying Alys along the footpaths they'd dawdled down to get to the pond. Without bothering to go inside, she and Darren packed Alys into the car and jumped in themselves, doing their best to ignore the still-assembled press pack. As they drove the few short miles to the hospital, Helen's conviction grew that her theory must be right. That it was the only explanation. Neil had told her about the pack of documents found in the house, how the police had tried to twist some of Barbara's research into an allegation that he was a paedophile. Suddenly she realised why the stuff had been hidden; it wasn't research for a story at all, it was research for this – Katy Clery's elaborate scheme, her life's work dedicated to destroying the man who had destroyed her.

Alongside her growing certainty, Helen's incredulity blossomed into anger and finally sheer rage. How dare Barbara involve her grandson in this? How could she put her own daughter through the horror of her son going missing?

'Mr Marsden is there, already,' said the receptionist at St Aeltha's, 'and another lady.'

That would be Sonia, Helen thought. She nodded a distracted 'okay' to the lady on the desk. Darren was already several steps ahead of her, seemingly not hampered at all by the weight of Alys squirming in his arms. She struggled to close the gap, breaking into a half-jog and wondering if she should have made him stay in the car – not that he'd have been likely to agree to it. To Helen, the rage in Darren was palpable. Even though she could only see the back of him, she could sense it rising from him and filling the corridor like steam. She prayed they weren't about to make a horrific mistake.

She had managed to catch him up by the time they reached the doorway, and the three of them almost stumbled through it together. Barbara seemed to be asleep, and Neil and Sonia were sitting silently by the bed. They both rose when the door opened and, before either Helen or Darren had opened their mouths, Neil quickly suggested that, if Helen didn't mind, he and Sonia would go and grab a bite to eat together now Barbara wouldn't be left alone. She nodded, blankly, unable to speak. Sonia swiped mascara away from her eyes as she gathered her things.

'She keeps trying to speak to us,' said Neil. 'But it means nothing. I don't even know if she was happy or angry about me bringing Sonia in.' His cheeks were wet with tears that he wasn't bothering to try to hold back.

'Could you take Alys?' Helen blurted, as the pair of them made to leave the room.

But Darren shook his head, drawing the girl close to his chest. 'She's staying with me.'

Neil paused in the doorway, a puzzled frown on his face. He looked as though he was about to speak, but Darren got in first, softening his tone with an effort that was visible only to Helen.

'Sorry, didn't mean to snap, Neil. She's really sleepy, that's all. We're all on edge.'

Neil's puzzled expression didn't change, but after a moment or two he gave a slow nod and went to join Sonia in the corridor.

Forcing herself to sit, Helen chose Neil's chair, and she could still feel his warmth in the upholstery. Barbara's hand lay still on the blanket, and when Helen picked it up, she wondered if the faint heat that she could feel there was a residue of Neil as well. For a few moments, Helen said nothing, just sat watching her breathing and looking for a flicker of her eyes or something that might tell her Barbara knew she was there. She could feel Darren's eyes drilling into her, but she ignored him, making herself take the few extra seconds to try to do this the best way she could.

'Mum?'

There was no response.

'Mum, it's me – Helen.' She tried a little louder and this time Barbara's lips moved, though no sound came out.

'Barney's still missing, Mum. I think ... I think you know where he is.'

For a moment, Helen wondered what she was doing. What if Barbara could hear and understand but wasn't able to reply? And what if she had nothing to do with taking him? Would Helen kill Barbara herself, accusing her like this? But she didn't have any choice.

'Please help me, Mum, please. You've got what you wanted. They've arrested Gardiner. It's all over the papers, just like you planned. I need my boy back, Mum ...'

Barbara was resolutely silent, her eyes closed.

Helen tried one more time. 'I don't know if you can hear me, but I suppose if you can't, it doesn't matter anyway. I think you are framing Simon Gardiner. I'm going to tell the police. I think they need to know.'

Barbara's eyes snapped open, fixing her daughter with a penetrating glare. She didn't bother to even pretend that she was only just waking up and Helen stifled a gasp at the change in her.

'He's been arrested?'

'Yes.' Helen nodded.

'Have they charged him?'

'I don't know, Mum. Are you saying I'm right? What the hell have you done?'

'I've done what I had to, Helen. I'm sorry I had to drag you into it, but I've done what I had to do.'

'*Drag us into it?*' Darren finally exploded, his loud voice – then Alys's wails – shattered the careful tranquillity of the room. 'Our son is missing. You've sent your own daughter to hell and back, and you make it sound like some minor inconvenience! Well, it fucking ends now, Barbara. Where is he?'

'He's safe. I won't patronise you both by telling you not to worry, but Barney's safe. I promise.'

Darren shoved Alys across to Helen before leaning over the bed.

'You think I can't make you tell me? You think I won't hurt you because you're ill, or dying? I'll cheerfully break every bone in your fucking body if I have to, you twisted, evil ...'

'Pah!' Barbara spat her derision into his face, her eyes gleaming with more life than Helen had seen in them in weeks. 'You think any of that matters to me? If you had the slightest clue of what I've suffered, you wouldn't waste your breath. Yes, I'm dying. So you go ahead and break every bone. It'll get me there sooner – but it won't help Barney.'

Helen was on her feet too now, every part of her shaking. She could barely recognise her mother in the hate-filled woman in the bed. Had Katy always been here, lurking under Barbara's placid, rather cold, exterior, biding her time? The thought turned her cold. She still held Alys with one arm, cuddling and comforting her but also trying to turn the girl's face away; desperate to protect her and determined that she should not be tainted by the raw hatred in the room. With her other arm, she reached out to Darren, praying he wouldn't lose control. Not for Barbara's sake, not any more, but for his own sake, and, above all, for Barney.

'He's not safe, Mum.' She tried to keep her voice low and calm. 'Barney's not safe because he's not with me. He's with strangers, and I'm begging you ...' she glanced at Darren '... we're both begging you, to end this mad scheme and tell us exactly where he is.'

But Barbara shook her head. 'Soon. But not now. I've come this far, Helen; I'm going to see it through.'

'You're not leaving us any choice, Mum. We're going to have to go and tell DI Nelson.' She made to stand up. Thankfully, Darren took a step away from the bed too – Helen had been far from certain he would.

'Slow down, Helen, think.'

Her mother's voice was soothing; the voice that had calmed her in moments of childish frustration, soothed her when she was bumped or grazed. But Barbara's ability to comfort Helen had evaporated. The words grated on her and her skin crawled.

'The plan doesn't involve Barney getting hurt, Helen. I wouldn't do that – you know that in your heart. If you go to the police, it goes out of my control. As you said yourself, there are others involved. Barney is not hiding under my bed. I can vouch for him as long as things go according to the plan. If they don't ...' Barbara tailed off with a shrug.

'Are you threatening him?' said Darren, his fists bunching as he stepped close to the bed once again.

'No. I'm pointing out the realities of the situation.'

'So when then?'

'When the time is right. We'll make sure he's found, Helen, and when he is, he'll be found with evidence to incriminate Gardiner. It's all worked out.'

Helen's mind was racing and she felt her cheeks grow wet.

'Look.' Barbara's tone grew warmer again. 'Go into the

bedside locker. There's a phone in there. In a sponge bag.'
Helen did as she was told, pulling out the floral plasticky bag
in a daze. 'Give it to me. Lock the door.'

Barbara's fingers fluttered agilely over the keypad.

'Look I have photos. They aren't great, it's an old phone,
but he's here.'

Helen gripped the plastic case as if she could squeeze her
son out of it. Darren pressed close to her, his greed to see
the images every bit as strong as her own. Barney's cherubic
face, slightly pixelated, gazed up at them. There were two
– the first a close-up of his face, and then the second showing
him sitting at a desk with some colouring pens in front of
him.

'When—'

'Taken yesterday. He's okay, darling, you'll have him back
soon.'

She could see no injuries. In the close-up there was almost
a smile on his face. She caressed the image of his face, tears
pouring harder than ever.

After a minute or so, Barbara gently pulled the phone from
her grasp and fixed her gaze on both of them in turn.

'Run off and tell DI Nelson if you like – I can't stop you.
Trust him or trust me. It's your choice.'

*Barbara*

The three of them left the room, dazed and silent. They
wouldn't go to the police yet, Barbara felt reasonably sure, but
soon. She cursed inwardly. That second photo – she knew it
was a mistake as soon as it flashed up. A small risk perhaps,
but a risk nonetheless. There was a back-up location. And it

wouldn't be for long. The net was closing in on Simon Gardiner. She allowed herself a small smile before her brow furrowed in concentration as she tapped out a message on the tiny keypad:

*MOVE HIM*

# May 1958

*Katy*

It had been a heart attack. The morning that he died, Hugh Clery had slipped Katy a mint humbug under the breakfast table, squashed her in his dieselly embrace and promised to take her to the pictures on Saturday afternoon. Built like a bull, everything about Hugh from his bristly moustache to his hair-sprouting yellow-nailed toes was full of life. Katy didn't believe he was dead until Joyce eventually relented and took her to see the body laid out at the funeral parlour. They'd shaved his moustache and put his best shoes on him.

People were nice to her at school. The girls saved sweets for her that tasted of nothing; she knew the last sweet she'd be able to taste was her dad's mint humbug. The boys didn't try to knock into her or hit her with the football. Her teacher, Mrs Cook, pretended not to notice when she stared out of the window rather than getting on with her work.

At home, all anyone could talk about was the funeral. Hugh would have the best and the Clery family would make sure of it. They would hold their heads up for all the black-hatted visitors who came to see her mum and drink endless cups of tea.

Now it was here and Katy was sitting in the front pew with Sonia and Terry and Kevin. She felt exposed, without another pew to knock her knees against. Sonia kept recrossing her legs and smoothing down the fabric of her new black skirt. Maybe she felt the same. Only Terry sang the hymns. Katy thought he was glad. He was sixteen and since he'd started work he'd been arguing a lot with their dad. Saw his chance to be the man of the house now, Katy supposed, and hated him for it.

She thought of the hole waiting in the graveyard, the mounds of earth stacked beside. They all knew where Hugh was going, but what about them? Nobody had talked about after the funeral. Would they have money? Would they be able to stay in their house? Who would take Katy to the pictures now? There was no one she could ask, and her future seemed as dark and uninviting as the new grave waiting outside.

When they trooped out, Katy and her siblings were at the front again, following the coffin. She was close enough to see the sweat on the necks of the pallbearers. He'd been a big man, Hughie.

As they passed through the back of the church, the organist slipped down from his stool to join the procession. It was Mr Gardiner, from school. He winked and she broke step for a moment, shocked by this little glimpse of cheerfulness. She liked Mr Gardiner, but she'd be leaving him behind in a few months when she went up to the high school. Sonia started last year and hated it. Katy felt the tears start to come again.

'S'okay,' Mr Gardiner whispered. He was walking beside her now. 'It'll get better, you'll see.'

He fumbled in his pocket and a moment later handed her

his cloth handkerchief. She managed a weak smile of thank you and began to open it out to wipe her eyes. There was something folded inside. She glanced at Mr Gardiner and he winked again. It was a humbug.

# August 2017

*Helen*

She left Barbara's room with her eyes blurred with tears and every limb shaking. The glossy parquet floor stretched down the corridor and her legs were so weak she felt she would slip on it like ice. If she couldn't even make it out of the hospital, how could she help Barney? Soon, it would be seventy-two hours. Three full days. He must believe that she'd abandoned him. How could a five-year-old think anything else?

She placed a hand on the cool, smooth plaster of the wall and forced herself to breathe. Breathe first. Then walk. Then the lift. Then walk again. Get to the car. She wouldn't think any further ahead than that.

'Helen!'

She flinched at the sound of her name as she exited the lift, but it was only her father. He and Sonia were still sitting in the plush ground-floor coffee lounge where they'd gone a few minutes before, although it may as well have been a lifetime. Helen moved carefully towards them, but paused on the threshold, leaning on the arched doorway for support.

'Finished already, love?'

'Barbara's still asleep.' Darren's voice behind her sounded staccato and alien to Helen, but Neil didn't seem to register anything wrong. 'Alys was getting noisy.'

'Oh, my little ducky.' Neil held his hands out towards Alys. 'Why don't you stay with Granddad for a bit?'

Helen opened her mouth to accept, but one look at Darren's face told her he wasn't about to leave Alys here.

'Thanks, Dad,' she blustered quickly, 'but we just need a bit of time to ourselves. I'll call you soon.'

*

They reached the car, secured Alys in the car seat and fastened their own seatbelts automatically. Helen spoke first. 'So what now? We can't go to Nelson, can we? We've just got to wait and hope she's right.'

They sat like that for a moment. Suddenly claustrophobic, Helen opened her window and the car filled with the scent of cut grass and the sound of a distant radio. The sun's warmth on the exposed skin at her neck felt wrong and absurd. She was thinking how crazy it was to be noticing the sun, when she saw Darren reaching into a pocket for his phone.

'No! You can't tell the police.' She kept her voice low, for Alys's sake, but the force was obvious.

'What do you mean?'

'Barney's safe.' She gulped back the sobs to find the words she'd been unable to speak a moment before. 'You saw photos. The people he's with are going to release him when Gardiner's ...'

'And I heard you tell Barbara exactly why he's not safe. For God's sake, Helen, she's psycho; we've got to do something. How long does this carry on for if we don't?'

306

She ran over what Barbara had said in her head. Barney would come home soon. He'd be found when the time was right. Along with more evidence against Gardiner. There was no more than that – Barbara had dodged it, or else Helen's head had been too fuzzed by rage to pin her down. Wasn't it enough that Gardiner had been arrested? Had Barbara seen the papers and the web reports? Surely she must have, Helen thought. Now it was clear that she wasn't nearly as sick as she was making out, she'd have made it her business to get hold of that stuff, wouldn't she?

She slammed a hand into the dashboard, enraged by the arrogance of the woman. Alys merely turned her head for a moment, so used by now to her mother's violent emotions. It was clear that Barbara's plan was not just to scare this man, not just to make him feel the breath of the law down his neck and suffer the ignominy of trial by tabloid, but to actually make it stick. And that surely couldn't happen. And what would happen to Barney if Barbara's carefully constructed game finally fell apart?

'I don't know, Darren. When he's charged, when he's bailed, when he falsely confesses? I don't know and I'm not sure if she does either. It's an obsession that's been consuming her all these years; she believes Barney's safe because she can't conceive that it could fail. But you're right – I was right – he's not safe and we need to get him.'

'So we take this to Nelson.'

'Just let me think for a minute … If the police believe us – if they give up the Gardiner line – that unleashes chaos. We don't know who's actually got him or how much hold Barbara has on them. If they are prepared to kidnap a child in the first place, then God knows what they'd be capable of in a panic.'

'So what do we do?' Darren's frustration was palpable, and Helen felt hopelessness threatening to overwhelm her. She put her fingers to her temples and rubbed, trying to conjure some sense, some inspiration.

The picture that swam into view behind her closed lids was the photo of Barney. Not the close-up, the other one, with the desk and chair. Part of a window in the background, and a narrow strip of curtain. It could be anywhere. But it wasn't.

'I *know* the room that was in the picture,' she said. 'I've seen it before.'

'Where?' urged Darren. 'Think ... is it Julie Hendricks' house after all? Or one of your mum's friends – what about Jackie from the paper?'

She shook her head. 'Nobody's house.' She spoke slowly. 'It was an office ... no, that's wrong, not an office.' There was a hunger in Darren's eyes as she turned to him, and she knew that he was fighting the urge to press her further.

*Breathe*, she told herself, *breathe and think*.

There was the sound of their breath, and the plastic clicking of a toy that Alys had in the back.

'Not an office,' she whispered. She was clutching at him now, the adrenaline sending her jubilant. 'A hotel. Well sort of. Mary Gardiner was buried in the construction site that became Moreton Chase services. That's where Barney is too.'

\*

They drove the few miles in silence. The country roads taking them back towards the village were almost deserted on a lazy August afternoon. Eventually, Darren swung off the road, past some 'No Entry' signs and over through the defunct barrier. This was the access road to the motorway services.

Moreton Chase. Mary Gardiner's body had never been found. The trial papers eventually retrieved from the police archive had showed that Barbara had confessed to burying her there, but the place had been a building site, with the motorway services under construction. By the time the police had the information to go on, there'd been over a month for the heavy land-moving equipment to carve up the place and rearrange the landscape to suit the motorway planners. The bones of the main structure were starting to rise out of the ground. When Katy Clery was taken back in handcuffs to try to find the burial spot, she couldn't begin to piece it together.

Etta Gardiner campaigned for the project to be stopped and the buildings that had already gone up to be dismantled. She wanted to sieve through every last shovelful of dirt on the site – with her own bare hands if necessary – until Mary was found. The coroner was sympathetic, but ultimately the cost and delay could not be afforded, and after a short hiatus the construction went on.

Barbara had always had an attachment to the place. An attachment that Helen had blindly read as fondness. She liked to walk and would often tramp the farmland footpaths that skirted it, perhaps slipping into the site for a cup of tea if the car park didn't look too busy. When Helen was little, she would occasionally take her to the restaurant on the bridge – the same restaurant where Barbara had been working on the night she met Neil. It was a Little Chef by the time Helen knew it, and she would have pancakes or a sundae and they'd both gaze at the patterns the car lights made streaking through the dusk below. Barbara had been angry when they closed the restaurant up there and it just became a corridor, and Helen, who had been a Saturday girl there herself for a short time and felt no such emotional attachment, had smiled at her whimsy.

If she thought about it at all, she must have assumed it was nostalgia for the place where Barbara and Neil had met. Perhaps for the freedom of a first job and first pay packet – especially one that came with a sprinkling of glamour that seemed difficult to associate with the services these days. It wouldn't surprise Helen either, if her mother was attracted to the liminality of it, to a place where no one stayed, where everyone was a stranger.

Now she knew that it was far more than that. Was Barbara simply drawn to be near Mary, as a type of penance perhaps, or did she actually hope to find her one day? Helen wondered if that was what had brought her to Moreton Chase in the first place. Without Mary, perhaps she would never have met Neil. Was Mary, ultimately, the reason why Helen existed? Would Barbara answer that question? Would Helen ever have the chance to ask her?

The road they were on took them onto the northbound site, which was the bigger of the two. All the locals used this as an unofficial junction, but what felt odd was slowing up, pulling into the car park, rather than joining the steady flow of traffic heading for the slip road.

They looked at each other. Now they were here, what *could* they do? They could hardly barge into the motel and start demanding to see in the bedrooms.

'Let's just look around,' said Darren. 'We won't be too obvious because we're parked away from the hotel. We can skirt round the back, to that wooded area. We might be able to see in some of the rooms, or at least get a sense of how many are occupied. Whoever is keeping him must be coming out for food and stuff.'

'Okay.' Helen unbuckled a sleepy and complaining Alys from her car seat. Darren would carry her with them. There was no way either of them would leave her alone.

They didn't get far. There was a dog-walking area, but most of the woodland that Barbara used to walk in was sealed off now with wire fencing. It didn't look much from the car park, but close up it was clear they wouldn't get through in broad daylight without attracting attention.

'Let's go inside,' suggested Darren eventually, motioning away from the motel and towards the main services building. 'Maybe we can see more from the bridge.'

A few minutes later they stood together on the bridge, gazing at the flow of traffic below, deflated and morose. They had a good view of the flat roof of the motel building, but that didn't give them any clues as to whether Barney was inside.

Helen started to talk, thinking out loud, about trying again to speak to Barbara. What they could say to make her realise that she had to bring this thing to an end. After a few moments, she realised that Darren wasn't listening to her.

'Darren?'

'What jacket did Barney have on, Hels?'

'The dinosaur one. Bright orange.' She didn't have to think – the details tripped off her tongue.

Darren nodded, and shifted Alys's weight to point with a finger. Helen followed his gaze to the edge of the carriageway, to the high mesh fence that separated the southbound service area from the motorway verge. Crumpled at the bottom of the fence, caught against one of the concrete fence posts, was a bundle of orange. Her heart started hammering. Even at this distance she could see that the fabric was identical. It wasn't Barney himself – whatever was there was no bigger than a carrier bag. But it might get them closer.

They both hurried down to the southbound car park and tried to get their bearings, to pinpoint the spot where they'd seen the fabric. They picked their way across the HGV parking area, ignoring the questioning looks of a few of the drivers taking breaks in their cabs. When they got to the fence, they could suddenly see the vivid flash of the orange again. Helen started to run. There was a tideline of litter against the fence, a foot or so wide in places. She could feel the wind pushing her up to the fence and it was clear that the microclimate of the site meant that this was where any discarded detritus would end up.

Helen grabbed at it, and as she plucked it from the ground it opened up just as she knew it would. The green dinosaur on the back winked at her. Instinctively, she buried her face in the fabric, desperate to smell her boy. All she got was diesel and leaf mould. She coughed and Darren gently eased the jacket from her fingers.

'It's his, Hels, look!'

In faded biro, because she knew what she was looking for, Helen could just make out her own writing. *Barney H.* Of course, they'd bought this whilst he was still at nursery. Thank God, thank God, thank God. Unlike so many of his other out-of-school clothes, the place for his name had been filled in.

'Should we be touching it?' She was suddenly worried. 'What about forensics and stuff?'

Darren shrugged. 'The main thing is we've found it. I don't think touching it'll make much difference – it's been here for a while. Let's go straight to the station. We'll insist on seeing Nelson. He'll get men into the motel before Barbara knows anything about it.'

Helen nodded, and they turned back towards the car park, but she couldn't tear her eyes from the motel building. What had been a hunch a moment ago now seemed a certainty. She paused, ready to duck into the passenger seat, as Darren secured Alys in the back. She gazed at the portico entrance with flags fluttering and concrete planters. She gazed at the rows of windows made blind by gauzy curtains.

She gazed and saw a woman carrying a child.

The entrance was cast into shade by the portico. At first, she saw only a movement, a glint of light as the glass doors opened, a shift in the shadows as the burdened figure emerged. The boy was big to be carried; his head flopped drowsily. As they emerged into the sunlight, Helen was already moving towards them. A toy rabbit dangled from the boy's hand.

She ran.

Without noticing the traffic in the car park, without any thought but to get to Barney. Her mouth was open, gulping air, but she had the presence of mind not to cry out to him. She had to get there before the woman knew she was coming.

As she got closer, Helen could see the woman glancing around. She looked quite old. She had sallow, wrinkled skin with some sort of birthmark or tattoo blotching her neck. But there was a smoothness to her movement, no sign of frailty or uncertainty, quite the opposite. There was a lone silver car at the far end of the parking area reserved for the motel. Family-sized. Helen pushed herself harder, forcing her lungs to burn. An irate driver blasted his horn. The noise drew a glance from the woman, though she didn't break her step. Their eyes locked and Helen knew that the other woman knew exactly who she was.

'Barney!' She could scream it now. She could let him know that she was coming for him. But there was no movement from the boy. The woman broke into a run. Where was Darren? He must have seen what was going on. The pair were only metres from the car now. Helen knew she couldn't reach the woman before she got to it. How quickly would she be able to get in and lock the doors?

Helen pushed through the scraggy bushes that bordered the parking area. She slipped on dog shit and something thorny scratched her face. She kept running.

She got there just as the woman wrenched open the driver's door and was bundling Barney across into the passenger seat. Hauling on her shoulder, she tried to pull the woman back from the car, to put herself between her son and his captor. There was a torrent of abuse flooding into the air. Helen recognised her own gasping, exhausted voice, giving vent to words she barely realised she knew.

The woman was silent, her body was tight and hard. Caught off balance, she turned in Helen's grip, but as Helen tried to grapple she found no purchase. Her opponent seemed to push her back easily, taking control with sparse, economical movements, using Helen's flailing to her own advantage. Helen felt the panic rising. This was wrong. She was fighting for her child; she couldn't let him down. The words had stopped. There was only her and her opponent. Then there was a pain in her stomach like an explosion, swiftly followed by a shove, which sent her sprawling to the ground.

'Your ma never taught you to fight then.'

Those were the only words the woman said. Helen heard the sound of the door slam and the engine rev, then a crunch of pain as the edge of a back tyre rolled over her wrist and thumb.

For a moment the world was black. It may as well have ended. She had failed her son. But almost immediately the footsteps and commotion flooded in. She tried to push herself up, testing the damaged hand, and opened her mouth to shout at the bewildered receptionist making her way across the car park to go back and call 999.

Her words were taken from her by the screech of brakes and the metallic thud of impact. She turned towards the noise. At the entrance to the slip road two silver cars were pushed up onto the banking. Noses crushed together – they could have been kissing. The woman was out as quick as a snake, using a back door because hers was jammed against the other car. A moment later, the driver's door of the other car opened and Helen watched Darren stumble out and run after the woman. He only took a few paces before realising it didn't matter; she didn't have Barney.

Helen limped towards the crash site. The car park was full of people staring now; they backed away silently as she passed, letting her through.

Darren had Barney in his arms by the time she reached them, blood from a cut on his temple mixing with the tears streaming down his cheeks.

'He's alive, Helen. Oh God. He's okay.'

# August 2017

*Barney*

At first, Barney had missed all his toys and wanted them, but later he wanted a picture of Mummy and Daddy so he could think properly about what they looked like when they smiled. He tried to think about Mummy's smile and how she had big lips that were a funny pink colour and she always wore lipstick every day so only him and Daddy and Alys knew the secret of what colour her big lips really were. He was thinking about that when the dragon-lady gave him more sleepyhead medicine and hissed at him to drink it quickly because they had to go.

He wasn't in the room any more when he woke up. He was in a funny metal bed in a room with bright white lights on the ceiling and Mickey Mouse painted on the walls. Sitting beside the bed was Mummy, with no lipstick on and proper-coloured lips. She hugged him tight and he could smell her Mummy smell. He thought that maybe he was dreaming because of the medicine, but he didn't think he could dream her smell so good and then she started crying.

'Don't be sad about Daddy, Mummy. Do you want me to

get you a tissue?' he said, because that was what he always said when she cried.

He didn't know where the tissues were, though, and his legs were too heavy to go and get them even if he did. But then Mummy started laughing and crying and telling him they were happy tears and Daddy and Alys had been crying happy tears too and Barney was her precious, precious brave boy.

'Yes, I am brave and can I have a sweetie?'

'Of course,' said Mummy. 'You can have lots of sweeties and I will never ever let you go again.'

*Helen*

Forty-nine hours and sixteen minutes. How sweet it was to be able to count the length of time she'd had him back for, rather than the time he'd been gone.

Everyone had been keen to keep the hospital stay as short as possible, and, after lots of checks, she'd carried him out of the General in her arms just before eleven p.m., meaning he didn't have to spend the night there.

Rebecca Evans had dropped in on Helen and Darren whilst they were sitting round his little bed, waiting for the sedative to wear off. She didn't say much, obviously in the dark as to how Barney had come to be taken, never mind how he came to be recovered. But it was clear she felt that being there was the right thing to do. It seemed like a million years since Helen had sat in that office listening to this woman explain how her mother had been the victim of an overdose. Both of them had been taken in. They'd been fencing each other, prickly and suspicious, whilst Barbara had lain elsewhere, the serene victim of her own machinations. Well, not any more – Veena had texted to say that Barbara had been arrested at St Aeltha's and taken into custody.

Now – after one blissful day yesterday with her children and Darren where they hugged and watched cartoons and she fought back all the thoughts of 'what next?' – Nelson was coming over to bring them up to date.

The atmosphere in the house shifted as the expected time drew nearer. Adam and Christine arrived to be with the children while Helen and Darren spoke to the police. Helen had been adamant that she was not going to let them out of her sight. The arrival of the grandparents, laden with sweets and new toys, was the compromise. Even yesterday they'd been texting Darren about coming over sooner. In fact, the whole glorious day had had the air of a Christmas truce, with the old battles very much waiting in the wings.

Neil, who had hidden himself away like a hermit in his own home since Darren, Helen and the children returned from the hospital, also came down from his bedroom as Nelson's appointment drew closer. Grey and broken, he lurked like a spectre, barely managing to raise a smile for the children and ignoring Christine's strained greeting altogether. By the time the doorbell rang, the air was already thick with tension.

After the pleasantries, Nelson cut to the chase. Barbara had admitted everything in the course of several long interviews over the last two days. In fact, she explained the whole thing with remarkable relish, the DI told them (with none).

'The plan was for there to be an anonymous tip-off to the police, and as a result of that information Barney would be found in a lock-up garage, tied up with strips from a bed sheet that would link the crime to Gardiner.'

'Link him how?' asked Neil.

'They'd stolen the sheet years before from Simon Gardiner's house and kept it wrapped in plastic to preserve the DNA.'

'What do you mean "they"?' Even as Helen asked the question, her eyes were locked on Barney's rumpled hair. The top of his head was just visible over the back of the sofa, where he was cuddled into Christine watching *Octonauts*. She could never thank her stars enough.

'Barbara had two accomplices, a woman called Maureen Stephenson who she'd met in the reform school and Stephenson's son, Dean.' Nelson paused to flick through his notebook. 'Stephenson persuaded Barney to get into her car and was the one you chased down at the services. Dean was backing her up. He's been known to the force locally for years – small-time burglary, that sort of thing. According to your mother, he placed a keystroke reader on Gardiner's computer and stole the sheet a number of years ago.'

'She's been planning this for years?' Neil's voice was choked.

'Yes, everything from the kidnapping, right down to the notes. She wrote them herself, although Stephenson kept the materials – that's why we never found them in the search. The cancer diagnosis meant they had to push the button. It also gave her the chance to come up with the gene-testing story to push us in the right – or wrong – direction. I suppose we'll never know what would have happened otherwise; maybe it would have remained a fantasy that they plotted but never carried through on.'

Helen's mind flashed back to that first phone call with Neil – Barney trying to comfort her and the feeling that her stable world was slipping away from her. Little had she known then just how true that was.

'So they did hack his emails? That's what the keystroke reader was about?' Darren remained pragmatic, still trying to understand the mechanics of what had happened.

'Yes. It wasn't watertight. A specialist technical forensics team might have spotted some irregularities if they'd looked closely. I'll be straight with you – I wouldn't have backed my team to figure it out if they'd not had the heads-up that the emails weren't kosher. Simon Gardiner came pretty close to spending a good time behind bars over this – very possibly longer than he's got left.'

Helen couldn't muster much sympathy for Gardiner and wasn't particularly inclined to try. Nelson's shrug suggested he felt the same way.

'So what will happen to him?' she asked.

He shrugged again. 'Too early to say. He can't be retried over Mary Gardiner's murder. The CPS could look at offences in relation to your mother, but there's her health to consider and ...' He left the fact that Gardiner's victim was herself likely to face trial in relation to the kidnap of her own grandson hanging in the air. Helen could see it might not play well with a jury.

'But what about the stuff you found on his computer?' asked Darren.

'Well ... looks like he was basically telling the truth over that. Most of it's legal. There might be a few dodgy sites he's downloaded from, but normally that'd only get him a talking-to and possibly a caution. Given what we know about these people, it's highly unlikely that Katy Clery was his only real-life victim. We'll be going over his history and associations with a fine-toothed comb. But I don't want to make you promises I can't come good on.'

Helen sipped at her glass of water. Nelson's words left a bad taste in her mouth. She'd never accept that Barbara was right to do what she had done; she knew it would take a long time to even get to grips with what had happened, never mind start thinking about rebuilding a relationship with her mother. But however much blame Barbara should shoulder, Helen could see already that she wasn't the only one at fault. As Barbara saw it (and it was hard to argue with her on this), Gardiner's actions had wrecked her life – and Barbara's own crimes were consequences rippling out from the horror that he'd bestowed on her. Why should he walk away with a 'talking-to' when he was the cause of so much damage and heartache over so many years?

Nelson was still speaking, reminding an irate Darren of the newspaper coverage and how Gardiner could hardly think that everything was going to carry on as before even if there weren't any charges brought against him. In the eyes of the great British public, Simon Gardiner would be a paedo from now till the day he went to his grave, never mind the legalities. A few weeks ago, the old Helen would have railed against trial by tabloid. Now she wasn't so sure.

'What about Mum? Will there have to be a trial? They wouldn't put Barney in court, would they?'

'It's just all too early to say, Mrs Harrison. She might plead guilty, and then it shouldn't need to go to trial. But if she doesn't, then there are other reasons the CPS might decide not to proceed – particularly related to her health.'

It was Nelson's turn to look questioningly at the three of them now. 'I don't want to pry. The info I have is that she's refused chemo? Do you know about that?'

Neil nodded and whispered, 'Yes', entering the conversation

for the first time. Helen couldn't understand how he didn't seem to get it that Barbara had sent her own daughter and grandson to hell and back. Even now, her sense was that his first concern was for his wife, and his dogged, unquestioning devotion felt like a sort of betrayal – one she didn't have the time or energy to deal with at the moment.

'Well, we'll talk about that more another day, I suppose.' Nelson seemed to sense the tension his question had provoked, and was keen to move on. 'You might not have seen, but there were motorway police based at the services; they managed to pick up Maureen Stephenson when she was still within the perimeter of the site. We got Dean a couple of hours later.'

'I didn't see those ones. I was tied up trying to explain myself to the couple who were about to arrest me,' put in Darren, with a quick smile to show he wasn't holding a grudge.

'Yeah. You gave that lot the most exciting afternoon that they'll have this side of retirement. Anyway, Stephenson's in custody. Dean's out on bail, but I think they'll both plead and both get custodial. These things take time to get through the system though.'

All three of them nodded. There was little relish to be had in the prospect of a legal process that would dredge up the memories of all this on a daily basis for months to come.

'So, um, we'll need to keep in touch with you, obviously. Have you thought about your plans yet? Are you going to take the children back to London soon?'

Helen and Darren glanced at each other. It had crossed her mind that morning, before Nelson arrived, and she was sure it had been in Darren's thoughts too, but they'd not spoken about it.

'No,' she said quickly. 'We've not decided. We'll let you know.'

Nelson let himself out; there were still photographers camped on the street and Veena went out periodically to chase them back. Only a few minutes after he left, the shouts and clatter of camera equipment heralded another arrival.

This time it was Sonia. The sight of this woman – the image of her mother – in the hallway, stopped Helen in her tracks. She'd still not got used to it; she doubted she ever would.

'Hi. I just came to say I'm so glad you've got him back.'

Helen didn't reply, and Sonia faltered.

'I'm sorry – maybe I shouldn't have come ...'

'You're here now, aren't you? Look, why don't you come into the kitchen?'

Barney was playing a card game with Christine when they went in. He glanced up, but if he noticed the resemblance between Sonia and his grandmother it didn't appear to bother him. He went busily back to matching his picture pairs.

'Can I make you a drink?'

'Well, only if you don't mind.'

'I wouldn't have offered if I did.'

As the adrenaline of the last few days had started to seep from her system, Helen was beginning to feel a crushing, bone-aching tiredness descending. She could quite happily have sent Sonia on her way, and everything about Sonia suggested she'd be more than happy to go. But another part of her wanted to hear what this woman had to say. Sonia wouldn't have intruded on them, now of all times, if her only intention was to trot out a few lines she could have put on a greetings card.

A few minutes later they were at the breakfast bar, hands curled around coffee mugs, leaning in for privacy as Helen sketched in the details of what had really happened to Barney.

'Did you know?' she asked when she was finished.

'No. I had no idea.'

She believed Sonia. She remembered the way Sonia had turned up at the door – two days and a million years earlier. Her trepidation, her worry for Barney, her deep and barely masked joy at the prospect of meeting her sister's family. All of those things had rung true, and even with the benefit of hindsight they still did.

Sonia shook her head. 'I knew she said Gardiner had framed her. I always believed her, though no one else in the family did. It upset me that we were barely in touch – we were inseparable as kids – but I told myself that that was the price she'd had to pay for making peace with her past and moving on.'

'Well, it seems that moving on was the last thing she was interested in.'

'Yes. If I'd had any idea … I wish I could have done something.'

Helen could find no response but a lump in her throat. She sipped her coffee and tried to will it away.

Suddenly, Sonia's face brightened a touch. 'She brought you to our Mam's funeral, you know – you won't remember.'

'What?'

'You were two or three – a right lovely little thing. We couldn't speak at the funeral, but I phoned her afterwards. She told me not to phone her at all, but she put up with it if I didn't do it too much. She even rang me once or twice. Anyway, I remember telling her how gorgeous you were. She said after that it didn't come naturally, being a mum. She said she was struggling, but that your dad was brilliant.'

'I suppose that's how I'd have seen it too, when I was a kid, if I'd stopped to think.'

'When she called me after the little one was born – your Alys – she said she knew she'd managed it. She must have been just good enough as a mother not to damage the mother that you were able to be. It was when she saw you with them and she could see it was different – like, it came natural to you – she knew you'd never let them down like our Mam let her down. She said your love for them was strong enough for them to cope with anything, and it was like the lifting of a curse.'

'And that made it okay for her to steal my boy, did it?'

Sonia patted her hand, and Helen flinched.

'Of course not, love, but maybe ... maybe in her head it did. And maybe in a way she was right. The horror that Simon Gardiner started, that blighted her and you, and even us. It's gone now.' She glanced across at the children, now sitting together watching a cartoon. 'Your Barney will be right as rain, Helen. I know it.'

\*

Darren had been in the living room when Sonia called around, keeping uneasy company with Adam and Neil and another pre-season football match none of them cared about. Later, when his parents had left, after Neil had retreated once more upstairs, and they'd put the kids to bed, they finally had the chance to talk about it.

'Well, as long as their long-lost great-aunt the psychologist – sorry, no, the checkout lady – thinks the kids will be fine, we obviously have nothing to worry about.'

His tone was gentle, not scathing, and he smiled as he poured them both a large slug of Neil's single malt. Helen smiled in spite of herself. They'd always had the same sense of humour. It played better with people who'd known them longer.

'Anyway, what do you think, Hels? He seems okay, doesn't he? Has he said anything to you?'

She shook her head. The whisky burned her mouth as she tried to frame her reply.

'Honestly?' she asked him.

'Honestly.'

'I think their dad leaving will mess them up more than this will.'

The smile died on Darren's lips. The little bit of light that had flickered to life between them as they began to accept that Barney was back and that life could return to normal vanished in a moment. Darren took a mouthful of his drink. 'Thanks for that.'

'You said honestly. That's what I honestly think.'

He drank again, refilling the glass carelessly so the liquid sloshed over the side. 'Would you have me back?'

She shrugged. 'Are you asking me to?'

'Fuck it, I don't know, Helen. Tonight can't we just be grateful for what we've got?'

Slowly, she nodded. 'We can. For tonight, tomorrow, for this week. But life has to start again sometime.'

'I know. You're right.'

'You know, Darren, I almost don't feel like I had a mother to lose. I mean, she went through the motions, but before now I'd never really stopped to think how far off the mark it really was.'

'Makes sense,' he said, obviously grateful for the turn in the conversation. 'You can't miss what you don't have – people normalise horrendous, abusive situations all the time. Especially in childhood.'

'Now it's you as well as Sonia with the armchair psychology?'

'Touché.'

'So what's hitting me hardest, every time a second creeps in when I'm not just thinking about how bloody grateful I am to have him home, what's hitting me hardest is ... is the feeling that now I'm losing my dad too.'

She didn't have a chance to fight back the tears as she'd done when talking to Sonia. She was engulfed almost before she realised, and once they started to come there was nothing she could do to stop them. Silently, her husband held her as she gasped and shook and made enough noise for both of them. She might have Barney back, but everything she had held to be true – about herself, about her family – had shifted. Who was to say she was any better at this than Barbara, or even Joyce? She'd misjudged her mother all these years. How could she be confident she had not misjudged her father too?

'Sssh,' Darren soothed her and stroked her hair. 'You'll work it out with him, I'm sure. It's early days.'

She nodded, embarrassed but at the same time grateful for his reassurance.

'I want our kids to have that,' she told him. 'Whatever happens with us, I want them to have a dad like I did – like I thought I had. Before this – you know what I mean.'

'I do know. And that's what they're going to get, Hels.' He stopped hugging her to look into her eyes. 'I swear.'

They held each other for a few moments more.

'I'll tell you something else, Hels. That stuff that Sonia said.

You *have* broken the mould. You're not like Joyce or Barbara – you're an amazing mother. It was the first thing I said to Veena and I'll stand by it, whatever happens with us. Barney and Alys couldn't have a better mum. Not in the whole world.'

And she held him and tried to believe him. And for now it was enough.

# Acknowledgments

As with a child, it takes a village to raise a book. (Or perhaps that's just when I'm the one writing it.)

I feel very privileged to have had the support of a great team at Avon, particularly my lovely editor, Victoria Oundjian, whose passion and enthusiasm for *If They Knew* has been an absolute delight. I must also thank Phoebe Morgan, who was instrumental in bringing the book to the imprint, and the rest of the hard-working Avon team for their involvement along the way. Equally, it's been wonderful to have the benefit of valuable advice and help from my agent, Peter Buckman at Ampersand.

The support of a committed and talented workshop group is invaluable and I'd like to thank James Aitcheson, Jonathan Carr, Lyndall Henning, Kayt Lackie, Liz Pile and David Towsey for reading and commenting on various parts of this novel as well as their help more generally. A special thanks must go to the driving force behind the group, Beverly Stark, for her organisational skills and hospitality as well as for her superb literary judgment. Separately, I would like to thank Jason Hewitt, who reviewed an early draft of this novel and provided welcome encouragement and also my good friend, Penelope Daukes, for everything she has done and for generally being fabulous in every way.

I was delighted to be long-listed for the Bath Novel Award in 2014 and 2016 which brought me into contact with the wonderful Caroline Ambrose. Along with her colleagues, she does great work in supporting new writing and it's been huge fun, and very encouraging, to be a small part of #TeamBNA.

Although my village may be mainly populated by wordy types, I'm very grateful that it also boasts a (retired) policeman, in the form of Andrew Osborne, formerly a Detective Sergeant with the Suffolk Constabulary, and a medic, namely Dr Emma Frampton. Their professional and technical expertise has been immeasurably useful. All remaining mistakes are entirely my own.

Turning to family... there is a cliché that writers should seek feedback from anyone but their mum. My own mum, Jean Dunlop, and also my mother-in-law, Pauline Sefton, are honourable exceptions to the rule that mothers will be blind to faults. Both cheerfully skewered early problems in my manuscript with very welcome (if occasionally bruising) ruthlessness. Their support and belief in me and in this book, alongside that of the rest of my extended family, has been instrumental in getting it written and published. I feel very lucky and grateful to them all. My two amazing children have also contributed (mostly unwittingly, but occasionally through helpful motivational remarks like 'why are you not famous yet?')

The final and most important thanks must go to my wonderful husband, Mike Sefton. He has been a stalwart supporter in this endeavour (as in every other), going to great efforts and exhibiting extraordinary self-sacrifice. If you don't believe me, just ask him.

In all seriousness, I am hugely grateful to everyone named and mentioned here, and also to many others too numerous to name. You know who you are. Thank you.